help yourself

rachel michael arends

DIVERSIONBOOKS

Also by Rachel Michael Arends

As Is

Diversion Books
A Division of Diversion Publishing Corp.
443 Park Avenue South, Suite 1008
New York, New York 10016
www.DiversionBooks.com

For more information, email info@diversionbooks.com

First Diversion Books edition March 2015.
Print ISBN: 978-1-62681-582-7
eBook ISBN: 978-1-62681-535-3

For my family

Chapter One

IN WHICH MERRY IS PRESENTED WITH AN UNEXPECTED OPPORTUNITY

As told by Merry Strand herself

Before you say I was crazy to listen to him, just try and put yourself in my shoes.

Ready?

Alright.

You're in your mid-twenties, but you're already starting to feel old. Since you graduated from college into a nonexistent job market two years ago, you've been back at home, spinning your wheels on the same stretch of rural mountain road where you were brought up. You enjoy your job, but your boss/boyfriend can be a real hothead. You love your family, but you have to admit what everyone else has seemed to know for ages: they're a bunch of kooks. Also, you (still being me for another second) have dreamed your whole life of getting to know your dad, and of finally seeing the ocean.

Keep all that in mind when you (as me) ponder the question the stranger asked:

Would you like to solve all your problems, transform yourself and your career, win money and an oceanfront home, and gain an understanding of the charismatic father you always longed for but never knew existed?

Now, I realize that everybody is different. Maybe you don't have any problems. Maybe you're pleased as peaches with your life just exactly how it is. Maybe you've got a great career and money has never been a worry. Maybe your dad has always been around. Maybe there's no question in the whole world that anybody could ask that'd make you stop right in your tracks and listen.

But me? I felt like the well-dressed British guy must've been able to see right into my heart. To come up with that exact set of items…I mean, what were the odds?

Would you, Merry? He asked, impatiently tapping one of his shiny shoes to show he wasn't going to stand around all day waiting on my answer.

Well, I was tempted to shout *YES.* Those prizes he offered seemed tailor-made. I knew that even if I lived to be 110, I'd likely never get another question like that put to me. And I confess that I'd been realizing, a little at a time over the past two years, that if I didn't make some changes soon I could be stuck here forever. I don't want to live the rest of my life on the side of this mountain, like a scrubby old tree trying to make the most of my small scrap of ground, trying to stay warm and cheerful in the few rays of light that reach all the way down to me.

Of course, I didn't answer right off because I didn't know what I'd have to do to earn the jackpot. Now that I've learned a few details, I'm even more confused.

But I'm still gonna say yes.

Let me back up a few minutes to give you a better idea where I'm coming from.

Picture it:

I'm under a table when the man strides right through the door, like it doesn't matter a whit to him whether the sign says OPEN or CLOSED. I'm familiar with pretty much everybody in this neck of the woods, and there's no violent crime to speak of, so I didn't lock up after I let myself into the restaurant.

The stranger's fancy shoes and the clip of his walk tell me he's not from around here, but I'm still not scared. I suppose people are either in the habit of being wary or they're not. I'm not.

"Pardon me," he says.

His accent likely blends in just fine in England. In the mountains of North Carolina, though? Not so much.

I push at the leg I just shimmed. It doesn't wobble anymore, so I crawl out from under the table. The man steps backward as I emerge, eyeing me like I'm a big, wet frog fixing to jump on his clean suit. He holds a briefcase with one hand and pats it with the other.

I don't need his expression to tell me I'm an awful mess. I'm here at the Mountainside early to get some dirty work done ahead of Phil's arrival. I want to make a peace offering because we had another argument last night. I know Phil will be happy when he sees that I steadied the eight-seat table with the best long-range view of the mountains. He'll also be pleased that I managed to make the stainless steel appliances shine again after Amy Jo cleaned them with the wrong spray yesterday.

Phil actually shouted at Amy Jo for doing that. He yelled at his own mother! I get angry all over again just thinking about it.

I admit that the streaks were awful; it looked like an acid rain cloud had opened up in the kitchen. And I know those appliances were expensive and all. I know. But Phil still shouldn't have yelled!

I came in early this morning to make Phil forget our fight. He started it all right, but I kept it going. I suppose I wasn't thinking beyond making up. If I had been, I'd realize that every time we make up it only lasts for a few days before something else sets him off. Then we make up again, and a couple squares down the calendar he gets angry again. And so on.

"Sorry, but the restaurant is closed," I tell the stranger. I'd like to get the soup started and the meat tenderized before Phil comes in.

"Right. I noticed the sign," he says. "Is Merry Strand here, by chance?"

Salespeople always ask for me because Phil won't give them the time of day. Though the guy doesn't look like a salesman, I figure he must be one. No one else ever comes around looking for me.

"I'm Merry," I say.

He stares me up and down like he refuses to believe it. "Are you *really*?"

I've still got on the plaid flannel pants and faded Dollywood T-shirt that I slept in. I came in straight from bed, planning to go home and shower before I open the restaurant for lunch. My unbrushed hair spills over my shoulders.

"Yes, sir, I am," I say.

"Sir?" he asks, in a way that makes it clear he thinks I'm a backwoods hick.

Well, saying 'sir' is a habit with me because of where I was raised. It doesn't matter if I'm talking to a salesman I'm about to turn away or that he doesn't appear to be any older than me. If he was a lady, I'd have said 'ma'am'.

"It's called politeness," I tell him.

He looks at me hard, and I stare right back. Finally, he sets his briefcase on the table I just came out from under.

"May I see your driver's license?" he asks.

A thought dawns on me that maybe my college parking tickets have finally caught up with me, two years late. I collected quite a few. But I doubt they'd warrant him driving up the mountain to find me. Plus, he doesn't look like a civil servant. He sniffs like he's bored, or irritated, or smells something bad.

I fold my arms over my chest. "So you just march into my *closed* place of employment and demand my license without first saying 'how-de-do?'"

I have always been able to tell when my accent isn't appreciated, when people think my IQ is lower than theirs just because I hold on to some syllables longer than they do. My Aunt Betty got rid of her accent altogether and sounds like a newscaster now, but I've never wanted to go lopping off parts of me to fit in. Besides, if blending into the woodwork was Aunt Betty's goal, she sure failed.

The stranger mouths *how-de-do* like it's the weirdest darn thing he's ever heard.

I don't have the time to stand around yapping with a rude stranger. "Just tell me what it is you want, or go out the way you came in," I say.

He frowns like it's a big decision. After a minute, he takes a piece of paper from his pocket and reads the exact question I told you about:

"Would you like to solve all your problems, transform yourself and your career, win money and an oceanfront home, and gain an understanding of the charismatic father you always longed for but never knew existed?"

I stare at him like he just fell from the sky. I try to absorb his whole question, but the word *father* keeps echoing in my brain.

"Would you, Merry?" The man taps his foot.

"What on earth are you talking about?" I ask. I have the weird idea that somehow I let a fussy genie out of a bottle, one who won't play by the regular rules because he thinks he knows what my wishes ought to be.

He sits at the table and opens his briefcase. Very matter-of-factly he says, "I have come to talk with you on behalf of your biological father."

I sit down hard in the chair across. "My *who*?"

Here's the honest-to-goodness truth: I have imagined a thousand versions of the moment when I would finally find out something, anything, about my dad.

I always dreamed he would suddenly appear out of nowhere, when I just happened to look my most beautiful. Like when I was four years old and dressed up in a new white dress for Lois Pretinger's birthday party.

Anytime I felt crushed or alone, I also imagined that my dad would suddenly arrive to cheer me up. Like my whole life until then had been a sad sack, made-for-TV movie, just waiting for a happy ending.

I remember hoping that my father would appear to console me when our old dog bit me on the cheek and had to be euthanized. I closed my eyes and yearned so hard for him to come…I knew it was my fault Carlton bit me because I had petted him in his twitchy sleep.

I also believed my dad would show up and lead me back home when I wandered too deep off the trail into the woods. I was dead scared and near frozen, and somewhere in the night I began to think he really was there with me. But in the morning, I woke up alone to the sound of a neighbor lady hollering my name.

And I watched out the window for my dad long after Phil called to say he wasn't picking me up for prom after all because he had gotten it into his jealous head that I liked another boy.

I dreamed my whole life that when my father suddenly appeared, he would say how sorry he was that it had taken him so long. He'd bear-hug me until I needed air, and we would instantly be best friends. He would whisk me away from Peaksy Falls, off to some wonderful place—I imagined so many different ones— where we'd make up for all our lost time.

But when the impatient English genie mentions my father, I know deep down that something is wrong. My dad wasn't supposed to send a messenger.

Maybe this will sound weird to you, but I never had a father figure at all.

My mom adopted me at birth; she's in pictures with me from day one on. Have I dreamed of my biological mother sometimes? Well, heavens yes! I've wondered if she's nice, if she's pretty, if she ever misses me. I wonder if her life has been better for having given me up. I wonder if she has a favorite color, and if it's pink, and if she loves peach ice cream the way I do. But I've always made an extra effort not to indulge in thoughts of the lady who brought me into this world, for fear of hurting my real, day-to-day mom's feelings. Or my grandma's. Those two have always been with me, so I suppose that's why I've never felt a gaping hole in my heart for a mom.

For the past two years, ever since my grandma had that bad fall and my mom begged me to come home to Peaksy Falls, I've been living with my mom and grandma again. I know lots of people move home after graduation these days. But when I went away to college (not too far away, just a few hours' drive), I had promised myself that I'd never move back home again. I figured that I had seen everything around here, and knew everyone, and done everything that could be done.

When Grandma fell, my mom seemed to want me back here more than anything. And Phil offered me the job and all.

As time passed, whenever I talked about moving on, Grandma complained about her new hip and started limping again. Mom fretted something awful.

I suppose that before the Englishman across the table marched into the restaurant, it must have seemed to everybody in the world, sometimes me included, that I'd be stuck in the same place, with the same people, doing the same things, forever.

"Your biological father, Claude Pershing," the man says. "May I see your driver's license to confirm that you really are Merry Strand?"

I get my purse from the shelf behind the hostess stand and hand over my license. "Why would I want to prove I'm his daughter if he hasn't cared this long? Maybe *I* don't care."

The stranger looks up at me and blinks twice.

"I wasn't clear," he says. "I'm talking about an inheritance, Ms. Strand."

"Oh," I say. So there it is: my dad is dead. I'll never meet him, never know him. And that's that. It's all I can do to keep from crying.

The stranger gives me back my license. I suppose it's wrong to call him a stranger now, since he obviously knows things about me that I don't know myself.

"Mr. Pershing wasn't aware that he had a daughter until it was too late to get to know you, Ms. Strand."

"Claude Pershing was my father's name?" I ask.

"That's correct," he says in a clipped, closed-off way. I wish he was more open because I have a million questions.

"Claude Pershing sounds like a name that should've belonged to an admiral or a duke. I always pictured my dad as Robert Redford in *The Horse Whisperer*," I say.

"I believe Mr. Pershing would have enjoyed all those images."

The way he says it, I can't tell if the comment was meant as an insult or a compliment. I open my mouth to ask a question, or maybe a whole mess of them, but I don't get the chance.

"When Mr. Pershing found out he had a daughter, he asked me to gather as much information about you as I could. He wanted me to help you fix your life."

"Fix my life? Did he figure it was broken?"

"From what he gathered… To put it simply, he thought you could use some assistance getting yourself together."

I stare at the man across the table, who seems about as different from me as anybody I've ever met. "Are you my brother?" I ask him.

"No, I am most certainly not. I was Mr. Pershing's barrister, and I suppose I still am." As he reaches out to shake my hand, he smiles at me for the very first time. "I'm Fritz Forth," he says. "How-de-do?"

I smile back. "There are your manners! I knew they had to be in there somewhere, especially with you talking so fancy and all dressed up like you're on your way to a wedding."

His smile turns into a wince. "Right. I have something for you. Let's call it a letter, shall we? It's from Mr. Pershing." He unpacks a stack of papers from his briefcase and shuffles through them. He makes two equal piles and starts to push one toward me, but stops.

"Let me first say that Mr. Pershing was blessed with many positive qualities. As you will soon see, however, he also had a stubborn streak of eccentricity. Please keep in mind that everything here is in legal order; I have seen to that. But your father's penchant for oddity grew more pronounced as he aged, and these pages, unfortunately, reflect that."

"My dad wrote those?" I ask, reaching for the stack of papers. Fritz puts his hand on top to stop me like he's not finished yapping yet.

I feel so many emotions; I honestly can't make them all out. Except excitement, and I suppose fear that Fritz will find his way back into his genie bottle and I'll wake up to find that his visit was only a dream.

"Mr. Pershing dictated them, yes. I typed them for him and encouraged him toward changes that would make the information as coherent as possible." Fritz rubs his eyes like he's got a tension headache. "But as I said, he was stubborn."

Before Fritz can stop me, I grab a stack of the papers and start reading.

Hello, Merry.

What a charming name! I do hope that it suits you.

Getting straight to business:

This document is to inform you that I, Claude Pershing, your biological father, regret having been unaware of your existence until very late in my life. When I discovered that I might indeed have a daughter, I was very sorry that I hadn't gotten to know you and perhaps to have been of assistance and support to you during your formative years.

With regret for having missed so much time and so many opportunities with you, my biological daughter (whom I most certainly did not know about), I sincerely apologize. As a token of my regret, I (Claude Pershing) bequeath to you (Merry Strand) a property of considerable value, which I hope you will enjoy as much as I did. There is also a sum of money, but we'll get to all that in a moment.

First, let me congratulate you on being my child. I have reason to believe that I am part of a fine lineage of good people. I only hope that hemorrhoids do not plague you, as they did me and my ancestors.

I must now take a moment to dispense with an important formality. It behooves me to explain that in order for the aforementioned property and money to pass to you freely and clearly, there are certain nonnegotiable conditions that must be met. Unfortunately, I cannot communicate them to you directly, being in no condition (i.e. dead), so you will have to depend upon the next best thing: my most trusted assistant in life, Fritz Forth.

The long and short of it is that Fritz shall give you a series of tasks, and he will advise you in completing them. You must live at the property in question for the time it takes you to fulfill the requirements I have entrusted to Mr. Forth.

I am (was) sorry if you feel the conditions of your inheritance are not very chivalrous on my part. I assure you that I believe they are for your own good and that in the end you might come to agree with me (posthumously, of course).

If you are unable to complete a task, Fritz will, unfortunately again, be forced to declare this proposal null and void. He will, in that case, turn you out of the house, and you will be left with nothing. Rest assured that Fritz would not enjoy this outcome; he is a most affable young man, and evictions aren't a hobby he would take up with any vigor.

I have been told that I am a long-winded meanderer. I believe it. Especially in the short time afforded to me between having discovered you and becoming ill-suited to making your proper acquaintance (that is to say: dead), I have been less straightforward in my logical capacity than I knew myself to be prior. I apologize. I would have liked to leave you with a sturdy impression.

Now to describe the property you stand to inherit. As you may know, native that you are, North Carolina boasts many long, thin islands along its acquaintance with the Atlantic Ocean. These are called barrier islands, and essentially they are sand bars. They are very large and very pretty (if my opinion counts anymore) sand bars, with trees and houses and roads on them. Between the barrier islands and the land is the intracoastal waterway, filled with brackish water—meaning a mixture of salt and fresh water, so that dolphins may appear as well as the occasional alligator. On the other side of the island is the Atlantic Ocean: the true love of my life.

I apologize for that insensitive remark. You might very well have been the love of my life, had I known about you.

I am sorry to say, if you are curious to know, which indeed you are if you have inherited my family's curiosity (though hopefully not our hemorrhoids), that your mother was not the love of my life. I can be sure of this because I remembered only fleeting impressions of her until a document recently came into my hands. That document was how I became aware that you might, potentially, exist. Because you're reading this now, Merry, I think we can both safely conclude that you do. Indeed.

I have left you at the edge of North Carolina, looking toward the barrier islands. Let me now land you on one: it is called Topsail. I don't claim it's the best, for I realize others are more famous, including one among the Outer Banks, where the

Wright brothers learned to fly. There are wild horses and giant dunes on others, if I remember correctly from things I have read, but I wouldn't know about any other barrier islands directly. I discovered Topsail Island first, you see, and it was enough for me.

Let me direct you more specifically toward the south end of the island. There you will find the home I loved most, though I didn't spend as much time there as I could have. My London house is far grander, to be sure. Becoming ill, though, it occurred to me to revisit my ocean home. To say that I'm glad I did would be a profound understatement. Somehow, I found it easier to contemplate death while watching the sea.

You might not be the sentimental type, so I'll tell you something else. The beach house is worth quite a lot of money. I hope that fact entices you to attempt to complete the tasks and receive title to it, along with a sum of cash that will not only help you maintain it, but perhaps help others you love maintain what they love.

I'll add quickly that if you don't earn the house, Merry my dear, then my brother Max will inherit it. He's a curmudgeonly old bastard, and I'd really hate to have him get it.

By now you're sick of my meandering. I am, too. I grow tiresome and tired simultaneously.

I'll move on to the conditions you will have to satisfactorily meet in order to solely inherit my beach house, along with the accompanying stipend.

1. *You live there for the time it takes to fulfill #2 below.*
2. *You complete the tasks, which will be communicated to you by Fritz Forth individually and checked off by him at completion. If a task remains incomplete to his satisfaction after a period of time determined by him, then I'm afraid he will be obligated to kick you out. (I assure you he won't like it.)*
3. *If all tasks are completed, you will receive the money as well as the free and clear title to the property. You could sell it, live there, or whatever you like.*

I think that is all. Again, to reiterate, I apologize for having been unaware of your existence for the vast majority of your life thus far. I would have liked to have known you. I wish I were more confident in the vice versa, but the end of life is full of regret and self-doubt. Dying is a terrible inconvenience.

Look to Fritz for assistance; he is an exceedingly good man.

Sincerely and belatedly, and with all the love one can give someone he's never known, which I have found at times to be rather more than expected,

I remain (though I'm dead)

Yours truly,

Claude Pershing

Honestly, what would you think of a letter like that?

I sit sort of stunned a while, until I notice Fritz take the papers from my hands and put them into his briefcase. When I look at him straight on again, I see that he's watching me closely. I watch him right back.

"If I agree to the proposal I just read, I'd have to live with you."

Fritz nods. "I'm gay, if that helps you feel more comfortable."

"I suppose it takes away the worry of you making passes," I say.

"It most certainly does. Any other concerns?"

"I'd have to believe that you're trustworthy enough to give me the goods if I earned them, since it would be in your power to say I didn't do something 'to your satisfaction,' and you could kick me out with nothing at all," I say.

Fritz nods again. "That's right."

"*Are* you trustworthy?" I ask.

"Yes."

He doesn't seem to relish his power over my destiny. It looks like it gives him a stomachache.

"You can say no," he suggests.

"Do you want me to say no?"

He doesn't answer. He looks at the same paper he read from originally. "I can help you change your life forever," he reads. "If you fulfill your father's set of challenges, strange though they may seem, you can save your family from financial ruin, solve an important mystery, and maybe even find love on your own terms. You can finally learn to help yourself."

Questions rise up in my mind, like bubbles when the stew starts to boil. I don't know half of what Fritz is talking about: A mystery? Financial ruin? Love on my own terms?

I can't form up any question well enough to ask out loud; they pop out of my thoughts too fast. I feel like I'm caught between two worlds. I keep picturing images I've seen of the ocean and remembering snatches of my father's letter one minute, and looking at the mountains through the window and imagining my Grandma and Mom alone in our cabin the next.

When I hear a pan hit the kitchen floor, I look up at the clock.

"Shoot!" I say, because I know Phil is here, and I know he's madder than a hornet.

Although I've already mentioned his temper a few times, I want you to know that Phil isn't just one of his attributes. He's also a good kisser, he fixes things around our cabin without being asked, and he's the best cook I know.

I suppose future beauticians get started by raiding their mom's makeup drawers, and future builders borrow nails and scraps from the piles beside their daddy's sawhorses. Me, I always knew I wanted to make good food. Phil was born knowing more about cooking than I'll probably ever learn, on account of his parents both being so culinary. Now Phil's an amazing chef, and he's taught me a lot of what he knows. We talk about herbs and spices like other lovers discuss their future plans and their dreams.

Phil pushes through the swinging door. "Nothing's been done!" he shouts.

"Now you watch your tone," I say.

He puts his left hand out like a stop sign to shush me. He raises the fingers on his right hand one at a time. I really hate it when he does that. It seems to me that even if he's only mad about one thing, he thinks of more on the spot just to get through all his fingers.

He puts his thumb down: "You didn't get the soup started." Pointer: "You didn't tenderize the meat." Middle: "You didn't get anything chopped," ring: "or prepped," pinky: "or... Who the hell are you?"

Fritz has left his seat and is standing directly in front of Phil. "It's really all my fault. I interrupted Ms. Strand's work," he says.

Phil stares at him hard.

I hope he doesn't scare Fritz away.

"I fixed the wobbly leg," I say.

Maybe I shouldn't have taken up with Phil again when I returned to Peaksy Falls. But he brought me over some brownies with little bits of salty toffee and chewy caramel baked in, and I just couldn't resist. I don't like to admit it, but Phil's cooking is to me what game shows are to my mom and grandma.

Phil is still sizing up Fritz when Amy Jo comes in the front door. She has on her uniform, which reminds me that I'm still not dressed.

"Are y'all sick?" she asks, putting one hand on my arm and one on my forehead.

She's heavyset and matronly, with knees that don't seem strong enough to carry her all day, but somehow they still do it. Amy Jo gives the whole place a homey feel when she's here.

Amy Jo and Cyril, Phil's parents, had a family restaurant out on the highway, which was open for decades. It wasn't "upscale gourmet" fare like Phil now serves here at the Mountainside, mind you. But growing up in his parents' place gave Phil so much confidence with ingredients and flavors that cooking now seems instinctual to him. I suppose he's like a dancer who began leaping when he could barely walk, or Yo-Yo Ma playing the cello from age four. Phil's comfort with food is just a natural part of him, like breathing.

I've always had the same sort of crush on Phil that freshman girls in college get for the professors who teach their favorite subjects. Last week there was a perfect example. He'd yelled at a delivery man in front of the entire kitchen staff, and I thought he was just about the biggest ass I'd ever seen. But then he gave me a taste of a new salad he'd put together. I chewed slowly and savored the flavors—tart and sweet fruity vinaigrette dressing, fresh textured mixed greens, dried cherries, salty nuts, and bitter, crumbly smooth cheese…well, I couldn't help but kiss him when I'd finished. I suppose I'm his one and only groupie.

"I feel fine. I came in early to do a few things and lost track of time," I tell Amy Jo.

"Would you stop babying her, Ma?" Phil says. "Lunch will be real easy today, since no one has done a single useful thing around here all morning! Now hurry up and get dressed, Merry."

He heads back toward the kitchen.

"No," I call after him.

Phil turns around slowly.

"I'm leaving," I say. I grab on to Fritz's hand, which he doesn't seem to like one bit.

Phil looks Fritz up and down, from his short hair, across his fancy clothes, to his shiny shoes.

"You're going off somewhere with this guy?" Phil seems to think the idea is a joke.

I don't speak; I let my expression do the talking.

"Who the hell is he?" Phil asks.

I pull Fritz toward the door, but Phil gets up ahead of us and stands in front of it with his arms crossed.

"You're not actually thinking of walking out of here."

"It's not forever," I tell Phil. "I just have to take care of some business out of town with this lawyer. I'll explain it to you later, once you've calmed down."

Phil looks as serious as I've ever seen him. "You better quit talking nonsense, go change your clothes, and be back here in time for the lunch crowd," he says.

It's so quiet for a minute that I swear you can hear the dust settle on the hostess stand.

Fritz turns to me and breaks the silence. "Are you sure you want to do this?" He looks nervous, like he's the one who'll have to pass a bunch of tests, not me.

I recall the most important parts of what I learned this

morning. While Fritz isn't a bona fide genie, he *is* offering to help me change my life, which I realize needs some changing. I look straight into his eyes. He's a prim and proper Englishman, who's just about the opposite of Southern-style me. And I know this is weird, but I trust him.

"Yes, sir," I say.

I give his hand a squeeze and march us right on past Phil and straight out the door.

Chapter Two

IN WHICH JACK MORNINGSTAR GOES SURFING

As told by the man in question

Katie's mouth tastes like summer: sweet from sangria and fresh strawberries, smoky from vegetables we grilled on the deck, salty from ocean water.

I inhale the coconut scent of her lotion, feel a fine grit of sand on my fingertips as her flat, tanned stomach rises up to meet my caress. A day of wind and waves spent under the blessing sun has left us tired, but not too tired for each other.

Chaser presses her cold nose to my neck. I push her off, but it's too late. The enveloping warmth I've been immersed in begins to fall away. I don't want to wake up.

What I want doesn't matter.

Reality creeps in. I reach deeper into the sheets, but it's no use. Heat and summer have dissipated like love grown cold. The air is chilled, the bed is empty. It's winter and I am alone.

Chaser whines. I look at the clock to see that it's after ten. The sun rising over the water didn't wake me like it did every morning during the sunny month that Katie and I spent together in this house. I keep dreaming of that time, only to wake again with a bitterness that wastes me. It was either last July or a lifetime ago, depending on how you add it all up. Today is gray; the ocean is daunting and wild. It looks angry. Like it has been betrayed.

Chaser play bows to me. She was Katie's dog. If Katie were

here, she would fall on Chaser's golden hair and kiss her muzzle, apologize for sleeping late while the poor "good girl" held her bladder. Katie would take Chaser on a five-mile beach run to make up for it.

If only she were here.

Freezing rain lashes against my face while I watch Chaser on the beach below the deck. I envy her resilience, her optimism. Or perhaps it's just her dog-sized brain that makes her able to forget the rawness of loss, at least long enough to run in the rain.

Chaser was a rescue from the shelter, a golden retriever/chow mix that seems to possess the best attributes of both breeds. She's loyal, quiet, and eager to please thanks to the golden side. She also possesses chow smartness, has a purple tongue, stand-up ears, a feather-duster blond tail, and a gorgeous coat. She was a breeze to train and never forgets what she's learned. The first time she jumped on our bed, we ordered her down, and that was it. When we tried to coax her up afterward, to warm our feet on cold Chicago nights, she'd look at us as if to say *I'm not allowed up there!* I don't know where she gets her speed from. She's the fastest dog I've ever seen, except the greyhound that was here last summer.

I remember Katie admiring that greyhound until Chaser started to pout. The greyhound's muscled elegance reminded me of Katie's own; she was always eager to run, too.

Trying to keep pace with my wife, though I never quite could, had kept me fit. If Katie ran up the beach now, or surfaced from the sea, or dropped from the sky, she'd scold me for growing soft, for letting my muscle tone go to hell. If she walked inside or appeared there suddenly, she'd see that I've let everything else go, too.

Chaser races along the edge of the water. She's clearly happy and blissful, like she thinks life is a game, like it's beautiful. She seems oblivious to the frigid wind pelting rain against her thick coat. She chases a bird, she jumps. It eludes her and she runs on. She looks up to see me and switches direction to race my way.

If it weren't for Chaser, I might have given up any number of times. I might have stayed in the water and not climbed back onto my surfboard, might have let the ocean erase my pain and memories once and for all. But Chaser seems to know when I need her, with a well-timed bark from shore. She watches all the while I'm out there, reminding me that she needs me, that we still have each other.

I pat Chaser's wet head when she reaches the deck, three flights of stairs and plank walkways up from the beach. I let her bolt into the house ahead of me, dragging sand, salt, and cold seawater with her.

Katie would have a fit if she were here. She always complained that I was too messy and disorganized, too laid-back. If she didn't keep after me, I would fall apart.

I fill Chaser's water bowl and give her fresh food. I dump last night's cold, half-empty pot of coffee and start a new one brewing. Though I know better, I open the fridge. I shut it again; there's nothing fresh in this house. I take a protein bar from a box in the pantry and eat it without tasting.

I check my e-mail and find a note from Martin.

I got the files you sent last night. Will you finish up today like we discussed?

Martin is my business partner, formerly my best friend. Six months ago, he would've called and hassled me instead of writing. He might have said, "You only sent half the stuff I need because you're too busy playing house to get anything done. Get out of bed and finish your end of the deal! We need to deliver on time; you know this client is our bread and butter. Or in your case, tofu and lettuce, or whatever Katie lets you eat."

He would have joked about my last-minute ways, confident that I'd come through in the end because I always did. Now neither of us ever seems so sure. And I can't stomach the sound of his voice.

What time do you need the rest? I type and hit send.

I turn and watch the rollers. The windows are fogged in sea mist.

Martin's response is in my inbox the next time I look back.

A minute or an hour might have passed; I honestly don't know.

> *We agreed on three o'clock. Remember? And I know you're sick of hearing this, but Sam and Varun are in way over their heads on the Langdon proposal. I wish you'd come back and do your real job. I could use some help keeping this company alive.*

Our firm thrived during the years when I designed the software systems for our Fortune 500 clients, employees built and implemented them, and Martin handled sales, support, and staff.

In college, I discovered I have an accidental talent for software design—it just fits my brain. Over the years, I've tried to train others to do what I do. No one we've hired seems to have the patience and discipline for it, though. It takes confidence and tenacity to eke out every detail of a client's business processes in order to design software that serves them fully and effortlessly. The design has to then be translated into specs, which the technical staff can use to build the software. My attention to detail has led to high customer satisfaction, which has led to a steady demand for our services. This has allowed Martin to bill the big bucks, which lets us pay generous salaries, which keeps everyone happy.

Unfortunately for us all, endless hours of design meetings are beyond my capacity now. I realize shit still needs to get done whether I'm in mourning or not, and that lots of our employees can code, but no one else can design like me. I can only do what I can do, though. And lately it hasn't been much.

Since October fifteenth, actually. Since that day, which is etched on my soul like a scar, I've had to take a step back from my old life. I have needed more space, a lot more space, to be alone. I've needed to be far away from everyone—employees, clients, family—everyone. After that first week of hell, I told Martin I would code for a while. He didn't like the idea, but he agreed. What could he say? He would've agreed to anything at that point.

. . .

A compelling numbness overtakes my mind when I'm coding. Time escapes me while I'm occupied with the complexities of syntax and logic so that I barely feel the dull ache that seems part of me now, like a canker sore or a bad elbow.

When I send the code to Martin, he e-mails back within minutes:

> *Files received. I'll get Steve on putting it all together, and testing will begin tomorrow. I don't like cutting everything so close, but we should be OK to deliver on time. Thank God you had this system designed before you took off! It's a real handicap not to have you here for the Langdon Logistics proposal.*
>
> *On a personal note, your mom says to tell you that their computer crashed, so she and your dad have been off e-mail and wanted to make sure you're OK. Can't you ever answer your phone? Seriously, they worry.*

I think of writing back:

> *What you like or don't like is as irrelevant to me as you are. I already know I'm letting the company down, so you can shove your whining reminders up your ass. And hell no, I won't answer the phone! I can't stand to hear anyone's voice; I'm sick of people crying in my ear and the worry woven into every sentence. So mind your own damn business for a change.*

But that would tell too much, open communication lines, and he'd try to weasel his way back in.

I order my parents a new laptop online. They needed one anyway, even if Martin manages to fix their old PC. He'll set up their laptop, of course. He's been a better organized, more responsible son to them since he moved to our street when he and I were five years old. My dad used to joke about claiming Martin as a dependent on his income taxes because he was always around.

Martin and I shared a dorm room freshman year in college. We shared a house with other students after that. We started our business before graduation, with a small project automating schedules for the school rec center, which we then replicated for the local Y. We grew our company together, incorporated it, expanded, and won bigger clients and more complicated projects. Now I wish I'd never shared anything with Martin, ever. I wish I'd never seen his face.

I take a pop from the fridge. I eat another protein bar and some chips, chewing and swallowing until the hollow feeling in my stomach lessens. I haven't made a meal in months. It just doesn't seem worth it.

The little grocery store on this tiny island has nosy checkout women. There are so few people here off-season that a thirty-year-old bachelor is apparently everyone's business, especially if he surfs alone in bad weather, has a tragic history, or both.

I was barraged with questions at the coffee house when I first arrived, so I never went back. The same thing happened at an island pizza joint and a seafood diner. So I order dry goods online and they come right to the house in cardboard boxes. I don't want to see anyone, or for anyone to see me.

I close the blinds on the window facing the house next door. Last summer, the owner and I became friends. I knew the old man lived in London, that he'd been diagnosed with terminal cancer, and that his place was usually a rental. Claude and I connected in a way that I hadn't really ever connected with an older guy.

My dad prefers talking to listening, and he acts as if he's on a perpetual lecture circuit. I'm a prop to him as much as I am a son.

Claude was refreshing because he didn't mind being a bastard sometimes, or saying something off-color or rude. Maybe it was because he knew his life was ending, or maybe he'd always been that way. He said he was going back to London at the end of the summer, and I was relieved that I wouldn't see him when I crawled back to the island without Katie. I didn't want to tell him what had happened. I didn't want to hear how sorry he was for me.

I wasn't worried about running into anyone else that I knew here on the island. Claude had been the only homeowner Katie and I befriended that month. Most of our fellow beach dwellers were vacationers in rental houses, including a newlywed couple from New York, a French Canadian family, and an Ohio group who took up three houses with a boisterous week-long family reunion and the cutest kids I've ever seen. When I came back here, I didn't expect to see a single familiar face.

One night after I came in from surfing, though, Claude's traveling companion from last summer knocked on the door. Fritz said he'd looked out and been surprised to see me. He asked how I was, apparently trying to seem nonchalant, while he clearly thought I was crazy to have been out in those waves. He asked about Katie, and I gave him the short version: she's gone. I didn't invite him in. I didn't even ask about Claude.

I realize that doesn't reflect very highly on me. Like being relieved that my parents' e-mail is down.

I know that I've shortened my reprieve by ordering their new computer, but I don't want to hurt them by cutting them off completely. It was hard for them to give me the space I needed in the beginning; I could see worry in their eyes and hear it in their voices.

Now they make it clear that they think my time for indulgent mourning is up, that I need to rejoin the land of the living. I get several e-mails to that effect every week. I don't disagree with their logic. There's only one problem: I'm not ready.

When everything crashed down around me, they had wanted me to stay with them. I tried. I went there and brought some of my things. But I couldn't stay.

I couldn't remain at the apartment either.

I tried several places. Like a nomad, moving on, and on, and on. I didn't realize that I was on my way here consciously until I crossed over the swing bridge and found myself on this narrow sandbar of an island, until I'd driven to this house, where Katie and I had spent the best month of our marriage. I called the rental company from the driveway and just stayed put.

I can feel her here; she's still close to me, somehow. I haven't had that feeling anywhere else. Only here. Moving on would mean losing that. And as I said, I'm not ready.

Chaser puts her head on my knee. I have a shorthand way to remember if she needs to go outside: if she's dry, she's got to go again. Her day is a cycle of running on the beach, romping in the water, then coming in to dry off—which takes hours. Then she repeats the process.

It makes me think of Katie and me during the time we spent here. The rhythms of our days were regulated by the need to eat, to surf or run, to make love, and to sleep. Life was so simple.

It seemed so simple.

It's hard to believe that the gray, churning ocean is the same water that was brilliantly blue then. That the thick, gray sky was clear and open, that the driving wind was a gentle breeze.

I'm drawn toward the chaos of the storm today. When I get into the water, the coldness will cut through my senses. I won't think; I'll only feel.

My wetsuit is hanging in the laundry room; Katie would have never allowed it in the house. Maybe I'm taunting her to speak, to yell, to talk to me. I struggle into my gear while Chaser follows me with expressive, worried eyes. She watches as I navigate the surfboard through the kitchen and living room.

When I open the door, the wind hits me like a shocking truth, like the rush of a truck braking too late. It threatens to blow me into oblivion.

Chaser runs down the many stairs ahead of me, looking back at every landing as if she's afraid I'll fall.

As I slowly descend to surf in the chaos of an ocean storm, I know that some parts of my mind will dull while others take over. This is what appeals to me. It's something like coding, except that it's violent, risky. The freezing water will awaken my senses and bring me to a primal state of survival, of board and strategy, of balance and failure. Afterward, I'll need all my remaining energy to drag my body through the rush and whorl of the current, back across the wet sand, and up the stairs. Every nerve ending will ache with fatigue and heightened awareness, from my freezing ears to my saltwater-reddened eyes, to my shocked and overburdened lungs, to the muscles that will keep me upright, barely, until I can divest myself of all my gear and fall into bed.

And dream of Katie.

Chapter Three

IN WHICH FRITZ IS AMBIVALENT

As told by Fritz Forth, Esquire

Little Miss Dollywood, my pajama-clad project, must be somewhat woo-woo. Why else would she agree to come away with me, a man she barely knows, on such a bizarre pretext? And not only agree, but to practically throw herself at this absurd bargain, like she might dive from a car just before it careens off a cliff? Actually, thinking of Merry's present life, perhaps I have just answered my own question.

Her yee-haw enthusiasm seems to be waning a bit, however, as we make our way across the Mountainside's parking lot toward my rented SUV. I put my hand on her back in an attempt to hurry us along. I even open the passenger door.

I'm not accustomed to making this sort of chivalrous gesture. In the normal course of my life, Victor and I would get too many odd looks from passersby. I have risen to the occasion during exceptional circumstances, though, like when he sprained his ankle last winter. He would rather have had me carry him everywhere, but as Victor has thirty pounds of weight and about ten inches of height over me, and I have (and need) enough self-respect for the both of us, he hobbled along with the aid of the crutch he'd painted black and decorated with rivets.

I cast a worried glance over my shoulder. I'm afraid that at any moment Merry's boyfriend, Phil, will come after us. He stared forlornly when Merry walked out the door, like an old hunting dog told he had to at stay home this time. But I'm concerned he'll start barking and howling at any moment.

"Go on, then. Get in," I say.

Merry stops in front of an old truck and folds her arms across her hideous T-shirt. "Where are we going?" she asks.

"Not far. I'll explain on the way." I make another go at coaxing her into the car.

"Don't take this the wrong way," she says, as slowly as it is humanly possible to say the words, "but I don't like riding with people who aren't used to driving in the mountains. Y'all can ride along with me, since we're not going far."

I wonder if elocution lessons could eliminate the obnoxious twang from her voice? Even if it were possible, though, there is no time to spare—a sad fact that I'm reminded of almost constantly these days.

"Don't take this the wrong way, but I'm not getting into your filthy vehicle," I say.

The enormous Chevy pickup behind Merry is muddy and rusted, and frankly provides what Victor might call an "artistically perfect backdrop" for her present state of personal disorder.

I know from photos that she cleans up rather well, but right now Merry looks like she could almost blend into a depressing documentary chronicling the poorest inhabitants of Appalachia. Merry's teeth are quite perfect, though, even by America's impeccable dental standards. And while she's curvy, she thankfully lacks even a trace of the slovenly fatness I've come to associate with indigent Americans. So she doesn't fully fit the ramshackle documentary profile.

Still, in this particular setting, and wearing her particular outfit, it isn't difficult for me to imagine her going either way. She could fail Mr. Pershing's tests and fall victim to inertia, driving her muddy truck until it rusts itself away to nothing. Or she could succeed and thereby claim her inheritance. And then who knows? Perhaps when we go through the final papers, we'll find that she has also inherited the London house, and then I'll simply be her poor neighbor across the way.

"I made it up the mountain in one piece. I'm satisfied we'll make it down one way or another," I say, growing impatient. I point to the SUV's passenger seat through the open door.

"Merry!"

I turn to see Phil coming toward us.

Let me just say that I am not a large man. Phil is, quite. Especially now, when this unfinished business of Mr. Pershing's has Victor and me strained nearly to the breaking point, I can't risk being swollen and ugly for our next Skype rendezvous across the pond. A broken nose would certainly test V's love for me—he recently admitted that the symmetry of my face factors into his equation.

In order to preserve my own features and also to defend the stalling Dollywood, of course, I gear up for a briefcase assault upon Phil. I plan to model it after that of a spry old woman I once saw defeat a thug on the streets of London. She had used only her purse. It was a triumphant performance.

As Phil approaches, however, I begin to panic because I don't see Merry anywhere. I think perhaps she's given me up for dead and has gone back into the Mountainside through a side door.

"Get in!" I hear her call from within my SUV.

I jump into the passenger seat and slam the door. Merry squeals the tires on her way out of the lot.

I'm still breathing hard and looking behind us when Merry states the obvious. "Here we go!"

I sigh long and loud before echoing her, under my breath: "Here we go indeed."

"Where are we going?" she asks.

"First, you're pulling off the road so that I can drive."

"I like to drive," she says.

"That's irrelevant."

When she has found a suitable spot a bit further up the road and we have switched positions, I breathe somewhat easier. I turn the SUV around and head the opposite way we'd been going.

"Are y'all gonna tell me where we're headed?" she asks.

Because I agreed to it, and I always keep my word, I try to sound like I believe this entire enterprise is perfectly reasonable.

"We are going to your house so that you can explain to your mother and grandmother that you'll be leaving them for a while."

Merry is quiet for approximately three kilometers before she graces me with her twang again.

"To get there, you need to make a right at the next stop sign."

"I know where to turn," I inform her. I crack my window for some fresh air. Merry smells strongly of pine-scented aerosol cleanser.

"How do you know?" she asks. "And how did you know I live with my mom and grandma?"

"I know everything about you," I say.

That is only a slight exaggeration.

For the past several weeks, I have studied Merry's life like a subject I'll be tested on at the end of term. For example, I know that Phil dominated her high school existence. He switched to a girl named Sarah while Merry attended college, then picked up with Merry again when she returned. That left Sarah heartbroken, but, I have to assume, better off.

I knew these facts about Phil before I met him today, and I had also seen photographs of him. But now I must concede that some details have to be experienced for full comprehension. For example, I didn't realize that Phil is, quite literally, a red neck. Actually that sells him short because he's red all over: from his shock of hair well above six feet off the ground, to his bear paw hands, to, presumably, every other extremity.

"You do not!" Merry says.

"Well, perhaps not everything, but I do know quite a lot about you," I reply.

"Like what?"

I check the time before turning on the radio. I tune it to a program that will help me prove my point.

Merry rolls her eyes as distinctive music plays. "*The Betty Answers Show?* Big deal. So you know my aunt is weird. Everybody knows that."

"Everyone knows she's your aunt?" I ask pointedly.

"Well, no. She changed her name forever ago, and now pretends she has no family anywhere. So no, nobody knows that she's my relative. And that's fine with me because everybody knows she's a nut job."

Merry's aunt's voice comes through the stereo speakers.

"Listen, Jenny, I don't know how many times I have said this over the years, but you don't have to explain anything…"

Merry talks over the program. "I could figure out how many times she's said that if I knew how many shows Aunt Betty's done altogether. She says, 'You don't have to explain anything,' about once every half hour, probably to reinforce the title of her book. She also mentions the whole title once in every two-hour show."

"What's the title?" I ask. I already know it, but I suppose I have a cruel streak.

"It's awful," she says.

"What is it, though? What's the title?"

Merry stares at me defiantly for a moment. I'm rather glad, on one hand, to see that she has a backbone. On the other hand, things will go much more smoothly if she simply does what I tell her without arguing.

"You said you knew everything about me," she says.

"You said I didn't," I counter.

She shrugs her shoulders. "Ask my mom or grandma when we get to my house. They never seem to have gotten the memo that Betty is a loon. They'll probably give you a signed copy of her book if you ask."

The title of Merry's aunt's book, in case you're curious or have a cruel streak like mine, is *POPPINS! Why You Should Never, Ever Explain Anything.* I don't blame Merry for not wanting to say it out loud.

"You don't know how long your aunt has been doing her show?" I ask.

"No," Merry says, like she couldn't care less. But her cheeks are bright red.

"I do," I offer helpfully. "Eighteen years."

As I said, I know a great deal about Merry and everyone in her life.

Betty Answers asks her radio caller, *"Why does your husband need to know everywhere you go and everything you do, Jenny?"*

"He doesn't, I guess, but I don't really mind him knowing. You know? I think it's awful nice that my husband cares where I am and what I'm doing and all that."

Jenny sounds indistinguishable to me from the other people who live in this vicinity. She was clearly born and reared nearby.

"What's the problem, then?" Betty Answers asks.

I happen to know that Betty spent her childhood here, too, but she's completely inflectionless. No one would ever guess that she was a mountain girl like Jenny if they happened upon *The Betty Answers Show* while driving through the area, scanning channels.

"He thinks I spend too much money."

"Is it really his business what you spend, Jenny?"

The caller hesitates. I imagine her setting a heavy kitchen table, in one of these wooden houses we keep passing, on one of these tree-shaded mountain lots that flash by outside our windows. Jenny is likely waiting for some down-home fare to finish cooking in the oven, for her husband to come through the front door and shout, "Honey, I'm home!"

"Yes, I think so," she finally says, *"because I've never had a job, and he pays all the bills."*

"Have you ever thought of getting a job, Jenny?"

"Why, yes! That's why I called you. Your housecleaner is in my prayer group, and she said you're looking for someone to paint your living room. I do a real nice job painting and all. I tried the number she gave me, but it said to call this one. I didn't know I'd be calling in to your radio program."

Betty clears her throat before she replies. *"Oh, that's nice, Jenny. You can go ahead and leave your number in my voicemail. Listeners,* The Betty Answers Show *will be right back after a short commercial break."*

I turn the volume low. "Your aunt Betty doesn't answer her home phone?" I ask. I knew this fact, but I'm curious to see how Merry explains it.

"Aunt Betty doesn't get nearly enough calls to her program to fill the air time, so she never picks up the phone at home,"

Merry says, as if it's neither fine nor wrong, but simply true. "Her home message says to call another number between nine and eleven on business days, which is when they do the show."

"What about family? If you call her at home, does she answer?" I ask.

Merry shrugs. "Same rule applies."

"Do you ever call in to the show?" I ask.

"No, sir."

"What about your mother?"

Merry blushes anew. "Yes, sir. She can't say she's related to Betty, though. It's another one of my aunt's rules because she doesn't go by her old name at all. Plus she says it wouldn't look good to the audience to have her sister calling her on air for advice all the time."

"The audience might wonder why she doesn't call her at home instead?" I can't help but ask.

"I suppose so. Mom pretends she's just a regular old caller, and they only know each other from their on-air talks over the years."

"Your mother calls for advice?" I have to admit that I find this quite fascinating, like driving by a gruesome car wreck.

"She has called the show asking advice and giving updates about me for years now, ever since the show began. Veteran listeners sometimes call up just to ask about me."

"Really?"

"Yes, sir. I suppose they've heard so much about me while I was growing up, they wonder what's going on now. Aunt Betty runs a highlight tape every year on my birthday. It's sort of sweet, in a weird way." Merry's blush is at its reddest.

"They feel invested in what happens in your life, like Truman from *The Truman Show*?" I ask.

"I suppose so. Except in that movie, everyone was lying to Truman, the poor sucker."

After a few more twists and turns in the road, Merry points to a scenic overlook ahead.

"Do y'all mind stopping a minute so I can collect myself before we get to my cabin?" she asks.

I slow to a crawl and park where she requested. I step outside to give Merry some space.

The view is quite lovely. There's a little village in the valley below, where the houses look like hand-painted toys, and there's a white church and an old-fashioned storefront downtown, with tiny cars parked outside, and a handful of miniature cows grazing in a field just out of town.

The scene reminds me of my extensive model train collection, which I'll unfortunately have to get rid of soon. Mr. Pershing added to it every birthday and Christmas, to the point where I could no longer fit it into my room. Then he gave over a large attic space to house it, with murals painted on the walls to enhance the illusion of villages, and hills, and streams, and even a little lake.

As the son of his longtime maid, I grew up in Mr. Pershing's home. I began to handle some of his sensitive correspondence when I was only twelve and apparently considered too young to know what was really being said. I handled sticky matters for him even earlier—my whole life, I guess I might say with some truthfulness. I used to pretend he wasn't at home when tiresome visitors called, I snuck vodka into his lemonade while my mother wasn't looking, and I pretended he'd been out walking with me for the exercise his doctor ordered, when really he'd lounged in a hammock hidden by trees at the bottom of the back garden.

The old man has done far more for me. In addition to gifts like the train set, he provided me with a wonderful home and the best education money could buy.

It was my mum's dying wish that I help Claude Pershing to the end, since he had done so much for us. Of course, I couldn't refuse her, no more than I could refuse him. As this project is the last use I can ever be to either of them, I won't shirk my responsibility, nor complain about it more than is strictly necessary.

I don't fear developing the family hemorrhoids, obviously, because I'm not a blood relative. But I confess that I always wished, with my entire heart, that Mr. Pershing was my father. The selfish old goat.

Merry smiles over at me with dewy eyes when I get back inside. "It'll be hard to leave my people, but it's about time I got out of here. You're like a genie, or an angel or something, Fritz."

Her trusting expression makes me exceedingly uncomfortable. I don't need more emotional complications on top of what I'm already juggling. I start up the car again.

"Or something," I say under my breath.

I thought I understood Merry's situation because I had collected as many facts about her history, her family, and her friends as I could. I should have realized that everything would be more complicated than it seemed from afar. Things always are.

I secretly wished she would refuse to come with me. I certainly didn't foresee how quickly she would leap at this chance, how desperately she would want to change her life once she knew she had the option.

"When do I need to get myself down to that beach house?" Merry asks when I park in her cabin's driveway.

"We'll drive down today," I say.

"Today?" she ratchets up her twang to an almost intolerable level.

I unbuckle my seatbelt, but Merry stays put.

"You know, that paperwork didn't look very official," she says, excruciatingly slowly. "No offence to your lawyer skills, but I always thought that wills were supposed to be way more formal. Maybe I shouldn't trust it at all."

"Maybe you shouldn't." I feel a glimmer of hope that she'll refuse to come with me.

"Phil might not give me my job back, even if I went there right now," she says, staring out the window.

"Would that be such a loss?" I ask.

"I love cooking, and I love the people who work there, and I love the people who eat there…"

"What about Phil? Do you love him?" I'd never ask a new acquaintance so personal a question in ordinary life, but this situation is surreal, and Merry seems to take it in stride anyway.

"Yes," she says, sounding a bit equivocal. "I don't believe he could make food taste so good if he wasn't a good person."

37

"So you're in love with him because he's a competent chef?" I ask. I also volunteer an opinion: "That's a stupid reason."

"No," she says. "I've known him most of my life…"

"That's so much better," I say.

She laughs a little and smacks my arm. "Shut up," she says.

"He's a horrible bully," I helpfully point out.

"He's more than that," she says. "But he can be that, too. I know it. The way he shouted at Amy Jo yesterday and stared you down today—which just about made you pee your expensive pants—well, I sometimes wonder if Phil and I really are meant to be together."

"But he cooks well and you've known him for quite a long while," I say, reaching for my door handle.

She grabs my arm to keep me in place. "Wait a minute. Back at the restaurant, you said I'd be able to save my family from financial ruin if I got that inheritance."

"I did."

She studies me. "Is my family having money troubles?"

"Indeed they are," I answer.

"You know that, but I don't?"

"I told you, I know everything."

"It's all those eBay auctions and QVC, isn't it?" she asks.

I don't answer; frankly, I have already shared more than I should. But between you and me, Merry is partially right. There's also the online gambling and various lotteries. I know from some investigative digging that they've had to surrender all their credit cards, so at least they can't dig themselves in any deeper while Merry is away.

"I suppose that would make my choice for me if I was on the fence," Merry says. "My small wages can't help with real money trouble. I'll go with you and do my best. And even if I fail, at least I'll have an adventure. I'm way overdue for one of those! I've never even seen the ocean."

"Never?" I ask. It's so hard for me to believe. She lives only six hours from our Topsail Island destination by car and closer to other beaches. I think of all the first-class traveling I have done over the years, accompanying Mr. Pershing throughout the world…it almost makes me feel guilty.

"No, sir," she says.

"If you like the ocean even half as much as your father, you'll be glad you made the trip," I say.

She looks toward the house, and I follow her gaze to see two women peeking out a front window.

"When Amy Jo came in and hugged me, I realized how hard it'd be to tell my mom and grandma that I'll be leaving them for a while. When I went away to college, and mind you, they'd seen that day coming for years ahead of time because Aunt Betty and I had been reminding them, they still acted like it was such a shock to their systems they almost keeled over."

"You can help them save their house if you earn that money, Merry. It's already in foreclosure," I say before I can stop myself. I'm not technically authorized to disclose those kinds of details, and nudging her toward taking the bargain means I'll be stuck with her for perhaps months on end.

She nods thoughtfully. I find it exceedingly strange that she appears to trust everything I say.

Victor often teases me about my innate skepticism; he says I must have had my frown lines since infancy. I honestly don't think Merry and I could be any more different from each other.

"How long will I be gone?" she asks.

"That depends. Maybe a few days if you hate it and give up. Maybe three months if you get through all your tasks. Frankly, I haven't the slightest idea how long this will take," I admit with a sigh.

"Well, I'm going to try my hardest," she says with a stubborn determination that reminds me of her father. "So I better gear up for the long haul. But it'll take me all day just to pack my clothes."

"We're not bringing your clothes," I tell her, looking down briefly at her Dollywood T-shirt. It suggests its inspiration in more ways than one: Merry's accent, her breasts (though thankfully only a fraction of the infamous pair), and her disarmingly easygoing manner are all reminiscent of the iconic country singer.

She looks down, too. "These are my jammies, by the way, so you don't need to be so snooty. I suppose you sleep in a three-piece suit?"

I don't admit to her that I do happen to wear very posh pajamas. Victor got me in the habit by blowing his budget on a sumptuous silk button-front pair a few Christmases ago that he'd seen me admire in a shop window. I have become hopelessly addicted to good loungewear as a result. Last time I visited my favorite store, I almost splurged on a velvet smoking jacket. It was shamefully expensive, but I would've bought it if Victor hadn't balked at the price tag.

I'm afraid that Victor judges me for spending too much because he's never had much at all. He lives in a studio apartment across the street from Claude Pershing's grand house, where I have always resided (and most of my belongings still do), in London.

"You're kidding about me not bringing my clothes along, right?" she asks.

"No, I am most certainly not kidding."

"You expect me to run around naked?"

I suppress a shudder. "No. Your first task is to cooperate through a makeover, all expenses paid. We'll visit shops on the way down to the island in order to get you some new things."

"My clothes aren't fancy enough, I suppose?" she asks.

"Well, we're not going to a fancy place. The island is virtually unpopulated during the off-season. It's cold and wet and quite miserable." I rub my eyes, trying to get the image of the ocean out of my head.

"Why won't my old clothes do, if it's so bad there? I have some pretty things."

I raise my eyebrows to this, which I realize is rude, but I can't help it. Perhaps if she hadn't said *purdy*.

"You're reminding me of the man on TV who teases people about their outfits, the one whose partner has a skunk stripe in her hair. I only saw it once, and I thought I liked it at first, until they made fun of some clothes just like mine," she says.

I take a cleansing breath before replying. "Listen, Merry,

this is the first task of several. It is by far the easiest, as it simply involves shopping for new clothes. If this seems too difficult, we may as well give up right now and save ourselves the frustration of going any further."

"I didn't say I wouldn't do it," she says, a touch petulantly, and I am grateful that I never had a little sister. I watch her face while she seems to consider the matter: it makes a slow and alarming trip from skepticism to jaunty confidence, while mine travels in the opposite direction.

"Alright, I'll go for it," she says. "I'll get some new clothes and shoes, and it'll be fun. I've never had two nickels to spend on clothes, but if it's on my late dad's dime, I'm game. We'll get you some new things, too, Fritz. Something beachy. OK?"

I stare at her a moment. "I also made an appointment for you to get your hair slashed off," I say. "I mean styled."

"You did? Well, hmmm. OK."

"OK?" I expected a fight.

"I'm probably overdue," she says. "But why bother with a makeover if there's no one there to impress?"

"There aren't many people on the island, to be sure, but a tidier look will help you make the best possible impression, which may help you accomplish your other tasks."

She looks down at her scuffed kitchen clogs.

"I have always been a jeans and T-shirts sort of girl. My grandma has worn old-fashioned print dresses ever since I can remember, and my mom does, too. My grandma makes them out of huge reams of fabric. I used to think they were pretty because I heard people complimenting them. I was around ten when I realized that those dresses were just the kind of thing that's hard to ignore, so people can't help saying *something*, and so they give a compliment. That couple on television would laugh hysterically and throw the dresses in a garbage can."

As merely the son of her father's maid, I had nothing but the best of everything throughout my entire life, while Merry grew up never enjoying a single benefit of being his actual child. If the tables were turned, I'd be quite irked, to say the least. I'm glad that Merry will have something nice for a change, though I don't relish the idea of being the one to take her from *before* to *after*.

"I bet you like to shop," she says with a knowing expression.

I blink at her. Merry is an odd combination of implicit trust and spunk, of formal and familiar. I have been discomfited in the past by American women who have tried to kick my ass in litigation and then acted overly playful with me afterward, as if we were puppy littermates who might bite each other's ears one moment and romp happily together the next. She addresses me as *sir*, yet in the short time that I've known her, Merry has already taken the liberty of hitting me and insisting that I *shut up*.

"You think I like to shop because I'm gay?" I ask pointedly.

"No!" She turns a pretty shade of red. "Because you're dressed so nice."

"Oh," I say. "Well, frankly, I do like to shop for myself. But shopping with you isn't my idea of a vacation, Merry. Nor is any other aspect of this project."

"You don't want to be here?" she asks, looking suddenly worried.

"No, I don't," I answer. I feel badly for hurting her feelings and alarming her so early on. But I'm a bit relieved, too, because I want to be as honest as the situation will allow.

Her eyelashes have an auburn tint that I hadn't noticed before. The sunlight filtering into her window makes me wonder how her unruly mop of dirty blond hair would look dyed a sophisticated shade of red. Once it's chopped off, obviously.

I wish Victor were here to help me. He'd enjoy the role of fairy godmother far better than I do. But he'd likely fashion her after his Bandmaidens, with tight black clothes and combat boots, black fingernails, and eyeliner enough for a dozen. Merry will undoubtedly be better off with my more conservative sensibilities.

"You won't quit halfway through, will you?" she asks.

"No. I'll see this project through to the end," I tell her, not only renewing the commitment I made to her father, but also making a new promise to Merry. "Whether I want to or not."

I take my briefcase from the console, remove a few sheets of paper, and hand them to her. "Here is your first official task. You'll see that your father fancied himself to be a bit of a philosopher. I apologize in advance."

Merry takes the papers and reads the following letter:

Hello again, dear Merry.

Forgive me for conducting business before pleasure, but time is (was), as you might imagine, of the essence. Here is your first assignment, which by the way is the only optional task you'll receive, my dear.

Task #1: Let the past fall away in order to fully embrace the next epoch in your life. In other words, get some new clothes and a haircut. Fritz will assist you.

There; now that that's settled, I want to more fully prepare you for your destination. I mentioned in my previous missive that I truly loved the home you may, with hard work and perhaps a bit of luck, inherit. In fact, I mentioned that I actually found it easier to contemplate death while looking out from it upon the sea. I'd like to expound upon that a bit now. Perhaps I can sufficiently explain what I mean; more likely I'll only muddle it. Nevertheless, here I go.

It occurs to me that a city house, even one that has stood for three hundred years, may fall apart or burn to ashes. The entire city that contains the home might be ravaged by bombs and rebuilt again. Certainly an ocean home can be leveled or carried off in a hurricane, and the truth of the matter is that it probably will be at some point in time. But the ocean house isn't the point, really.

It is the ocean itself that calls to me. Of all the wonders, natural or man-made on this earth, the oceans seem to be the most enduring, the least changed by time, the strongest, and the most captivating. Oceans comprise the pulse of the planet, the churning lifeblood. I believe that they are the mirror of our collective souls, the home of mine. As you see, I rather liked it before I died.

I'll digress further to say that my mother (how she complained of her hemorrhoids!) used to tell me tales of heaven. She made me cower with the idea of that unremittingly perfect place, where one would live on and on, forever. And ever, and ever, and ever.

I always felt nauseous at the idea of so much sameness. If I thought of it for too long at a stretch, I would invariably vomit.

My mother said that to get to heaven, I must behave well on Earth. Though I never considered myself truly bad, I admit that goodness wasn't something I pursued very doggedly. Heaven was never the lure to me that Earth was, and I blamed my mother's description of that high holy place for containing altogether too many "and evers."

Then, somehow, as an old dying man coming back to the dune on Topsail Island, where I had built a house long ago, I found myself looking out at the ocean one day. This is what I thought: if I could watch this water, even for that nauseating span of forever, I would never get bored of it. It changes every day, every hour, every second. It grays up and then blues and greens and aquamarines. It reflects the sun or absorbs the clouds; it flattens out, ripples, rolls, or roils mightily. I could watch it forever, and ever, and ever, and ever.

If I could choose my heaven, and if I weren't deemed too earthly a man during my lifetime to gain admittance, you would find me standing on my deck now, a happy shadow, looking out at the water and waiting to finally meet you.

I'm afraid that my ramblings have stolen my energies, Merry, and I must go.

Godspeed on your first task, my dear. Fritz has impeccable taste, so fear not. He has accompanied me on more trips to the haberdashery than I can count, and I believe I have been a better man for it.

Yours sincerely and posthumously,
Claude Pershing

Chapter Four

IN WHICH MERRY SAYS
GOODBYE AND HELLO

As told by Merry Strand (a.k.a. Cinderella)

By the time I finish reading the papers Fritz gave to me, Mom and Grandma have shuffled outside to stare at Fritz's SUV in the driveway.

I wave to reassure them as I climb down from the passenger seat. Looking very relieved to see that it's me, they inch closer, twitching like timid white mice, until they get to the edge of the porch. There they stand so close together they look like a two-headed, four-legged, tent-dressed lady.

The house I grew up in is made of unpainted cedar. It has a green metal roof, which starts out high but angles down sharply to hang low over the porch. I've lived here all my life, so I can't even try to imagine how it all looks to Fritz. I suppose the house seems pretty worn-down when viewed by a stranger who never laid eyes on it before.

But I see the old place as a whole series of memories. Every pine tree, rhododendron, or azalea, as well as every deckboard and windowpane, recalls a story or two. Not just for me: my mom grew up here, and my grandma did, too. So did grandma's mom, my great-grandma, who I only know from faded pictures. This little house has stood for a long, long time, and there has always been a female who stayed on here. Right on down the line. I always thought I'd break the chain, since I'm this generation's only child and I knew I didn't want to stay.

On occasion since I moved back, though, I have had the same unsettling dream. I think I'm waking up as usual, but then I look in the mirror to find that I'm suddenly old and gray, wearing a big cotton dress, and trying to wedge another UPS box into a closet or under a bed. In my dream, I realize that I stayed on here at the house. Not because I meant to, or wanted to, but because I never seized the chance to leave.

Fritz's shoes are sure to be a terrible mess by the time he reaches the path. Every step he takes in the dusty driveway steals a little of the shine away. He tries to pick his route carefully, but it doesn't matter; he can't keep the dust off. It just goes to show that you can't stay perfect around here even if you try. I suppose Fritz wouldn't be so fussy if he had grown up in this house.

My mom and grandma seem to think that Fritz has come here especially to slice them up into tiny pieces. While I'm not in the habit of being wary, my mom and grandma are just about the wariest set of ladies you'll ever see. They seem downright terrified of a stranger appearing out of the blue, even if he did bring me along. I might tease them about their lack of hospitality if I wasn't about to break the news that I'm leaving.

"This is a friend of mine," I call.

I motion for Fritz to follow me into the gate and across the flat front yard. It's knitted in by a split-wood fence, which sort of zigzags along. It used to make me think of skipping, so I'd skip along it, tracing a dirty rectangle path in the sparse grass that's always been too shaded to grow vibrant. I'm told that my grandpa used to keep a beagle out here before I was born, and when I was a kid, our big old dog, Carlton, slept out here on a nice day. The fence stops on either side of the house because that's where the flatness ends. The back yard is open air, the house being perched on the side of the mountain.

Fritz makes an effort to smile at the ladies, and I'm glad for it.

"Mom and Grandma, this is Fritz Forth," I say.

"What'd she say?" Grandma asks Mom.

Grandma has grown hard of hearing. It's gotten so bad recently that they crank their game shows, and my nerves along with them, right up to the brink.

"Francis Ferdinand, did she say?"

"Fritz Forth, ma'am," my mother says. She's got good manners. "His name's Fritz Forth. That's what Merry said."

"Oh, I see. I see. Fritz Forth. But *who* is he?"

"He's a new friend of mine," I tell them, loudly enough for Grandma to hear. "Let's go on inside and I'll explain."

We walk through the doorway in a line: my grandma and mom in their cotton dresses, me in my pajamas, and Fritz in his city clothes and dusty shoes.

As soon as we reach the kitchen, my grandma brightens up. She claps her hands together. "Is he here about a contest?" she asks my mom.

"Y'all aren't trying to sign me up for game shows again, are you?" I ask. They look guiltily at each other.

I shake my head, but try and calm down quickly; I don't want to make a fuss only to turn right around and leave. But, so help me, these ladies have gotten stranger and stranger over the past few years. They've filled every nook and cranny with items from eBay and QVC, making gifts of them to anybody and everybody, without ever even opening the boxes. I suppose I should have asked more questions, but they called it their hobby, and it seemed harmless. They always bragged about the bargains they were getting and made it sound like the packages arrived practically free of charge.

Especially over the recent months, I should have sat them down and had a serious talk. They've become downright fixated on how they can get money—actually not them, but me—by winning this contest or that one. They also scratch off as many lottery tickets as they can get. I thought they were just having some innocent fun, but since Fritz said the house is being foreclosed, I know it's a lot more serious than that.

Since my mom and grandma spend almost all their time together, and I'm not at home much anymore, I suppose they don't get enough reality checks. It might be like twins developing their own language since they're never apart, or Tarzan being raised by gorillas and picking up their habits, or what have you.

These ladies may have created their own fantasy story, based on the hope that some windfall will come along and save their home.

This train of thought makes me very uneasy about leaving them.

When I went away to school, I worried like crazy. Don't get me wrong, my mom and grandma can manage the house chores just fine, and they know where to find Grandpa's old hunting rifle if they need to scare a bear. But they've always been so nervous about anything and everything beyond our little town—I have been their ambassador, messenger, gopher, and adviser on all things relating to the world beyond Peaksy Falls, certainly for the past two years, but before I went away to college, too.

I remember being scared for them the first time I ever left for more than just a sleepover at a friend's house. I was set to attend a two-week summer camp in Asheville that my Aunt Betty had given me as a fourteenth birthday present. I almost backed out, but Aunt Betty convinced me to go. She told me not to worry and promised that she'd watch out for the "old girls," as she always calls them. I remind myself now that she did watch out for them. Then as well as during the four years when I was away at college. I suppose she'll watch out for them this time, too.

"I can explain the situation to your relatives, Merry, while you collect your things," Fritz says, like it'll just be as simple as that. He has his smile back on, but it looks like a mighty big effort to keep it there.

My mom and grandma exchange frightened looks. Grandma wrings her apron.

"Remember not to bother packing clothes," Fritz adds.

My mom puts her hand to her heart like she's about to drop dead.

"I'll explain things, don't worry," I tell my mom and grandma.

I put the teakettle on the stove and take the cookie tin down from the top of the refrigerator. That's the signal for everybody to sit at the table. I remember the cookie tin used to be kept high so that I couldn't reach it, but I don't know why we still put it up there. I suppose it's out of habit, like so much of life around here.

I set some pretty dessert plates and napkins on the table and get the teacups ready. All the while, I'm thinking about what I should say.

Mom and Grandma sit on one side of the table and stare at Fritz without blinking.

He looks at his cell phone. "I've got to make a call, Merry, so I'll step outside. But we shouldn't dally too long."

I give him some cookies and watch him walk out of the kitchen. When I hear the front door shut behind him, I know I have to start talking.

The teakettle whistles before I've thought of anything to say, though.

"Who is that man?" my mom whispers. Then she has to shout it anyway because Grandma didn't hear.

"His name is Fritz, like I said."

"What's he doing here?"

"Well, he came to find me. He told me some really great news. I might actually get a beach house and some money."

"In a contest?" Mom asks.

"No!" I reply. I'm sick of them being so fixated on game shows. "Ma'am," I add quietly.

"How then?" Grandma asks.

I look at the ladies. One, then the other, and back again.

I could tell them everything I know, right now. But they used to get so upset every time I asked about my real parents that eventually I just gave up asking questions. I don't want to worry or upset them and then walk right out the door.

I'm not a natural liar; my ears turn bright red, and I start to stutter something awful.

"I guess you could say that it's s-sort of like a contest," I tell them.

"A game show?" Grandma asks, lighting up like she's had two beers.

"Not exactly…"

The ladies exchange concerned looks.

"What kind of a contest did you enter, Merry?" Mom asks in the tone she usually uses when she wants to say my jeans are too tight or my shirt is cut too low. I believe she'd prefer me wearing cotton dresses that match her and Grandma.

"I didn't enter a c-contest so much as I was picked," I say.

"What do you have to do?" Mom asks, leaning in and smiling brightly.

"Well, I go to this house that I could win, and I l-live there while I complete certain tasks," I say.

"Are you sure it's not on TV?" Grandma asks. She looks very skeptical.

I shake my head a little so that my hair falls over my burning ears.

"P-pretty sure."

"How do you know it's safe, then?" Mom asks.

That's a good question, except the 'then.'

I realize that I don't have any proof that Fritz isn't an axe murderer, but I can't see why he'd make up a complicated story to lure me away from Peaksy Falls, first knowing that I never had a father and everything. It's too strange to be a lie, is what I keep telling myself. Plus, I want the letters Fritz showed me to be real. I want to believe that my own father—a man who wasn't an admiral or a duke or a horse whisperer, but a Londoner who loved the ocean and wished he'd been able to make my acquaintance—wrote them especially for me.

Maybe that shouldn't be enough reason for me to go running off with a stranger. But honestly, I never felt like I had less to lose, and I've never won anything in my whole life.

"Why don't you need clothes?" Grandma asks.

"I get to buy new ones. It's the first task." That part is true.

"Oh!" The women look at each other with raised eyebrows, like it's starting to seem real to them.

"It must be on TV. You had to have misunderstood that part, Merry. They aren't giving you new clothes if you won't be on TV," Mom says. "That wouldn't make any sense at all."

"M-maybe you're right," I say.

"Probably next season, though. They're likely keeping it

hush-hush because this game will be all the rage next season," she adds.

"You said there's a cash prize?" Grandma asks.

"Yes, and a house. But now I'd better get going or I'll miss my chance." I get up from the table and push in my heavy pine chair.

"Can't you tell us more, though? Like exactly what the tasks are…do you have to swallow bugs whole, or answer trivia questions? I hope you don't have to lose weight, because you're already thin," Mom says.

"I don't think I'll have to do any of those things. Fritz hasn't given me many details, but from what he's said, the tasks are more about helping me to improve my life," I say while brushing cookie crumbs from the table into my hand. I drop them in the sink as I pass through the kitchen to the stairway.

"Oh, it's all top secret, I bet," Grandma tells my mom. They both nod thoughtfully. They sip their tea and look at each other. I can see that they're trying to decide whether this is all a very good turn of events or a very dangerous one. I know I'm clear to go, if I hurry, when they start talking about whether Drew Carey or Chris Harrison might host.

I climb the spiral stairs to my loft while they chatter like magpies. I gather a few books, my computer, shampoo and makeup, and some shoes.

Fritz rings the doorbell, but no one answers until I holler down, "Please, for heaven's sake, let the poor man in!"

I look at the duffel bag I packed. I'm sort of amazed to see how few things I want to take with me. Over the rail I see Fritz standing with his hand on his hip, holding a small UPS box I'm sure my mother forced on him as a parting gift. Mom and Grandma seem to be coming off their game show excitement. I can tell from their faces that I'd better hurry if I want to get out of here without a fight.

I bet my mom will call into Aunt Betty's show today for advice. As if Betty ever really helps anybody anyway. I remember thinking that she was wise, but that was a long time ago. Betty's one of those cult personalities who still gets good local ratings, but only because people like to laugh at her. My mom and grandma don't seem to get the joke or know that they're sometimes part of it.

I pick up my bag and hold it over the rail while I climb down the spiral stairway.

My mom bursts into tears when I get to the bottom. My grandma does, too. I drop my duffel and hug each of them tight.

"Imagine her winning the prizes, though, Fanny," Grandma says. They both nod bravely.

"If there are any more of those cookies, Merry, I wouldn't mind a few for the drive. They are insanely good," Fritz says before stepping out the door.

I can't believe I only met him a few hours ago. It seems like my whole life has changed, or is about to. I head back into the kitchen, take down the cookie tin, and wrap a few cookies in a paper towel. My mom and grandma stare after me, hopeful yet worried-looking, like they might have done when I was a newborn baby and they first brought me home.

I wave to them as I climb back into the passenger seat of Fritz's SUV.

My mom puts her hand over her heart, and my grandma wrings her apron.

Fritz turns on the radio after about half an hour of silence. He must've had the same idea as me, because he doesn't seem surprised at all to hear my mom on *The Betty Answers Show*.

"I'm worried sick, Ms. Answers."

"Now here's a perfect example of knowing where you end and others begin, listeners. You may recall that Darla's daughter Gladiola is a grown woman now. If you've been listening long enough, you've witnessed her growth. Now she's a college graduate, isn't she, Darla?"

My mom goes by Darla on Betty's show, and my code name is Gladiola.

"Yes, ma'am, you know she is," my mom says.

"Yet she still lives under your roof, if I remember correctly?"

"Yes, ma'am, you know she does!"

"And she can't even run off for a few hours without having the whole world told about it! Listen, Darla, why don't you let Gladiola have a little adventure?"

"Did I tell you he has an accent? He sounds like Simon Cowell."

Fritz scoffs.

"Well, Darla, maybe this Englishman is like Fred, Mary Poppins's friend. You all remember Fred, don't you listeners? Fun-loving, wise, interesting, played by a young Dick Van Dyke in the film? Well, Darla, perhaps Gladiola and this Englishman have only gone on a jolly holiday. Maybe they're dancing on rooftops."

Aunt Betty laughs a little; it sounds fake to me. My mom doesn't join in.

"Just like I say in my book, POPPINS! Why You Should Never, Ever Explain Anything, *'The road to happiness is self-paved, and the only person one need pay a toll to is oneself.' Remember that, Darla?"*

Fritz shakes his head like he's never heard anything so crazy.

"I remember it, though I'm not rightly sure what it means."

Aunt Betty laughs again, and it sounds even faker.

To me, laughter is like sugar versus artificial sweetener. The real thing is good, pure, and delicious, and anything else just falls short and leaves a bad taste behind.

"Luckily my readers and listeners understand what I mean. Please call in later if Gladiola returns with smudges of chimney smoke on her cheeks!"

"I told you I'm worried, Patience!"

I put my hand over my mouth. I have never heard my mom call Aunt Betty her real name. I'd almost forgotten she was christened as Patience. Once, when I was younger, I found an old box of memorabilia in the attic, with a high school yearbook and academic awards in it. I didn't know who on earth Patience was. Aunt Betty looked as different from her old self as she probably sounded, if she ever sounded anything like me and everybody else around here.

I hope my mom hasn't gotten herself in trouble.

"Listen, Darla, I hear that you're worried, but I am actually in favor of a jolly holiday for Gladiola! Do you agree, listeners? Let's move on to someone else now. Hello caller, are you there?"

I feel bad that Aunt Betty just cut my mom off like that. I think it serves her right when the new caller giggles and says:

"*Good answers Betty has not.*"

"That's a decent Yoda impression," Fritz says.

"Somebody does a better Scooby Doo," I tell him as I switch off the radio.

We've been listening to Fritz's boyfriend's "glamour indie-punk" band, Cryptodynamite, for the past two hours, and my head is pounding something awful.

"Can you please tell me more about the island?" I ask in between songs.

Fritz turns off his iPod and looks over like he forgot I was even here. Maybe he did; he's been singing along with his boyfriend and not paying me any mind at all.

"Let's see. For starters, it's cold this time of year. The wind rarely stops. Sand gets into everything, whether you walk down to the beach or not. There is no more disagreeable feeling in the entire world than sand in your bed, unless it's sand in your teeth. Both occur regularly, no matter how diligently you fight against them." He sighs.

"Isn't the ocean pretty, though?" I ask.

He sniffs. "In bad weather, a filmy haze builds up on every window. All color drains away except the dull blues of the sea and the sky and the gray-gold of the beach. In good weather, the sun is so bright it threatens to blind you. There are no gardens to speak of on the island, no beautiful buildings of any significance whatsoever, and the monotony of the entire existence there is enough to drive an otherwise sane person absolutely imbecilic."

"Are there any restaurants I could work in?" I ask.

"There are greasy pizza places and greasy deep-fried seafood establishments. In terms of real food? I don't believe there is a single good restaurant on the entire island."

"Come on," I say.

"You *come on*," he echoes me, but stretches the words out a country mile.

He does that every once in a while, repeats a word or phrase I just said, but in a very mocking way, like a bratty brother might. I still haven't had the chance to ask if he actually is somebody's brother or any of the other questions I've got waiting.

"Unless you like fried foods and conversing with locals, you must drive into Wilmington for anything even approximating civilization, and that's forty minutes away."

"I should've brought my truck down," I say. "I wish I had thought of it sooner. I guess too much was going on to think of day-to-day details, like what I'll do for work, and how I'll get to and fro."

"You'll have this vehicle at your disposal for getting *to and fro*," he says.

I look at the spotless leather seats and think of my pickup's worn fabric ones. "It's more than I'll need, but I suppose it'll come in handy for getting to work."

"Your work will be your tasks, Merry. You'll have cash at your disposal to get started. Remind me when we stop, and I'll give you some."

"But I like to work. I've always had jobs, ever since I can remember, from babysitting when I was only a kid myself, to working in any restaurant that would have me. I'll get a job and do my tasks, too."

"Before you decide, you should see how busy the tasks will keep you," Fritz says.

"What are they?" I ask.

He suddenly gives all his attention to the road ahead. "I'll give them to you one at a time, like the document states. I already gave you the first one: you're getting made over."

"That first one is optional," I point out. "It said so in my dad's letter."

"You'll still do it, though, correct?"

"Yes, sir. I want the works. But what about the second task? What's that?"

He sighs. I notice he does it a lot. "Please don't be tiresome, Merry. Trust me to follow your father's wishes."

"I'm sorry. I didn't mean to be *tiresome*," I say, clipping through the word like he did. He frowns, and I can tell that I'm getting on his last nerve.

"Let me focus on driving us to our hotel. Tomorrow we'll get you some new clothes and a new look, then we'll drive the rest of the way."

"You mean we're not getting there tonight?"

"Tomorrow will be soon enough," he says.

When I woke up this morning, none of this was even on my radar. My dad was just a wisp of a dream that had been real once, but over time had faded into almost nothing. The ocean seemed so far away, it may as well have been the moon. But now…

Tomorrow doesn't seem nearly soon enough.

I feel out of place in this fancy hotel, too homegrown to blend in. Fritz, on the other hand, marches across the lobby like he owns it. Everybody looks up and falls all over themselves trying to serve him, like he really is in charge just because he acts like it.

I want more than anything to sit down and have a nice long chat with Fritz, without him blaring Cryptodynamite every chance he gets, without him looking at the road instead of me. I'd love to hear about Fritz's family and friends, and all about the beach house, and get some hints about what my tasks will be. Most of all, I want to learn everything I can about my dad.

Fritz acts like he can't get away from me fast enough, though. He hands me my room key. "Right then. See you in the morning."

"Don't you want to have dinner together?" I ask.

"Not particularly."

I suppose it shows that I'm disappointed.

"Please don't pout; it's indulgent and unattractive. I simply need to spend some time on the telephone tonight. My significant other is feeling rather insignificant lately. I'm afraid this assignment of mine was, shall we say, inconvenient for my love life."

"It's too bad he couldn't have come along," I say.

"Victor has his own scheduling constraints."

"His rock band?" I ask.

"Yes," Fritz answers in an annoyed tone, like I said something to offend him again, when again, I sure didn't mean to. "For your information, Victor is a talented musician and so are his Bandmaidens. They'll likely never achieve fame or make their fortunes, but they're doing what they love every day. At least he didn't throw away a business degree to cook in a restaurant, like you, or dedicate his law career to the whims of a selfish old man, like me. Not only is it impossible for Victor to be here, he doesn't forgive the fact that I am."

"I'm sorry," I say.

Fritz rubs his eyes like his head is about to explode.

"It's not your fault. Bill dinner on your room; the restaurant here is lovely," he says, glancing up and motioning toward my clothes. "You should order room service."

I meant to change before we started our drive, but I forgot. I feel my face turn red.

"Tomorrow we'll get you some things that will be appropriate in any setting. One day you may look back on your Dollywood era and laugh. I know I will."

"I like Dollywood," I say.

"That doesn't mean you have to wear the T-shirt. You don't see me wearing a Cryptodynamite T-shirt, and I've been in love with their lead singer for five years."

"Do you go to their concerts wearing that kind of thing?" I suppose I'm sick of him criticizing me and want to show him how it feels. I thought he'd have a better sense of humor about it.

"Meet me here in the lobby at eight tomorrow morning, and we'll continue on this delightful journey."

Fritz and I are back on the road. He looks so tired, I wonder if he slept at all.

"Tell me about your family," I say. I know that people usually like to talk about their loved ones, and I'm curious as all get-out.

"I have none," he says.

"Really?" I ask.

"Oh no, that's right, I do have a right jolly, happy family. I simply pretend that I don't, for fun, you see. I make believe that my father died before I formed any memory of him. And that my mother died last year. And that I never had any cousins, aunts, uncles, or siblings. It's a laugh a minute."

"Remember, I have a very small family, too," I say.

He doesn't answer.

After a while, I try again. "How is Victor?" I ask.

More silence. From Fritz's frown, it's clear that their talk didn't go well last night. He waves my question away like a pesky fly.

"I feel bad, because you're here on account of me, and it's causing you trouble," I say.

Fritz sighs heavily. "I had trouble before I met you, Merry, and I'll have trouble when I'm back in London. Not everything is about you."

"Victor probably just misses you like crazy," I say, ignoring his bratty comment along with his bad attitude.

"Are you seriously going to give me relationship advice? Victor isn't a Neanderthal like Phil."

Well, so much for friendly conversation! I wish Fritz would have left Phil out of it. When I checked my messages last night, my whole mailbox was full of his voice. He started by saying he was sorry for being a jerk yesterday morning. Then he branched out and was sorry for being a jerk back in high school and all the time in between that he'd been jerky. After that, he got extremely weird and said he wants to marry me.

You could've knocked me over with a feather. We'd never even joked about marriage before!

Fritz hasn't said a word to me for hours, not since his mean comment about Phil. I hate riding along in silence, but I'm too anxious to be on Fritz's good side to complain. Especially when he parks outside a cluster of boutiques.

"Are you still planning to help me?" I ask. I'd rather kill a kitchen mouse than put together an outfit in front of Fritz.

"I've seen where your fashion inclinations have led you. So yes, I am indeed going to help."

I laugh a little. It was an insult, I know, but this time he didn't say it mean. Plus, I know I'm a fashion disaster, and I can admit the truth just fine.

Fritz waves away the very thin, very elegant lady who rushes forward to help us in the first store. "I have everything under control," he says. She nods and goes back to her paperwork.

Fritz is a whirlwind shopper. He goes around the boutique, picks up items, and hangs them on the rack beside a hot pink wing chair outside the dressing room. When he's finished gathering everything he wants, he stands in front of the rack and groups items together for me to try on.

"Green tea?" he asks the clerk, who trips over her feet to get it for him. He sits in the pink velvet chair and motions for me to go change.

"Don't look at the price tags!" he warns after I catch my breath loudly in the zebra-striped dressing room.

"OK," I say, but Jesus Jenny! I didn't know a pair of jeans could cost so much.

It takes three stores and way more misses than hits before we get everything Fritz says I'll need. He has me leave on the last outfit I try. The clerk cuts the tags off me.

"Throw away the clothes she wore in," Fritz tells her. "Or donate them, if anybody's that desperate."

When he's not looking, I sneak my Dollywood shirt into one of my shopping bags.

I go over to a big floor mirror while Fritz pays the bill. I like my dark-wash jeans, stylish leather ballet flats, flouncy cotton blouse, lightweight cardigan sweater, and the bright silk scarf around my neck.

"I would never have chosen anything like this for myself," I tell Fritz when he comes up behind me.

"You didn't even look like a girl before. You wore T-shirts and jeans that were cut for a man three times your size." He turns me to the side. "You actually have a cute little body, Merry. Let's just pray that Helena can work a miracle on that hair."

What girl hasn't imagined starring in a real-life Cinderella story?

Fritz discussed me with Helena when we got to the salon after a quick lunch stop. Their ideas sounded pretty radical, but I was game. I pretended to be unsure so that I could have a little leverage with Fritz. In exchange for me getting the haircut he wanted, he had to buy an outfit he could wear walking the beach—even though he said he's never gonna wear it.

Now a brand-new person looks back at me from the salon mirror. My former long, wavy hair has been shorn, and I've got a pixie cut dyed darker than even the darkest shades in my old hair, which held every color I ever had—from baby blond, to college apartment well-water brassy, to I'm-getting-older mousy yuck—because it had been with me for so long.

My new color is snazzy; everyone in the salon is raving about it. It's brownish reddish blond. It was picked to bring out my blue eyes, which have also been helped along by new makeup. I swear if I didn't know it was me in the mirror, well, I wouldn't know.

My head feels so light!

Fritz walks through the door and comes up behind me in the mirror. He pretends he doesn't know who I am.

"Pardon me, stylish lady," he says. "I'm looking for a frumpy mountain girl with twenty pounds of dull, straw-like hair, who has apparently never heard of tweezers. Have you seen her?"

We share a smile in the mirror.

"Y'all are such a flatterer," I say.

I drank two glasses of wine during the three hours it took to get my hair cut and colored and my makeup and nails done. That's probably why I turn and throw my arms around Fritz.

"Thank you!" I shout.

He squirms away.

"See my nails?" They're dark blue. I hold my hands out for Fritz.

"Hmm," he says, and what with his frown lines and tired eyes and all, I swear he looks like he could be 100 years old for a minute. He shakes his head like he plum gives up. "Well, Victor would like them."

"I'd love to meet him," I say. I never met a glam rock-and-roll guy before. It's hard for me to picture someone like that with fussy Fritz.

"Maybe you will. He lives across the street from your father's house in London."

"Is it still his house?" I ask. "With him passed on and all?"

"Yes, it's still his. I actually don't know what will happen to it. Those papers haven't been made available to me yet, which is inconvenient." Fritz rubs his eyes again.

"Why?" I ask.

"Because until I came here, I lived there, too."

"You lived with my dad?"

"Indeed."

"For how long?"

"Ever since I can remember," he says.

"Wow." I shake my head in wonder. "What was it like?"

I meant what was it like living with my dad, but Fritz must've thought I was asking about the house. He misunderstands me so often that I'm beginning to think he does it on purpose.

"It's really a gorgeous place," he says. "I suppose it'll be sold off, with the proceeds going to Mr. Pershing's pet charities." He sighs heavily.

"I want to hear all about him," I say.

"There'll be time for stories later. Now we have to get back on the road; if you're ready to see your father's favorite place in the world, that is."

Thirty minutes later, we have to stop and wait for the swing bridge to turn before we can drive onto the island. Fritz is impatient. I know, big shocker, right? He doesn't like to wait for the boats to pass by before the bridge can swing back and we can cross over it. I don't mind waiting, not at all. I'm glad for the chance to sit here an extra few minutes and take in the scenes.

"Can you shut the window?" Fritz asks. "It smells like fish."

I notice a fish smell, too, but it smells fresh, and it takes a backseat to the wonderful salty smell of the ocean. There's a seafood market to our left. I can't wait to go in and see what I can get.

"Don't you like fish?" I ask.

"To eat, yes. To breathe, no."

"You won't believe my bouillabaisse. Especially with all the kinds of fresh seafood I'll be able to get here...oh my. Can we stop now?"

"No. You can come back without me; I'm not the fish market type. And you said, only fifty or sixty times so far, that you want to see the ocean before the sun sets. We'll be cutting it close as it is. Please shut the window; it's too cold, and you're messing up your hair."

My goodness, he's a grumbler. I see myself in the side mirror, and I know he's lying about my hair. It's like it was cut just for this wind! I roll up the window for Fritz, though, so he doesn't grouch at me again. Or sigh.

As we cross over the swing bridge, I crane my head around to look both ways, up and down the intracoastal waterway. It's like a wide, calm river in some fairytale land, with green, odd-shaped islands popping up in the deep blue water. The sun, fixing to set, shines on everything, like there's a fun-loving wizard in the sky changing things from pink to orange and back again. Any seabird that happens to fly under his wand glows dazzling white—like a falling star, or a wish, or a blessing.

The wine still makes my head seem overly light, along with my crazy-short hair that I can't help but touch every few seconds or so.

I have never seen houses like the ones on the island. They're all built so high. Some of them show exposed stilts, some cover them up with garages, like modest ladies in long skirts. The houses are all sorts of faded colors: beige, sea foam green, pale yellow, soft white. Most are tall, windowed rectangles, three stories high. A few are shorter and look older, more weathered.

The street runs down somewhere near the middle of the narrow island, like it was drawn by a child's crayon, and she didn't keep it exactly straight, but pretty good, with the ocean on one side and the intracoastal on the other.

On the intracoastal side, I catch glimpses of the green fairytale islands, now in deepening shades of sunset colors, like the wizard is getting tired of his game and is nearly ready to call it a night. On the ocean side, the houses form a more solid wall and are harder to see past. I watch closely for a view of the ocean. We pass a stretch of land where no houses are built on the ocean side because the road was drawn too close, and for a fleeting second, I see it!

I catch my breath.

Fritz points up ahead. He slows down and pushes a button on his keychain, which makes the garage door open on a very tall and beautiful green house with white trim. We pull in.

"We'll worry about bags later," Fritz says. "A more pressing point is the sun, which is about to disappear. I'll show you to the deck, where you can see the ocean properly."

He unlocks the glass door from the garage into the house and leads me up four half flights of stairs to the top. The stairs end on the level where the kitchen and living rooms are located. They're big, pretty rooms, but I don't really take them in because my eyes are drawn to the view beyond the windows.

Have you ever built something up in your mind until it became a hundred times bigger and better than it actually was? Like when you were a little kid, did you ever see a certain park or building or waterfall, and it just seemed so gigantic that it nearly boggled your mind? And when you thought about it later, you just shook your head in wonder?

It used to happen to me. But when I've seen those same things again as a grown-up, I've had to laugh and say: *That? That's what I thought was larger than life?*

I suppose I'd been a little worried that the same thing would happen when I saw the ocean. Although I'd never seen it in person, I'd studied pictures, and glued myself to the television during sea-centered nature shows, and dreamed about it enough so that I could have sworn that I'd actually been there before. On the drive out, I wondered if maybe I'd built it up too much.

Well, let's just say I shouldn't have worried.

Oh my *Lord*.

Fritz opens the patio door to the deck, and I feel a rush of cool air. I follow right away, skipping fast across the big room. It feels wide open when I step outside. There are no trees overhead, just endless sky.

The prettiest shade of pink catches on the rolling whitecaps and crowns them like jeweled tiaras over the mild blue color of the water, which is already fading away into darkness, becoming harder to see. I hate to have it happen—I want to keep watching!

Fritz points to the intracoastal side of the island, visible through a vacant lot beside us. We watch the orange/red sun sink down, and I want to cry at the beauty of it, or laugh. Or both at once.

On the far side of the wide deck that spans the entire house, I hear a noise that isn't part of the roaring ocean. It sounds like a man chuckling—a pure sugar laugh, not aspartame. I turn toward it and can't make out anything but some outdoor furniture in the fading light.

I figure that I must have imagined the laughter. Fritz would have told me if someone else was here. But then I make out the silhouette of a man standing at the rail.

"So there you are, Merry."

I put my hand to my heart, and if not for Fritz's arm going around my waist and steadying me, I'm sure I would fall over.

The lines from the letter I read yesterday morning play in my mind, in the voice of the old man I just heard, or maybe only imagined:

If I could choose my heaven…you would find me standing on my deck now, a happy shadow, looking out at the water and waiting to finally meet you.

Chapter Five

IN WHICH JACK IS
DISTURBED AT DAWN

As told by a shivering Mr. Morningstar

Awakened by the sound of a telephone ringing, I stumble into the kitchen and answer it.

"Jack? Hey buddy."

It's my father on the line. He's been calling me "buddy" since Katie's accident, like I'm six years old again. I squint out the window and discover that it's dawn.

"You woke me up. Is something wrong?"

"Not anymore. It's so good to hear your voice. It's been awhile, hasn't it? It's really good to hear you, to know that you're right there on the other end of the line."

My father, a PhD psychologist, has had a private therapy practice since before I was born. Friends of mine always thought he wasn't necessarily cool, but pretty cool for someone's dad, until they found out what he did for a living. Then they were very guarded around him, apparently under the impression that he could find out anything they were thinking, or what they'd been doing, just by having a casual conversation about English Lit or basketball. Martin was my only friend who wasn't discomfited by my dad. I thought it was because Martin didn't have anything to hide.

"Did you need something specific? Or did you just want to wake me up and hear me?" I ask. I'm standing barefoot in my boxers, shivering.

"Your mother and I would really like to come see you, buddy," he says.

Dad mentions this fact constantly—in e-mails and voicemails and, in this case, live on the phone since he caught me so off guard that I answered.

I can't agree to a visit, which would just be an excuse for him to lecture me, or try some quack new therapy he read about, or devised himself, that he's sure will shock me out of my gloom. He has always been game to try new approaches when his tool kit doesn't seem to have just the right wrench.

My eyes have adjusted enough to see the squalor I'm living in. This house is beautiful, but you'd never know it if you walked in now. Before I married Katie, I had someone come in to clean twice a week, to make sure rats didn't invade my apartment. My only saving grace against infestation now is that I don't cook. I live off power bars, chips, coffee, and soda, so at least I don't have food rotting in pans all over the kitchen.

There's dog hair and dust everywhere, though. And enough sand to fill a sandbox, if someone swept it all up. I'm sure it smells terrible. It's not the main reason I won't let them visit, but it's on the list.

"We want to bring Marty down. You two need to talk," he says.

My dad has always spoken at interminable length of our *family interconnectedness—how we count on each other, and depend on each other for support, for encouragement, for the steadying ballast that keeps us all on course.* He actually says shit like that.

"Not happening, Dad."

"I know you're going through tough times, son. But Marty is, too. He fears that you hate him, and he's also been traumatized by the accident."

I know my dad thinks that I want him and Mom to sever ties with Martin, their close-second son, who they all but adopted because we were inseparable friends. I've told him it's not true—that as far as I'm concerned, they can all keep each other. I just need them to let me go. I refuse to be part of their dysfunctional family unit anymore.

"I do hate him," I say.

"I know you don't mean that, buddy."

"Nice talking to you, Dad." I hang up the phone.

I'd challenge anyone who thinks I'm a jerk for cutting off my dad to sit through one of his lectures. They loop and repeat, so if you happen to miss something, you don't have to worry because it's coming back around again.

Since I'm up, I open the folder of design documents for the Langdon Logistics project that Varun and Sam sent for my review. I try to focus on it. I know I need to. But I find myself rereading the executive overview for a third time and still not absorbing it. My dad keeps intruding.

I am well aware of what he would've said on the phone if I had given him the chance. He has said it all before.

He'd say that Katie is gone. As if I didn't know that, as if every time I wake up, I don't spend my first sentient moments reestablishing that truth in my mind. A fact being obvious doesn't stop my dad from stating it, though.

He'd say that Katie is gone.

He'd say that sequestering myself hundreds of miles away from everyone I love, trying to commune with my wife's memory, is indulgent and defeatist. He'd say that life is for the living. He'd say that he and Mom are here, and that they love me so much it kills them to see me suffer alone.

He'd say that Martin is here and needs my support and forgiveness to get through these dark days. He'd say I'm the only one who can really help Martin understand that it's OK to be alive, even after such a terrible tragedy.

My dad would actually think he was helping me while he tore open the tremulous scab I've formed over the gaping hole in my heart. He'd think he was fixing my problems while instead he was opening me up to a tidal wave of pain and fury that might drown me for good. He would say the very last words that I want to hear.

He'd say that Martin loved her, too.

Chapter Six

IN WHICH MERRY TWIRLS
IN THE MOONLIGHT

As told by the newly renovated Ms. Strand
(a.k.a. Dorothy)

I'm not squeamish, but I tell you what: I nearly faint when I see that ghost standing at the deck rail. Lucky for me, my grumpy genie is there to catch my arm and hold me steady.

"You're still here?" Fritz asks, which means he sees someone there, too. Thank goodness. I'd sure hate to lose my marbles just when life got interesting.

"Hiya Merry, I'm Max," the ghost says. But when he steps out from the shadows into the moonlight, I see that he's actually a live old man. He kisses my hand like we're both royalty.

Fritz sighs—maybe his heaviest one yet. "This is Mr. Pershing, Merry. He's called Max. You read about him yesterday in your father's papers. I believe he was referred to as a 'curmudgeonly old bastard.'"

It dawns on me—Max is my dad's brother, the one who will get the beach house if I don't. I think it's pretty rude of Fritz to tell Max what his brother called him, but I suppose that's Fritz for ya.

"Yes," Fritz says, more to the old man than to me. "This is Max the black sheep, who has unceremoniously descended upon us here. Though it complicates matters considerably, it looks as if he means to stay awhile."

When Phil gets mad at his mom, or one of the busboys or waitresses, he does this type of thing. He explains to me, in front of them, what they did wrong instead of just telling them directly. I hate it when he does that.

"Thank you for such a fine introduction, you pompous little ass," Max tells Fritz under his breath. Turning his back on him, he takes my hand again. He comes closer, until I can see his face in the light coming from inside the house. "How are you, dear?"

Oh, he's perfect! He's got twinkling blue eyes and white hair. He's the very picture of a kindly grandpa. Or I suppose, in this case, old uncle.

"So *you* are Claude's daughter?" he asks.

"Yes, sir. That's what Fritz here says," I reply.

He smiles and squeezes my hand tighter. "You look so very stylish; you're quite a fashion plate! I'm afraid Fritz had rather prepared me for a barefoot, backwoods, illiterate girl. I wasn't expecting a sophisticated young lady like you."

"Don't listen to the old fool," Fritz says. He turns to Max. "If you remember correctly, I prepared you to *leave*."

Max ignores him. "I understand that, with Fritz's help, you're trying to steal away my beach house?" he asks me. "I felt as if I should stay around and protect my interests. You don't mind, do you dear?" He laughs quietly, but it soon turns into a coughing fit.

Fritz looks at him with that frown I'm already used to because he puts it on so often. This morning I thought he looked tired, but now he looks downright exhausted. Sure, he's still dressed to the nines, and from far away he probably looks like the handsome young man that he is. But the closer you get, the more Fritz appears to be carrying the weight of the world on his shoulders.

"Have you gotten much rest today?" he asks Max.

Max shakes his head and waves him off. "You're so very solicitous. My brother must have been a helpless old coot at the end if he needed constant reminders to rest and whatnot."

"Claude Pershing was unwaveringly generous to me throughout my entire life. I felt it was not only my duty, but my pleasure, to help him in any way I could," Fritz offers his arm to Max, who looks weaker and smaller after his coughing episode.

Max accepts Fritz's help to get inside. "Well, I did rest quite a while. I think the sea air does me good."

Fritz turns on a lamp, creating a little golden pool of light. He delivers Max to a seat in the center of it. "Here you are: the shabby chair you've adopted."

"A bit like my brother, am I? Adopting shabby things."

"If you're referring to me, I was never adopted," Fritz says. He points to the side table. "I see that you have a very full ashtray here, which proves that instead of resting, or leaving as you were supposed to do, you sat and smoked like a stubborn chimney for the past two days."

"Henpecker," Max says under his breath. His frown looks like a deeper, more practiced version of Fritz's.

"Merry, here's a matching chair to your relative. You two can sit in this horrible conversation area and get acquainted."

"It's not horrible," I say. "It's so pretty here!" It really is such a nice, big room. I still hear the ocean, even with the door closed. If Fritz doesn't even like this place, I can't imagine what would ever be good enough for him.

"Everything's always *so purdy*," he mocks.

Max reaches over and pats my arm. "It's a bit faded here and there, and scratched, and so forth. You don't have to pretend it isn't, Merry. Claude knew it wasn't perfect. It made a lot of people happy, though, lots of families. It was used as a vacation rental during his long absences."

"A few scratches don't worry me," I say. "I'm not used to anything fancy. Besides, the ocean is right out there."

Max smiles. "Here, here. Could you pour me a whiskey, dear? The bottle's on the counter."

Fritz shakes his head. "Why don't you skip the whiskey tonight? You look pale."

Max's hand shakes as he lights another cigarette. "No ice, Merry. I like it neat," he says.

"Have you eaten anything?" Fritz asks him.

"Look how familiar you are! It's as if you're transferring all your overzealous ministrations for my brother right over to me. How charming a bullying nag you are, Fritz. What a lovely stay we'll all have here together…"

"Did you eat?" Fritz repeats.

Max acts like he didn't hear.

Fritz marches into the kitchen, where I'm fetching Max his drink; it's open to the living room. He takes a casserole dish out of the fridge, opens the cover, and puts it down hard on the counter.

"I wasn't hungry," Max mumbles.

"Are you hungry now?" I ask brightly. The mood in here is so darn tense! I want to lighten it up.

Max shoots me a skeptical glance. "I don't think there's anything in the house worth eating."

"Let me see about that," I say.

I skip over to bring Max his whiskey and head right back to the kitchen. The appliances are new, the countertops are wide and long, and there's plenty of lighting. Patio doors must show views of the intracoastal waterway side of the island during daylight. And on the other side of the house, past the big sitting area with the furniture Fritz thinks is so ugly, patio doors open to the oceanfront deck. I love this kitchen!

I take an inventory of the cupboards, the spice rack, and the fridge. I come up with only one meal that wouldn't need a supply trip first.

"I can make you an omelet, Max. First thing tomorrow I'll go shopping, and then I'll be able to make anything you like."

Fritz sniffs. "You overestimate our local grocery store," he says.

I smile even brighter. I have to really turn up the wattage to cut through his gloom. "You underestimate me," I reply.

Max laughs. "I like that. Spunky."

"Can I make you one, too?" I ask Fritz.

"No. I'm going down for the bags," he says, in a sort of kick-the-floor boyish way that makes him seem about nine years old for a second. I wonder if he was always so serious or if that came later. I still can't imagine him dating a glam rocker!

"I'll help," I offer.

"No. You stay here and wait on your relative. If he extends the same delicate treatment to you that I've been getting, you'll be thanked with repeated insults."

When Fritz is halfway down the stairs, Max calls after him: "Henpecker!"

Max eats his omelet like it's his first meal in months. I watch him the whole time. I want to ask so many questions about my dad. I want to hear how they spent their childhoods, if they went to fishing holes the way boys do in Peaksy Falls, or if maybe they sailed model boats in London parks like I've seen in movies.

The way Max shovels his food doesn't leave much chance for talking, though. And once he's done eating and drinking his second whiskey, he's sleepy.

"That was delicious, Merry," he says around a yawn while I clear his plate. "If you weren't trying to steal my inheritance, I think we'd be good friends."

I can't help myself: I kiss him on the top of his white cotton candy head. He doesn't seem to mind. He reaches up and pats my arm.

"Better friends than you and my dad were, sir?" I ask.

"What a question!" he says.

"I'm sorry if it's impolite to ask questions, because I have a whole mess of them."

"Right. Well. It's a long and complicated story, my dear, and I'm a tired old man who is in need of a rest. Maybe we can take it up another day?"

"OK," I say, trying not to show my disappointment.

"You must think that my brother was quite strange to arrange for you to come here?" he asks.

"I'm glad to be here, and meet you, and stay in this wonderful house. I'm just sad that I didn't get the chance to meet him—I wanted to, my whole life."

A sniff at the top of the stairs makes us turn our heads to see Fritz standing there, frowning as usual.

"Here's some company for you, Merry," Max says, yawning again. "You young people can stay up and chatter if you like. I must retire, though. I'm overdue."

Fritz gives Max his cold medicine and then excuses himself to go back down to his room, making it clear that he's no more interested in chattering with me than he was last night.

I busy myself by washing the dishes, but I can't stop there. The whole kitchen needs a good going-over! I pause often, as I scrub and mop, to make an arm-long list of things I'll need to buy.

When I finally finish scouring and scribbling, I'm still too wound up to even think about going to bed. So much has happened in such a short time! Plus, the ocean is calling to me. It's muffled on account of the closed doors and windows, but I can still hear it well enough to know it's out there.

When I can't resist a second longer, I open the door and feel the rush.

It's chilly now, but I'm used to cool mountain nights. The wind is strong; it whirls around me, and I feel something like I used to feel when the fireflies were out in numbers, like I'm invited outside to be part of the night.

Though it's dark, I'm not scared. There aren't any bears around here, I'm guessing, and if there were, I'd see them fine because there are no trees to hide behind. The houses are all perched high on their dunes like quiet watchtowers, and down below there's only sand and water. The moon makes a shining path on the sea and a narrow slice of beach. It's like a beacon, or a path. Or a yellow brick road that you can't take very far, only to the water's edge. But that's OK. Dorothy's path wasn't even real at all—it was only a dream—and she still learned a lot by following it.

Though it's chilly, I want to feel the sand and water on my toes. I walk down the wooden steps, all the way down, until I'm level with the water.

The sand is very cold, but soft. I walk through it toward the water until I feel it wash over my feet.

I laugh out loud; I can't help it.

I go to the edge of where the moonlight shines like gold on the sand. I smile because it points toward my father's house, the place he loved best in the world. Dorothy's path ultimately led her home. I love that story.

I step into the moonlight spotlight. I twirl in circles, like I'm a little girl again. Like life is just starting for me.

I think I might be able to describe this house better than my mountain home. Since I'm new here, I haven't put too many of my own feelings and memories in it yet.

I have three rooms, and they go from the front of the house to the back. One room is on the street side; it has white bunk beds, bright linens, and an assortment of toys and games which must come in real handy when families rent the house. There are patio doors to a covered deck overlooking the intracoastal waterway. Pocket doors lead to a full bathroom, which also opens up to an oceanfront bedroom with a queen-sized bed, where I plan to sleep.

I'm tickled about how much space and privacy I'll have while I'm here. I don't know how long that'll be...I've got a thousand questions lining up, just waiting their turns.

There's a knock at my door. I open it to see Fritz wearing fancy pajamas.

"Were you actually outside? In the dark?" he asks.

"Yes, sir." I can't help laughing. It was such a wild rush to be out there. I still feel pink and windblown. "It was so pretty! Want to go out? I'll go again."

He doesn't have to say no; his frown leaves no question about it.

"I brought up your bags and put away your new clothes," he says, crossing the room and opening the closet door. "You'll see everything is arranged by clothing type. Please take note of how I hung up the various articles. And for God's sake, read the tags before you toss things into the laundry willy-nilly. The same goes for the things in the drawers."

"Yes, sir," I say. The bag I packed from home is still full, leaned up against the wall like a homely girl, watching everybody else dance at a cotillion.

"Did the cosmetologist teach you to apply your own makeup?" he asks. His arms are folded, and he looks like he doesn't trust me to do anything right, not a single thing. "What about your hair? Do you know how to style it?"

I sit on the edge of the bed feeling like the wind's been knocked out of me, along with the confidence boost I'd had from getting all gussied up, meeting my surprise uncle, and finally feeling the ocean breeze blow through my hair. It's like I was brought high only to be knocked low again.

My shoulders sag; I'm worried that I'll end up ruining all my new clothes, doing my face wrong, and my hair, not to mention all the tasks he's going to give me. He'll send me home without anything; maybe I won't even be able to keep my new outfits. And when I get back to Peaksy Falls, Phil will forget his apologies and lock me out of the Mountainside, and me and my mom and grandma will be homeless.

Fritz is staring at me like I'm already a big disappointment, when I haven't even gotten a chance to prove myself yet. I feel like Dorothy must have felt when she finally got to Oz and found that the wizard she thought would help her was only a man after all.

It's like I'd been riding high up on one of the waves I glimpsed at sunset, and now I've just plumb crashed. But I make myself stand anyway and try to raise my spirits as part of the motion. "Yes, sir. They taught me," I say.

Fritz unfolds his arms and sighs. I know he doesn't want to be here, so none of this is fun for him. He's not riding up on any waves; he's just in a permanent crash.

"Did you notice the house next door?" he asks.

"The one that was lit up?"

Fritz nods. "There is a man staying there whom your father liked."

"Didn't he like all his neighbors?"

"No," Fritz says, like he could say a whole lot more on the subject if he had the time or inclination. "The people your father liked, he truly adored. I'm afraid everyone else escaped his notice."

"Oh," I say. I wanted to think of my dad as a neighborly person. I wanted to think he was a nice guy.

"Mr. Pershing wasn't often here," Fritz says. "This house was mostly a summer rental, which is true for many of the houses along the ocean. The man staying next door doesn't live there permanently."

"When did my dad meet him then?"

"Last summer, after he was diagnosed with cancer, your father wanted to come and stay here, and I came along to help him. The man next door was vacationing at the same time with his wife."

"So you all became friends?" I ask. I sit on the edge of the bed and pat the next spot over for Fritz to sit, too, but he keeps standing.

"Jack—that's the man's name—and your father got on quite well. They spent hours sitting in the sunshine talking," Fritz says, frowning a little.

"And y'all like to sit in the shade?" I ask.

"Indeed. I got to know Jack a bit, though. He and his wife were a lovely couple."

"That's nice," I say, wondering if anyone thinks of Phil and me as a lovely couple. "Maybe we can have them over here. I like the idea of making some new friends right away. I know *everybody* in Peaksy Falls."

"I spoke to Jack when I saw that he was back at the house," Fritz says. "He told me that his wife had died in a car accident."

"My goodness." I shiver. An image of Phil holding a casserole pops into my head. The idea of him being dead, and me knowing I'd never see him again, or never taste even one more bite of his cooking? Ever again? Well, I feel awful for the man next door, who made one half of a 'lovely couple' and is now alone.

"Jack had been so vibrant last summer…" Fritz shakes his head. "It was depressing to see him so altered. I knew your father would be affected by it."

"But by then he'd passed on, right?" I ask. I'm not clear on the whens of all this—they're on my list of questions.

"Right. Your father and Jack had enjoyed each other's company. They whiled away hours upon hours discussing politics, and sports, and several other subjects that I found exceedingly boring. Your father genuinely liked Jack, and he didn't necessarily get on with everyone he met."

"I suppose not," I say, "Especially if he couldn't even be friendly with his own brother. Max seems like a teddy bear to me."

Fritz sniffs. "By the way, your aunt called."

"She called you?" I ask. "Why didn't she call me?"

"She did. She said your voicemail was full."

"Oh." Likely more messages from Phil. "How'd she get your number?" I ask.

"I left it with your mother, as a backup way to reach you, in case there was an emergency."

"Was there an emergency?" I ask, thinking of the wary ladies all alone.

"No, no. She simply asked for you to call her." With his eyebrows raised, he adds, *"At home."*

As I finish unpacking my bag from Peaksy Falls, I notice that my new bed looks like it'll be mighty comfortable. I yawn wide and long and discover that the bed is as cozy as it looks. I stretch out, kick my feet around a bit, and make myself at home.

I turn on my phone and listen to my new messages first. They're all from Phil. In one, he describes a new soup, and I can almost taste the ginger. It's hardest to stay mad at Phil when he's in a sweet mood, calm and tender. He gets that way when he brings things to a simmer or when he bakes. I could live for a year exclusively on his bisque. And, I tell you what, Phil can be downright irresistible with a cheesecake in his hands.

I dial Aunt Betty at home.

"Hello?" she answers right away, like she'd been holding the telephone ready to push the green button.

"This is Merry," I say.

She pauses for a long time. I picture her sitting in her sterile townhouse. She has it painted white every few years. It never needs it, as far as I can see, but it must make her feel better somehow because she keeps bothering to have it done. She is likely sitting in her white leather rocking chair. Aunt Betty only has one comfortable chair in her living room, and that's where she always sits. The other seats are hard as planks. I don't think she wants anyone there but her.

"Yes. Well, I spoke to a young man earlier who was quite rude to me."

"That'll be Fritz," I say. "Sorry he was rude, ma'am. I don't think he really means it."

"Who on earth is he, Merry?"

I don't want to get into the particulars with Aunt Betty. I'm pretty sure she wouldn't buy the game show explanation; she's more streetwise than Mom and Grandma, and it'd be pretty hard to hide my lying stutters over the phone. Plus, I'm bone-tired. "I can't really explain now, ma'am. How are Mom and Grandma? Are they well?"

"Of course they are. I'm watching out for them."

She sounds like she's half-focused on something else. That's how she usually is, even in person.

I cover the phone while I yawn big. I rest my free ear on a soft pillow. "Well, thanks for taking care of Mom and Grandma while I'm away. Tell them I'll send some goodies soon."

My grandma's hearing is so bad that talking on the telephone with her is like a Laurel and Hardy skit. My mom isn't fond of phones either, except when she calls into Aunt Betty's show. When I was away at college, we communicated the old-fashioned way: letters and boxes of cookies shipped through the mail.

Aunt Betty doesn't answer. I wonder if she's still there. Sometimes she'll hang up on callers to her show, but usually only when they insult her, like the boys who do impressions.

"Exactly where are you, Merry? And exactly what are you doing?" she asks, just when I thought she was gone.

Two 'exactly' questions in a row from Aunt Betty? The words I've heard her say to callers at least a hundred times come into my mind and right out of my mouth: "I don't have to explain anything."

A few silent seconds pass.

"Ma'am," I add.

She laughs. It sounds like saccharine and aspartame.

"No, of course you don't," she says. "But the old girls are worried, and your friends will wonder where you've gone. I hoped you would tell me what's going on so that I can reassure them."

"I'm fine, Aunt Betty," I say over the biggest yawn yet. "I'm going to go now because I'm mighty tired. Just tell anybody who asks that I had an opportunity I couldn't pass up."

"Can you at least tell me where you are?" she asks.

I stretch out my legs and pull the comforter higher. I'm anxious to hang up the phone so that I can hear the sound of the ocean better, so that it can sing me a lullaby as I shut my eyes on the longest and most eventful day I've ever had.

"I'm exactly where I need to be right now," I say.

And somehow, in my heart, I know that it's true.

Chapter Seven

IN WHICH MR. MORNINGSTAR TRIES TO BE A GOOD BOSS

As told by Jack, from the edge of the world

During my months spent staring at the endless ocean, I have rarely thought of civilization at all. Sometimes I've found my rental house on Google maps and zoomed out, further and further and further, taking comfort in the fact that ahead of me was an ocean so vast that it made everything else seem pitifully insignificant by comparison.

Having dropped out of society, I was surprised on an unavoidable trip to Chicago last week that I still remembered how to put on shoes, and walk through airport security, and make small talk with strangers. I suppose everyday life is like riding a bicycle. I know driving is; I navigated my rental car without consciously signaling to turn, behaving as directed at traffic signals, and safely getting into the lanes I needed to occupy.

I must have because I found myself parked in my old space at the office without really understanding how I got there. I punched my code into the office door and was surprised when it worked. I felt like I hadn't been there in a hundred years and that the suite within its high-rise building was a relic of another life. It didn't seem possible that I had worked there, day after day, for years.

"Jack?" I looked up to see Jaycee Hayes staring at me like I was a ghost.

"Hi, Jay."

She's the number three person at work, a right hand to both Martin and me. She agreed to meet me after hours. It was easiest for flight times, so I could get back to Chaser quickly. Plus I wouldn't have to see a bunch of people.

"I barely recognized you. You look like a caveman," she said.

I reached up and felt my scraggly chin and ran my hand through my long hair.

"How is Martin?" I asked. He had taken a sudden and unplanned mental health leave. Though my dad had offered to fill me in on the particulars and has repeated his offers several times since, I frankly didn't care beyond what it meant to the company.

"It sounds like he'll be all right," she said.

I felt relieved hearing it there. Martin found the space and talked me into signing the lease, even though it was much more high-end and expensive than we needed. I looked up the hall at the doors leading to the darkened offices of people whose livelihoods depended on their jobs with us.

"What about you, Jack? How are you doing?" Jaycee asked.

I didn't answer.

She patted my arm in her familiar way.

I took a step backward.

"Will you be able to help me until Martin returns to work?" she asked.

I respected the skepticism in her voice. I appreciated her cutting straight to practicalities and getting right down to business.

"That's my plan, Jay."

"Are you coming back here?" she asked.

"No. I'll work remotely."

I knew that I should come back, that the team probably wondered what kind of freaks they signed on with, tag-teaming their way through loss while their lives disintegrated and hopefully their business wouldn't follow.

"And I'll have to handle all the client face time?" Jaycee folded her arms across her chest.

"Will that be OK?" I asked.

"Only if you give me your apartment."

She smiled, and I knew she was going to stick with me.

I was relieved for that, but I wished she hadn't mentioned my home. I pictured the rooms in Katie's and my place gathering dust. The furniture my wife had chosen, the dishes, and vases, and artwork. The rugs, countertops, and floor-to-ceiling windows overlooking the lake.

I didn't reply to Jaycee's joke. I didn't trust my voice to stay even. The truth was, I honestly didn't know if, or when, or how, I'd ever be able to move back and try to live within the colorless shadow of my former life.

She stared at me, and I could tell she wouldn't try to make light anymore. "Will you work with Sam and Varun on the Langdon design? They need help."

I nodded. I wasn't sure how I'd be able to focus on it enough to add value, enough to make sure we weren't trying to sell a valued client something subpar, or impossible to implement, or charging them too little or too much for it. But I knew that, without Martin around, I had no choice but to try.

"Let me catch you up on Martin's projects," Jaycee said.

She led the way up the hall to his office, across from mine. When she turned on the light, I felt like I was seeing it for the first time.

I was struck by the photos on his bookcase. They were mostly pictures of either me and Martin or my parents. I guess I hadn't realized that we were truly all he had. Before the accident, I was on a men's softball team, I golfed regularly with my uncles, and I had always been friendly with Katie's family. I'd never noticed that Martin had failed to branch out.

There was also a picture of my wife.

The photographs on Martin's bookshelf had never seemed strange to me before. I stared at them, feeling as if gravity had doubled and everything had become impossibly, unbreathably heavy in a moment.

"I can only spend another two hours here before I have to leave," Jaycee said. "I want to tuck Graham into bed and go over some things with his nanny before I pack for an early flight tomorrow. So let's focus and get through this."

I nodded and repeated: "Let's focus and get through this."

I worked through much of last night, and now I'm sleepy. The sun comes through the window with stubborn bravado; I turn toward it with my eyes closed, drinking it in through my skin like a plant. I know it's cold out today and that there's a driving wind. When I let Chaser in, she was coated from nose to tail with fine sand, like a husky dusted with snow in the Arctic. I still try to pretend that it's warm outside as I doze off to sleep. I try to believe that it's still summer.

The phone rings and I ignore it since I don't recognize the number. I'm hosting tonight and have a decent buzz going. It's good to be with the guys again. The ones who knew me before I got married razzed me, as they always do, when they came into the apartment. This high-rent space in this high-rent building used to be wasted on me: a slob who utilized only a quarter of it.

Katie changed all that. We live not only neatly, but fashionably. Finger foods are set out on nice plates tonight, and the guys sit in real chairs instead of the college-era folding ones I used to have. The single men look at Katie's picture and ask if she has a sister I can fix them up with. I answer the same way I always do: there is only one Katie.

Martin isn't here winning my money tonight because he has a date. I joked that he must be in love to miss poker for the first time in years. He got so quiet that I guessed I hit the mark, so I teased him harder.

The phone rings again, and this time his number comes up.

"Martin must've struck out on his date, guys. Maybe he'll make the last tournament."

My voice is almost a shout, which is typical during these poker games—we all get louder and louder as we drink beer and argue over who's playing like an asshole and who's winning all the money. Somewhere around eleven, I usually get a softly reprimanding phone call from the mother in the apartment just below ours, reminding me that her kids need their sleep. This building is a favorite with families because of the park across the street and the high-performing schools nearby. Jaycee Hayes from the office has been on a waitlist for years. I fold my cards and step out to the balcony to answer the phone. It's an unseasonably mild night, October fifteenth.

"Hey, Martin. You coming after all?" I ask.

He is crying.

"What is it?" I sit heavily on one of the sleek steel stools that are high enough to see over the balcony rails, giving an unobstructed view of Lake Michigan and the path where Katie and Chaser like to run.

I know that this can't be about my wife. She's working late on a project that has kept her out most evenings for the past month. She has been coming home so late that I'm usually asleep. If anything happened to Katie, it wouldn't be Martin who called; it would be a colleague of hers, or a policeman, or the hospital. The thought shakes me anyway.

"What is it?" I ask again. My voice is stronger because I know it can't be the worst. It's obviously very bad, from Martin's reaction, but it can't be the worst.

"Meet us at the hospital, Jack," he says. His voice chokes off. He hangs up and doesn't answer when I call back.

I have no choice but to go.

Chapter Eight

IN WHICH MERRY IS GIVEN HER BIGGEST TASK

As told by Fritz, who doles it out

I wake to the delightful smells of bacon frying and coffee brewing. It brings me back to a time when that was normal for me, when my mum would have done two loads of laundry, watered the English ivy in the streetside flower boxes, and overseen the heavy housework before turning her attention to frying bacon and brewing coffee. That would signal both Mr. Pershing in his posh suite facing the garden on the second floor and me in my attic room above to yawn, stretch, and greet the day. I have seen alarm clocks that mimic the sunrise. I want one that will wake me to the scent of bacon frying and coffee brewing.

I thought I may have heard a garage door open an hour ago, but as I have always slept with a sound machine to tone down the city rhythms of London, I can never be quite sure what I hear during the night. I used to set my sleep machine to Ocean, but having confirmed that I hate the ocean, I now set it to Peaceful Jungle. If I ever visit the jungle and find it obnoxious, as I probably would do, I'll be forced to try Desert Melody. When I get back to London, however, I plan to never leave there again. So eventually my memories of blowing sand and roaring waves will dissipate and I should be able to listen to anything I desire. Better yet, I can throw away the machine and sleep to the rhythm of Victor's peaceful slumber beside me—the most soothing and blissful sound on God's green earth.

I dress rather faster than usual, in light of the bacon. I take the divided flight of stairs to the kitchen two at a time. The old man sits at the head of the table. He smiles like a Cheshire cat at a stack of pancakes dripping with butter, whipped cream, and syrup.

He raises his fork to me.

I shake my head. He ought to know better than to start his day that way. I realize he won't listen to any health advice, however. The line of cigarette smoke still visible in the air makes that fact unassailable.

"How many?" Merry asks me from her station beside the griddle.

She's so unremittingly chipper that between her and the insanely bright sunshine in this room, I need my sunglasses. I keep a pair on top of the refrigerator because the light on this floor is invariably too much for me on sunny mornings.

I feel a bit better once I'm shaded.

I see that Merry doesn't have a stitch of makeup on, but her hair looks tolerably nice. She is wearing dark jeans, brown sporty shoes, and a casual pink shirt that fits well.

"Did I do OK?" she asks, touching the hem of her blouse self-consciously.

I realize I was staring critically, which of course no one likes because it's rude. "Yes, quite good. Well done."

She smiles bigger and flips the pancakes on the griddle. "So, how many?"

"Zero, unfortunately. But I'll have some bacon and coffee."

"He usually eats granola and yogurt. He tries to feed it to me, too!" The old man makes a face like a tattling child.

"Only because you apparently never learned to feed yourself," I say.

"More coffee needed here." He lifts his cup to Merry, ignoring me entirely.

"You'll spoil him, waiting on him that way," I warn.

Merry pours his coffee and wipes a drip off his mug with a napkin.

"Remember he's here to steal your inheritance away," I

remind her. "He's not your friend. He's your enemy."

"May I have some more syrup?" he asks.

Merry pours it from up high so that it flows prettily over the disappearing stack.

"Come join us," Merry says, reaching out to me. She sets a stack of pancakes down, with several strips of perfect bacon on the side. She places a cup of magnificently odiferous coffee beside it.

I pick up the cup and take a sip while standing. I wonder what brand Merry bought and how it can taste infinitely better than what I've been brewing and still be made in the same machine.

"Hey, what's that?" Merry asks, pointing out the window at the ocean.

The old man cranes his head to see.

"Come on, Merry! Dolphins!" he yells, heading for the door. He needs his bifocals to read anything at all, but he can spot dolphins from a mile away.

"Real dolphins?" Merry asks in awe, hurrying toward the deck after him.

They leave the door wide open so that cold wind rushes in.

The old man points out to sea, where the creatures surface, disappear for a while, and surface again. Merry squeals with delight and claps her hands. Together they laugh and cheer, apparently under the impression that the pod going past is putting on a show just for them.

I close the door and walk slowly back to the table.

Though I know I shouldn't, I sit down at the place Merry set for me.

Merry is a serious threat, I have come to realize. Every day that I exist alongside her I put myself in danger. Imminent danger. Grave danger. If I live with that girl day in and day out, for who knows how long this project will last, I will jeopardize my life as I know it. If I am not vigilant against it, I will slowly become, meal by meal, not only a tad pudgy, but certifiably fat.

We have just finished what was honestly the best home-cooked meal I have ever had. I'm sorry, Mum, may you rest in peace, but it's true.

"Does Max look much like my dad?" Merry asks in a whisper when she has finished tidying up the kitchen. She needn't be so quiet; the old man is in absolutely no danger of hearing her; he's snoring in his hideous pink chair, now in the extreme recline position.

"Yes, quite," I say.

"Oh, good! He's so *cute*. He seems like a perfect picture of a grandpa, with his white hair and his bright blue eyes. My grandpa died before I was born, and I always wanted one, almost as much as I wanted a dad. Is Max much older than my dad was?"

I become fatigued just being near Merry sometimes—she's constantly flitting about, neatening and straightening, cooking and serving. I realize it's ungenerous of me to complain, especially in light of the superb meals and the clean house, but she said her entire tribute to Max in one breath.

I sigh. "No, he isn't."

"He must've been old when I was born then. I always imagined him younger. Are there any pictures of him here that I can study?" She puts her hands on her hips and looks around, like she might discover a treasure trove of leather-bound photo albums among the hotel-spare furnishings if only she digs deeply enough.

"No. Sorry. All his personal things are at the house in London. When he made it down here, he used it much like any tenant might. His papers are all in London."

"Except the ones about me," Merry says.

"Right. Speaking of those, you're due to get your second task."

"Oh good!" she says.

I walk down to my room feeling very heavy after the meal, and perhaps in contrast to Merry's annoyingly spirited lightness. I open my briefcase to retrieve the page in question from the set of ludicrous documents pertaining to this project. A small fuchsia paper peeking out from a pocket catches my eye.

It's a note from Victor, written in tiny letters:

I love you.

He rants and raves on the phone like he's a world-renowned diva with an entourage fawning all over him instead of a talented-but-undiscovered glam rocker who has to carry his own guitar and amp to gigs. He melodramatically rehashes the story of how horribly I wronged him by leaving, but then he sends sweet little trinkets through the mail or instant love messages. And I keep finding the tiny notes he must have planted the last time I was home.

I fleetingly consider sending him the purple porcelain dog that Merry's mother forced upon me, which I think he might love for its kitsch. But, imagining it on the mantle of our future shared den, I discard the idea, along with the purple porcelain dog.

Love notes don't dull the ache of missing Victor for more than a moment. I miss him so much that sometimes it doubles me over like a gut punch. I bang my head three times on my bedroom door to clear it.

Whenever Victor tours beyond London for more than a few days at a stretch, I nearly go mad missing him. He struggles even more. He says that I am his sanity, his rock, his safe haven. He says that without me, he is liable to float off into the uncertain winds of chaos. He's a songwriter—when he puts music to those thoughts, they make far more sense and take on an urgency and pathos. Suffice it to say that I know what he means, and I worry about him.

I worry about me, too. Victor is a one-man man. Before he met me, he had only been in one other serious relationship. It lasted for years. Not only does he hate to be alone, he doesn't know how to be alone. And we have already been apart for months now, with only short visits to sustain us, and there's no end in sight.

Mr. Pershing warned me that I was too young to fall in love so completely, so overwhelmingly. He also wasn't thrilled that the object of my affection was male instead of female.

Until I met Victor, I had gone to dances with girls, had brought girls home to dinner, and had generally only dated girls in the open. I know I wasn't fooling the girls, who were invariably friends of mine who, for whatever reason, preferred spending time with me rather than more hands-on young men. I was, however, fooling my mother and Mr. Pershing.

Until, that is, Victor came along and I fell so hard I couldn't pretend anymore.

Mr. Pershing was right that I was young. I was only twenty-two when I first met Victor five years ago. My passion hasn't lessened at all. It has grown, rather, and I'm confident it won't ever fade.

If I lost Victor, I would lose what makes my life the most colorful, interesting, and happy. Of course, I'd also lose what makes it the most infuriating, painful, and frustrating. In short, I'd lose the brightness, the contrast. Everything would become monotonous and dull...like the sand on the beach outside, and the blowing wind, and the undulating waves that stretch out forever, between where I stand and London.

When I met Victor, he seemed so exotic. Having grown up in Paris, he was different from the English schoolboys with whom I'd spent my childhood and youth. Victor was as different as diamonds are to pebbles, as magenta is to beige, as London, England is to Topsail Beach, North Carolina.

V's mother is an artist; his dad is a writer. Most of the young men I knew were sons of businesspeople or politicians. Victor was fantastically exciting and interesting compared to everyone else. He still is. Actually, more so the longer I know him. He's like a bottle of fine Scotch that improves with time or a stone sculpture that grows lovelier the more it weathers in a garden. He's like Venice. I'm making him sound ancient, and he's still a young man, but I know he'll be gorgeous when he's gray. And I want to be right beside him to see it.

It would not be fair to paint Mr. Pershing as a rabid homophobe; he was never like that. He was simply uncomfortable in the way most men his age are with things that were formally hush-hush and are now supposed to be out in the open. Also, I think that he was scared for me. He didn't have gay friends, so he hadn't seen examples of how I could be perfectly fine, how

I might exist freely in the world without getting beaten up or harassed. How I could have a quiet life, not too dissimilar from his, if I chose.

Back when I began to fall for Victor, I thought that the few stilted and awkward conversations Mr. Pershing and I had had on the subject revealed him to be bigoted. Now, with a little more maturity under my belt, I see that he was only trying to help me in his own, convoluted way.

It was never easy to walk the line between Victor and Mr. Pershing. V complained that the old man was homophobic, that his wealth was ostentatious. Mr. Pershing said that Victor was a fool to follow his musical dreams instead of a lucrative career path. He always said that if V ever found success as a rock star, he'd leave me.

So it's very odd, when I reflect upon it, to think that Mr. Pershing actually brought Victor and me together.

"I decided something," Mr. Pershing said to me one day, five years ago.

"What's that?"

"I decided that I can love argyle and you can love stripes, and we can still think very highly of each other…which doesn't mean that we have to necessarily wear our argyle with our stripes or that either of us should wear leather pants to the club if it makes the other one uncomfortable. Now does it?" he said in his infuriatingly cryptic way.

"May I ask what in the hell you're talking about?" I respectfully inquired.

"I asked that young fellow to tea," he said, evidently quite proud of himself.

"Who?" I demanded.

"That fellow you watch through the window every afternoon when you sit in the parlor pretending to read."

I blushed because it was all too true.

Victor and his mother lived in a rented flat in the house across the way. The revolving residents of that particular house were a bone of contention to our neighbors, who all lived in posh, single-family homes. The house in which Victor dwelled had been divided into four units some hundred years ago, and though you couldn't tell that fact from the front, and though the parking access was from an alleyway behind, the neighbors on our street still found it abominable. Whether there was any evidence without or no, they knew there were altogether too many persons within that domicile.

Every afternoon, Clarisse, Victor's mother, brought out her easel or her drawing things and worked in the open air. And every afternoon, Victor followed.

I sat inside our home with the window open and a book or newspaper in my hands. I watched them and caught whatever snatches of French or laughter came through the window from their direction.

"Why did you invite him to tea?" I asked Mr. Pershing on that particular morning five years ago.

"Would you like me to cancel?" he asked smugly, knowing full well that I didn't want him to do any such thing.

I shouldn't have been surprised about his intervention because he always stuck his nose in my business. Whether it was arranging internships with his legal colleagues, or talking me up to the mothers of pretty girls, or a million other instances.

When I complained about it, sometimes rather loudly, and once with the added emphasis of a vase thrown down the stairs, my mother invariably pointed out that Mr. Pershing was only trying to help me and that I should be grateful.

Often I was, genuinely so. But at other times, like that which led to my pocket money being docked for a month to pay for the vase, I rather wished he'd keep his nose out. In the case of Victor, of course, I was, and am, sincerely appreciative of his meddling.

From that first stilted tea, to a quiet dinner with just Victor and me, to a heady, intoxicating affair took very little time. If Mr. Pershing regretted extending the invitation in the first place, which I have to guess he did at times, he never said so to me.

When Clarisse moved on from their flat in London to paint in other settings, first in Tuscany and more recently in Amsterdam, Victor stayed behind. He moved from their two-bedroom, second-floor apartment to the attic studio where he still lives.

By the time Clarisse departed, Victor had already assembled his Bandmaidens, and Cryptodynamite played enough bars in the vicinity to keep him fed. There have been months when I know full well that he's had trouble making rent, but he never lets me help him financially. Victor is very proud. As he likes to point out to me, he grew up without servants and elegant surroundings, and he can do very well without them. I have to remind Victor that my mother was Mr. Pershing's maid because when he introduces me to people after a few drinks, he makes it sound like I was Mr. Pershing's son instead.

Victor and I have discussed moving in together. Rather, I discuss it, and V says we need to wait until we're on equal terms. I insist he's too fixated on financial differences and that I wouldn't mind paying more to keep our household running. I point out that we'd be a team: our resources would be one and the same, and it wouldn't matter who brought in however much money.

More than anything, I want him to marry me.

When my mother grew ill, she continued on at Mr. Pershing's house, which had been her home for decades by then. He insisted she stay. I remember he was appalled when she suggested she should move out when she knew she would soon become too weak to cook and clean for him. Mum hadn't been gone long when Mr. Pershing was diagnosed with cancer himself. He said he needed me by his side, so of course I stayed.

When this project is finished, I'll have to let the bare-bones staff that remains at the London house go. I'll have to sell the place, ensure that the proceeds go where Mr. Pershing decreed, and move out. Maybe Victor and I can get a larger apartment in his building. I would sorely hate to leave that street altogether.

All this digression brings me back to Mr. Pershing's long habit of orchestrating my affairs, which is really nothing compared to what I'm attempting to do on his behalf.

Merry is cleaning the oven when I reach the kitchen again, task in hand. I motion for her to join me in the living room. She sits in the hideous companion chair beside the dozing old man, and I sit opposite them on the sofa. She smiles when I hand her the paper.

She reads it silently.

> Hello again, Merry.
>
> Because this document has reached you, it is manifestly evident that you have wisely taken me up on my posthumous offer and arrived safely at the beach house.
>
> I hope that you find my beloved ocean and home to your liking. I further hope that my most honorable and trusted barrister, Fritz Forth, isn't proving himself to be too much of an inconvenient pain in your ass. If he is, I apologize. Let me assure you that however annoying he may be, I am convinced that he will also prove helpful to you in many ways, which should balance things out.
>
> Remember to keep your eyes toward the goal my dear, trust Fritz to help you, and be sure to earn your inheritance so that my impossible old goat of a brother can't get it.
>
> You'll be surprised to learn that Fritz actually advised me against writing introductory notes to each task. The audacious upstart even suggested that my initial letters might better have been shorter and more to the point!
>
> Not because I concede that Fritz was in any way correct in his assessment, but because I am now ready to present you with it, here is your second task.
>
> Task # 2: Take stock and get on your own two feet. You must do more than earn your keep; you must begin to build a career. You must make a profit.
>
> Maintain patience with Fritz and allow him to help you, if for no other reason than the fact that he can kick you out at any time.
>
> Best of luck to you, Merry, my dear. I remain (which is all I can do now),
>
> Sincerely and belatedly yours,
> Claude Pershing (a.k.a. your father)

I watch her read it three times, with her lips moving. I fear a fourth.

"All right then," I say.

"I don't know what it means," she says.

The old man wakes up with a start. He is disheveled from his nap, and his hands tremble as he reaches for a cigarette. He lights it.

"Can I get you anything, Uncle Max?" she asks.

I hear myself mocking her without really meaning to. It's honestly too easy to resist, though I admit I could try a bit harder. She follows the old man's example and ignores me anyway.

"What's going on here?" he asks, after filling his lungs with poison and releasing some back for our edification.

"I was just reading my second task," she tells him.

"You may as well read it to me, too."

Merry, always eager to please, a regular perfect little Pollyanna, immediately complies with his request:

"Task number two: Take stock and get on your own two feet. You must do more than earn your keep; you must begin to build a career. You must make a profit."

"It seems perfectly clear to me," he says, after taking another drag and clearing his lungs by blowing smoke in my direction. "My brother was always remarkably clever with riddles," he adds.

"Is it a riddle?" Merry asks, staring down at the paper hard, as if she believes the confounding words are written in magic ink and will rearrange themselves into an answer. "What does it mean?" she asks, looking as innocently stupid as a kitten.

"It means you've got to make a career. It couldn't be clearer on that point," the old man says. He waves me away dismissively and leans toward Merry.

"What kind of a career?" she asks.

"'Take stock': that means you're supposed to figure out what you'd like to do, if I read my brother's words correctly."

"Gosh. I don't know…"

"Poppycock! I thought you had the blood of a Pershing in your veins, child!"

Merry stares at the old man. "But that doesn't mean anything about who I am, really. It's just blood."

"Pershing blood!" he shouts.

"You want me to fail so that the house will be yours. So what do you care?" she asks.

I look to the old man with my eyebrows raised, certainly curious as to what he'll answer.

"I do want you to fail, ultimately. But I see no reason why it should be so soon. Or that you should give up without a fight. I rather like getting to know my niece, who is so pretty and such an excellent cook," he says between long drags on his cigarette.

Merry stares down at the paper again.

The old man takes it from her hands and reads it quietly, moving his lips.

"I thought Fritz told me you had a business degree," he finally says.

"I do. And that, along with a dollar ninety-five, will buy me a scoop of peach ice cream down at the corner store."

"What are you saying?" he demands.

"My degree hasn't meant much to me, unless you count rejection and failure. I couldn't get a job with it, not even close."

"Why not?" the old man asks, in a *let's get to the bottom of this* manner. "The recession?"

"My mom and grandma blame the economy, and so does my Aunt Betty. But I don't know if that's all there is to it. I had a few classmates with lower GPAs who still landed career-track jobs. I suppose interviewers might have been able to tell that I didn't have a fire in my belly for business."

"What do you like to do?" he asks, clearly growing impatient.

Merry shrugs her shoulders.

He turns his face away and stares at the ocean.

She looks out, too.

What a pair they make. I wish I could fly back home to London now and let the two of them figure everything out.

"See the pelicans?" The old man points and Merry looks up.

"Wow! I thought they were gangly when I just saw pictures. Look how elegant they really are, gliding along right above the water," she says breathlessly. "They change direction with what looks like no effort at all."

"In their proper context, they really are quite gorgeous,"

the old man says. "Once you find a place where you belong, everything is easier, Merry."

She looks at him like he's a brilliant sage she walked barefoot for hundreds of miles to hear.

He notices and tries to deliver in style. He clears his throat and sits up taller in his ugly chair.

"A butterfly underwater is nothing; it's dead and doesn't possess even an echo of its former beauty. A whale on the beach is a municipal logistical nightmare, with stench that long outlasts the mourning. But in their proper contexts, in their natural environments, they are something else altogether. They are sublime, surreally beautiful, amazingly and wholly resplendent."

I roll my eyes at the superlatives, but Merry nods in mute agreement as she watches the pelicans soar away in perfect unison.

"Maybe this place is my 'proper context,' where I really belong," she finally says. "It feels like it."

"You worked in a restaurant, right?" the old man asks when the birds have traveled so far away that they are only dots on the horizon.

"Not just one; I've worked in a bunch over the years."

"And you like to cook? You said you did, and you're clearly wonderful at it."

"I love to cook more than anything. But I don't think working in a restaurant will count as completing my task. It says I need to make a career for myself."

The old man becomes impatient all at once. He grinds out one cigarette, grabs his pack, and shakes out another. He tamps it down on the table three times and lights it.

"I just don't see how working in a restaurant would count as making a career," Merry continues. "I'm sure there's not enough money set aside to open a café of my own. And I don't have enough experience anyway, even if there was."

"Are those the only choices?" the old man asks after a few long drags.

"No?" Merry asks.

"Oh, for heaven's sake, child, you've got to learn to

help yourself!"

He gets up and stomps off to his room.

Merry and I are left behind, breathing the smoke that trails after him. She stares at the sea again.

"I'm trying to memorize it," she says. "In case you kick me out and it has to last me forever."

"What on earth do you see out there?" I ask. For the life of me, all I see is water.

"Like my dad said in that letter: no two seconds are the same. The ocean changes and moves constantly, along with the clouds above it, passing over like so many blessings. It's wonderful to watch. It's so surprising and so pretty."

I shake my head.

"No, really, Fritz," she says, looking at me earnestly. "I feel what he felt. I know that we never met, but I feel connected to him when I look out there."

Her eyes actually fill with tears. Good God.

"My dad used to sit in this room and look through these windows at this same ocean. He really did. And I might have gone my whole life without even a hint of who he was. Thank you for bringing me here."

Before I can defend myself against it, she's got her arms around my neck in another one of her sudden hugs. I peel her off and push her back toward her chair, where she smiles at me like I just gave her a *purdy* birthday balloon. I rub my eyes. I think perhaps I've developed an allergy to smoke. Or sand. Or this whole damn project.

The old man, apparently finished with his temper tantrum, comes back out and sits down.

"Any inspirations come to you?" he asks.

Merry's face lights up. "What about a catering service? Just a small one, set out of this house."

"If you really don't want to do something with your business degree, which I think is a pity, I suppose your idea isn't so bad. What'll you make?"

"Whatever people will buy," she says.

"What'll you call it?"

She furrows her brow in concentration for a minute. "Maybe I'll use what you said to me. Maybe I'll call it 'Help Yourself.'"

The old man smiles like the cat that just ate the canary.

Merry smiles, too. She becomes serious again quickly, though, pointing to the ashes that hang from the end of his cigarette.

"I have a deal for you, Uncle Max: I'll feed you delicious food every day, but in return, you can't smoke in the house. If I'm going to use the kitchen for catering, you can't *ever* smoke in the house. Period."

"And where am I going to smoke?" he asks, outraged.

"The deck. Or one of the covered balconies on the intracoastal side—you can even smoke in bad weather."

"What if I say no? I shouldn't be helping you anyway. If you meet all your goals, you'll get the house and I won't."

"OK," she says, shrugging her shoulders. "If you're going to be stubborn about it, I won't make you any more meals. Fritz can cook for you again."

The old man makes a disgusted face and snorts, like I'm not even in the room.

"What's your very favorite thing in the whole world to eat?" Merry asks, leaning in close to him.

He answers right away. "Chocolate cake. I have my mother's old recipe memorized, but no one ever makes it quite right."

"Maybe I can," Merry says.

He looks at her hard for a few seconds.

"Maybe you can."

Chapter Nine

IN WHICH MERRY WORKS VERY HARD

As told by our very hardworking Merry

I try not to waste any time today. After preparing, serving, and cleaning up from breakfast, I go right down to my room. The very first thing I do is shut the curtains: there's no way I'll get anything done if I stare at the ocean. The second thing I do is dust off my laptop.

I see right away that Phil hasn't limited himself to voice messages. There are twenty-three e-mails from him in my inbox. I tell myself that I should just delete them all without reading a single one—I can't get distracted by Phil and still reach my goal. But I don't have the willpower.

I had forgotten that Phil can write a nice love letter when he wants to. Or twenty-three. He claims that my leaving made him see the light—that, as well as long chats with Amy Jo. He says he knows now that he's been a bully, and a hothead, and he wants to change his ways. He keeps mentioning marriage.

In note number six, he mentioned how he'd gone up to my cedar cabin on the mountain and brought Mom and Grandma a nice dinner. He said he fixed the leaking spigot on the house, too, and sat with the ladies through three game shows.

In note number twelve, he said he'd bought Amy Jo that new recliner she's been hankering for down at Swanson's Furniture. And I guess I did picture him in a tuxedo standing at the front of a church for a minute.

In Phil's last few notes, he begged to know where I am.

He said if I don't let him visit, he still wants to send me a care package or two. My stomach growls…but I know that if I told Phil the address, he'd show up here, even if he promised not to.

I put his notes in a new folder called *Food for Thought* and get back to work.

I create a spreadsheet to enter costs so that I can track my sales against my expenses. It takes me until lunchtime to finalize what I hope will be a good starting menu.

I try out a few of my ideas by preparing and feeding them to Max and Fritz for lunch. Then I clean the kitchen until it sparkles again. Then I get right back to work at the computer.

I had taken a few graphic design electives as part of my business school coursework. After some false starts, I remember how to use the software and mock up some menus, business cards, and labels.

Just when I think that everything looks nice, I hear Fritz in the hall. I call out to him, "Can you give me your two cents on something?"

There's only one desk chair in my room, so Fritz stands behind me and looks over my shoulder. I adjust the screen so he can see it better and launch right into showing him all the things that I've made.

"These actually look quite professional," he says, like he's surprised.

Actually. I always notice when people use the word like that. As in: that's actually a good idea, or you actually look really nice today. It's such a backhanded compliment!

"Except the font," he says. "You need something simpler, more elegant."

He tries to edge me out of the desk chair to take over my computer, but I stay put. Though he tries to, I don't let him touch the keyboard or screen. He tells me what he doesn't like, and he keeps complaining until I've tweaked things to his fancy. Nothing looks much different to me, but Fritz seems to think that it's all way better than it was before.

Just when I think we're done, he says, "Now switch that atrocious background color."

"It isn't that bad," I say. It's called ocean blue, which I think is just about the prettiest color going.

"It looks babyish to me. And this white scrolling border makes it look a bit like a wedding invitation."

"Phil wants to marry me," I say.

He stares at me like I just threw up on the floor.

"I didn't say I agreed."

"Of course you didn't! That would be insane, Merry. Absolutely insane."

"Thanks for your opinion," I tell him, and maybe I sound a bit bratty, but he did, too. "So what color do you have in mind for the background?"

"Well, you're trying to sell food, so you need something appetizing. You need to use green."

"Green?" All my life, I've been surrounded by evergreen trees and green vines and grasses. He says green and I picture Peaksy Falls. "I'm a little tired of green, to tell you the truth."

"Your materials should be appetizing," he says. "I challenge you to name a non-manufactured blue food."

"Blueberries," I answer. I cross my arms and feel like I got the better of him for once.

"Another?" he asks.

I try, but I can't think of more.

"By contrast, I'll name a few natural and healthy green foods. Asparagus, artichoke, arugula, avocado…" he looks at the ceiling like there's a list up there that he's reading from.

"Shush!" I say, but I can't help laughing a little.

"…bell pepper, broccoli, Brussels sprouts…"

I try to cover his mouth up, but he ducks out of my reach.

"…cabbage, celery, chives, cucumber…"

"Fine!" I yell. "You win. I'll change the background color to green if you want, but for heaven's sake, stop listing vegetables!"

The days fly past, like they always seem to do when I'm racing around as busy as a bee. Four are already gone.

Uncle Max acts like he's been half-starved for months.

Every time I put a plate of food down in front of him, he gobbles it up. He doesn't leave anything behind but the garnish. I feel guilty sometimes that I like Max so well, when I know from my father's note that he wasn't too fond of him. But my dad isn't here, and Uncle Max is.

Though he sometimes grumbles worse than an old lawnmower about it, Uncle Max has kept to his word and never smokes inside the house now. I have kept up my end of the bargain by feeding him like a king. He says my chocolate cake might be even better than his mother's. The sparkle in his eyes when he says it makes me believe that he's either the most sincere man I've ever met, or he's a darn good liar.

Uncle Max complains that I'm trying to steal away his beach house. What he doesn't seem to mind at all is me working my tail feathers off while he rests in his recliner watching the water or sits at the head of the table eating my creations. I can't say that I blame him for wanting this place, though. And I can't stay mad at Max, even when he's acting like a big old baby. He's just a lonely man, from what I can see. Maybe he wanted to be around people for a change, and this is the idea that struck him for how to do it, on account of how he'll get the house if I fail.

He shoos me away when I ask questions, but I've still managed to learn a few things. For example, Uncle Max never had a wife or kids. Maybe that meant he had a lot of freedom all his life, and he could do what he wanted without answering to anybody. But I think being alone must be pretty sad when you get old.

At least my mom and grandma have each other. Yesterday when I spoke to my mom on the phone, she kept yelling everything I said back to Grandma and shouting into the phone so Grandma could hear her side. It's a relief to me that Aunt Betty is nearby to keep an eye on them. She won't be cozy on the cabin sofa watching game shows like Phil did the other night, but I trust she'll make sure that Mom and Grandma are OK.

I think of Aunt Betty sitting all alone in her white living room every evening, and to tell you the truth, it makes me sad.

Out of the blue yesterday, Fritz asked me if I was lonely for my Aunt Betty.

"You claim to know everything about me, and yet you think I could be lonesome for someone I barely even know?" I said. "You're slipping, Fritz."

You can imagine how much he liked that, right?

I'm cleaning the bowls from Uncle Max's cake when Fritz comes up the stairs with his iPod.

"Listen to this," he says.

"Just let me check the cake in the oven first."

Naturally, I think it's going to be a Cryptodynamite song. They all sort of sound the same to me, honestly. When I start listening, though, I find out that it's a podcast of Aunt Betty's show.

"I didn't know you could hear it this way," I say. I sort of half listen to the opening while I clean the counter. I know the music by heart, and Aunt Betty always begins the exact same way. Boring so far.

The first caller comes on.

"Hello, caller. What's your name?" Aunt Betty asks.

I once sat in the studio and watched her record a show. I was about ten, and my mom had a doctor's appointment in the city. I think school had been canceled because the heating system went down or something; I recollect that it was a last-minute choice to drop me off there and that Aunt Betty was none too thrilled to have my mom and me show up. That was the only time I set foot in the studio.

I remember that the first thing Aunt Betty did at the beginning of each call was to find out the person's name. She wrote it down on a pad of paper in red ink. Then she circled it every time she said the caller's name, which was too often for my taste. When the call ended, she crumpled up that page of the pad and threw it away, like the caller was dead to her the minute they disconnected. I bet she still does it.

"I'm Claudia," a girl replies.

She sounds pretty young.

"Hello, Claudia. What's your question today?"

"Well, I've been offered a college scholarship, but it's far away from

home. My question is: I can't really turn it down. Can I?"

"So you're seventeen?"

"Eighteen," Claudia says, like it's a whole lot different.

"So you're eighteen. Let me guess: having grown up in a small town, you have easily beaten all your peers in test scores, gotten all the boyfriends you wanted, along with the head cheerleader role, and probably anything else that you set your sights on."

Aunt Betty sounds like she's staring off into space as she talks, like she does when she's off the air.

"Wow! How'd you know all that?"

"You think you're ready to conquer the world, Claudia, because conquering your tiny corner of it has been a walk in the park. So easy that you could have done it with half your brain tied behind your back. You think that's how it's always going to be, that your upbringing is reflective of the world at large."

This is weird. I've never heard Aunt Betty talk like this on the air.

"Well, I don't know…"

"You may be valedictorian, Claudia; you may be looking at a full-ride scholarship, but you're absolutely clueless when you get right down to it. You wonder how I know you so well? Because I was you, a lifetime ago."

"Pardon me, ma'am?"

"Decades have passed since then, Claudia, but I can remember all the emotion of being your age as if it were yesterday. Sometimes I feel that the girl in my memory must have been from a movie I saw or a book I read long, long ago. Sometimes I can almost believe that she never really existed at all. And sometimes she surprises me in the mirror."

Whoa. This is the weirdest show of Aunt Betty's I have ever heard. She's always odd, mind you, but she never talks about her old self like this.

"Huh? Are you saying I should take the scholarship then? I mean, I pretty much have to…"

"You're the one who will have to live with your choices, Claudia. What do you want to do?"

"I guess I want to take the scholarship."

Claudia sighs almost as heavily as Fritz.

"You said that like you were spelling too easy of a word in a spelling

bee, Claudia. A tedious contest that you know you'll ultimately win because you always do."

"*I never entered a spelling bee, ma'am. Maybe you did, but I didn't.*"

"*Why do you want to take the scholarship, Claudia?*"

"*Because it's the right thing to do. My parents don't have much money, and this is the best scholarship offer I have.*"

"*When I was your age, I was also offered a scholarship from a college far away from home.*"

I'm amazed Aunt Betty has said so much. She doesn't even talk about herself when she's sitting at a holiday table surrounded by family, let alone on her show.

"*What did you do?*"

It's quiet so long that I think maybe Fritz only downloaded part of the show by mistake. Then I hear Aunt Betty again.

"*I did many things; some of them were very unwise, some smarter. In short, I made choices, just like you'll have to do.*"

"*But did you take the scholarship and move away, and did it work out for you?*"

"*If you ever listened to my show before, Claudia, you might be able to guess my response to your questions. You might also recognize it from a certain film called* Mary Poppins. *The only answer I'll give is: 'I never explain anything.'*"

Aunt Betty seems to have woken herself up out of her trance and become her usual self.

"*Why do you call yourself Betty Answers then?*"

Go, Claudia! I've wanted to ask the same thing a million times. I would have if I thought I'd get an answer.

"*Because it's my name.*"

See?

"*But I still don't know what to do! I guess I'm afraid to go so far away and live somewhere I've never been, with people I don't know, and all that. I don't want to eat cafeteria food and put on my freshman fifteen and throw up at kegger parties or whatever.*"

"*Whether or not you take the scholarship and go away to school, you certainly don't have to gain weight or drink yourself sick, Claudia.*"

"*I like living at home. My parents are really nice, and they don't bug me like my friends' parents bug them.*"

"You're a lucky teenager then, Claudia. When I was eighteen, I hated the very sight of my mother, the woodsy nature of our house, the smell of the fireplace in winter. I hated everything about my home life when I was eighteen. I jumped at the scholarship I'd been offered like it was the last raft on a sinking ship."

I am sad to imagine Grandma and Mom listening to this when it aired live. And listen they surely did because Aunt Betty's show is the highlight of their days. The thought makes me want to cry.

"Good luck, Claudia. And call back to let us know what you decide, and then keep calling. I'm sure my listeners would like to keep track of your progress."

"OK, Ms. Answers."

"And if you'd like to leave your address in my voicemail, I'll send you an autographed copy of my book, POPPINS! Why You Should Never, Ever Explain Anything.*"*

I remove the earbuds and set the iPod beside Fritz, who's now playing chess with Uncle Max in the living room.

"Was it a good show?" Fritz asks without looking up.

"I didn't listen to the whole thing. It was weird," I say.

"Weirder than usual?" he asks.

"Yes, sir. Hey, since you claim to know everything about me…"

"You claim I don't," he cuts me off.

"Be careful of Fritz's claims, Merry! I'm sure he thinks he knows more than he does. For example, he thinks he knows what my clever brother had planned for his London house."

Fritz folds his arms across his chest and shakes his head in annoyance.

"Why isn't that settled yet?" I ask.

"Claude was very cagey." Uncle Max chuckles, but soon begins to cough.

Fritz gets up and brings him a glass of water, apparently forgetting he was mad at him just a second ago.

When Uncle Max is himself again, I make another try at

getting a straight answer.

"Fritz, just tell me: do you have any idea why my Aunt Betty is so strange?"

"Can you be more specific?" he asks. Fritz is so stiff and short sometimes; he reminds me of an English butler on TV.

"Why does she have to act so superior to my mom and grandma all the time? And why did she have to say such mean things on that show just now? Why is she so darn selfish?"

Fritz looks at me like he did on that first day, when I came to believe that he'd really help me if I went along with him. He looks like he might even care a little.

"The questions you ask are complicated and subjective, and I wouldn't attempt to answer them, even if I could. However, I will share some facts that you do not yet know. Your Aunt Betty remortgaged her house to save your grandmother's. Now she is nearly broke herself."

"Really?" I ask.

"Indeed."

I shake my head, trying to take that in.

"So the money I might earn, if I do everything you say while I'm here, could save my grandma's house and also help Aunt Betty?"

"If you chose to use it that way," Fritz says.

"Of course I would. Those are my people."

The oven timer buzzes. "And that's my cake!" Max says.

Chapter Ten

IN WHICH JACK MEETS A MERMAID

As told by Jack Morningstar,
man between two worlds

I stare at the violently churning water through the sea-misted windows. One night last week was mild, almost serene by comparison. I even saw a woman out there, walking alone along the water's edge. It was very late and I was bone-tired, so tired that I wasn't sure if she was real or if I only imagined her, like a sailor of old conjuring a mermaid to stave off his loneliness or perhaps to guide him into safer waters.

The woman I either saw or imagined was so different from Katie that it shocked me. In my isolation here, I had almost forgotten that other women existed. She must have been a mirage. No real woman would go down to the beach on a cold winter night and twirl in the moonlight.

In my exhaustion, though, I thought she might be real. And I thought that if I were another man, in another phase of his life, I might even go out and speak with her. But just as I imagined stepping out onto the deck and calling to her, she slipped out of the silvery stream of moonlight and disappeared into the shadows again.

I have put out several fires at work with Jaycee's help and have tried to assure the staff and clients that everything will be just fine while Martin is away. No one has asked me particulars about him—I guess they've heard enough of the story to know better.

I've had to throw out half of the design elements that Varun and Sam came up with for the Langdon Logistics proposal. I reviewed all their meeting notes and devised some better ideas, documented those, and plan to present the new prototypes to the customer once the guys have mocked them up. I know it's risky to change our plans at this stage, but if we can't do a project right, I'd rather not do it at all. Sam felt undermined and threatened to quit. I told him to go ahead.

I take a protein bar from the cupboard and eat it without registering the taste. I drink a soda that may as well be dust. I pull my wetsuit down from its peg. Chaser remains on her pet bed and follows me with only her eyes; her chin stays on the floor.

The ocean is wild and inviting. It looks like it'll clear my head or smash it. It calls to me.

Chaser rises and play bows. She waits while I suit up and follows behind as I carry my board down the three flights of stairs and across the walkways over the dune to the ocean. She watches from shore while I wade out into the frigid water.

I argue with Martin while I clamber up on my board and fall back into the freezing surf again moments later. I argue with clients, employees, my father, Katie, and then Martin again. I repeat the process until I can barely think or feel anymore. I try to keep the conversations in my head, but I know they escape sometimes into cries and screeches like the seabirds', like the foam flying from the waves, like the primal roar of the ocean itself.

Finally the time comes for me to either go back to shore, or not. It always does.

I lay back in my wetsuit with my head floating. I could let my surfboard go and simply turn over. I could let the waves bash me and not fight them. It would be harder to swim to shallower water and then to put my feet on the bottom and walk to shore, against all the forces and currents that would encircle me, weighing me down more and more as I got closer to dry earth again, as I lost the buoyancy of the water and the numbness of the cold. I would have to drag myself across the wide beach and up so many hard wooden stairs, only to be alone.

I sigh and roll over. The ocean begins to overtake me with the solemn earnestness of not giving a damn.

Chaser barks from shore. She barks again and keeps it up with increasing urgency.

"Jesus," I curse.

I'll go back to earth again, for no better reason than to feed my dog.

I swim with my board toward shore until I can put my feet down on the shifting sand.

Darkness has closed in by the time I get to dry beach. I can't see Chaser up ahead of me. I call for her when I have dragged myself across the cold, wide desert to my stairs.

"Chaser, come on!"

I still don't see her. I look up and down the beach for any sign of movement. There's nothing. She seems to have abandoned me, too.

"Chaser!" I yell, less kindly than normal.

Finally I hear her bark. I look around.

Through the darkness, I perceive movement first. For a fleeting moment, I pray it will be Katie. Somehow whole, and alive, and approaching…

Then I hear Chaser bark and see her white-gold feather-duster tail as she comes closer. She wags it happily, like life is inherently good.

I hang my head and turn toward the stairs. "Come on, girl," I grunt.

Chaser barks once and I look back. It takes me a moment to trust my eyes, to see that she's not alone.

She has brought a mermaid with her.

Chapter Eleven

IN WHICH MERRY EMBARKS
ON A CAREER

As told by Merry, who hopes everybody likes it

It has been a whirlwind week! I just put together another shipment of cookies and sundries for the two little ladies in Peaksy Falls. Mom and Grandma have each written to me twice already. Though the little ladies keep peppering me with questions about the game show they're sure I'm working on, it's still been nice to hear from them.

I've enjoyed getting the news of folks back home, too. Mom wrote to say that Harley Hancock's wife, Missy, had her twins, and they're just as healthy and cute as can be. Mom said she and Grandma were so anxious to see those babies that they went right on over there and knocked on the door. I was pleased as peaches to hear that; they sure do need to get out more! Mom said they brought over lots of presents in honor of the blessed event, which likely means they unloaded a trunk full of eBay and QVC items still in their shipping boxes.

This morning, I only have time to scratch out a quick reply to their latest letters to slip inside their box. I end it with:

I'm having the time of my life!

Maybe that seems weird, seeing as how I've been working like a dog and all. But, so help me God, it's the truth.

I got up at 5 a.m. to finish the salads, desserts, and rolls that I'm fixing to bring around to island realtors and shops as well as office buildings in the city. Today is the day that I launch my catering business.

Wish me luck!

The countertops are chock full of food. I'm packing sample sizes of every item into pretty cardboard containers I bought from the bakery near the swing bridge. The owner said business was even slower this winter than last year. She was tickled for the chance to get rid of her extra odd-shaped boxes before they yellowed in her store room, and I was just as happy to get them.

The printer did a really nice job on my menus. I also got business cards and some cute stickers I'll use to seal the boxes. Once I get everything packed up, I'll drop off my samples like little seeds and hope people will like them so much they'll order more, and my business will take root.

Fritz won't check off this task unless I'm in the black by the end of my time here, so I've got to start bringing in cash ASAP. I'm tracking all my expenses on my trusty spreadsheet, which will make it easy to see the bottom line. The things I learned in college are a lot more fun when I'm applying them to my own business than they were when it was some musty old case study from a book. Though I'm trying to enjoy every minute of it, I don't have to remind myself that this is the most serious game I'll ever play. And I'm not the only one who stands to lose if I fail.

I'm wearing one of my pretty new outfits, and I have my makeup and hair done just like the ladies at the salon taught me. I'm getting used to myself looking this way, but I tell you what, when I walk past a mirror, I sometimes still jump a little. If I stop a second, though, I have no doubt that I'm the same old me. My eyes are blue like they've always been, the scar over my left eyebrow hasn't gone anywhere, and my smile is still in place, even if it looks a little bit nervous today.

I hear Fritz sigh. He's been doing paperwork at the kitchen table for the past hour.

I know that he can be grumbly, and insulting, and bratty as all get-out, but I also know that I never in a million years would have tried to start my own business without a big kick in the butt. My dad has passed on, but he sure left a good kicker in his place.

I don't know how on earth Fritz knows so much about so many things! He has an opinion about everything under the sun.

"Are you going to get out for a beach walk today?" I ask him as I load the cooler. "I never did see the beachy clothes you bought when I was getting my hair done."

"I didn't buy any," he says, without so much as looking up.

"You didn't?" I ask.

"Nope."

"So you don't have to keep up your end of the deal when you strike a bargain?" I ask, maybe sounding saucy.

"Do you really want to argue with me about such a minor issue?" he asks. "I *am* keeping up my end of this horrendous bargain." He sweeps his hand around, indicating the room, the ocean, me, and pretty much everything.

He sets right back to work on his papers.

I don't want to fight, so I try to make up with him. "It was so pretty when I went out earlier."

"So *purdy*?" Fritz mocks my accent.

"A weird spiny fish had washed up on shore," I tell him. "Its eyes were so human! It wasn't decayed at all, either; it looked like it could just swim right away."

"Trust me, Merry, if it could have, it would have," he mumbles.

Fritz helped me get all my ducks in a row for this catering business. I was willing to follow the saying that it's better to ask forgiveness than permission, but Fritz said I had to do things the "proper" way. I suppose I can put up with his frowns and sighs and mockings and stubbornness after all he's done to help me.

"Do you know what kind of a fish it was?" I ask.

"Sounds like a deflated puffer fish. I can't say that I blame him for just dying and washing up. His last words were probably: *Screw it, I'm so damn sick of the ocean.*"

"I'm sorry you have to be here," I say.

Fritz sighs. "There's a book on the shelf that has all the shells and sea life you're likely to find here." He points to a white wicker bookcase that also holds a stack of battered board games.

"You really miss home, and Victor, don't you?" I ask.

He rolls his eyes and turns back to his papers. "Don't *ya*?" he mocks me quietly.

I don't give up that easily, though.

"I've never been to London. I bet it's just beautiful. What do you miss most about it?"

He puts down his pen and sighs again.

"Everything. I miss the city, the lights, the pavement on the streets, the traffic, the architecture, the people…" He looks up. "Shall I go on?"

"Oh my goodness, yes! I want to hear all about it. I've never been out of the country—not even to Mexico or Canada. I've always loved watching travel shows on PBS and dreaming about going on long visits all over the place. I want to see the buildings, eat the food, and hear the accents. Will you tell me all about London once I get back here tonight?"

"Sure, Merry," he says. He picks up a little scrap of bright pink paper and holds it tight in his hand.

I try to sound confident. "Now I've got to go off and see what I can do about task number two."

"Go on, then," he says.

"Want to come along?" I ask. I suppose I'm a touch scared.

"You'll do fine, Merry," he says with more kindness in his voice than I've heard yet, which I know isn't saying a whole lot, but still.

It was one thing to talk a big talk. It was nice to have an excuse to shop for all the ingredients I needed to make my favorite staples. I loved spending days in the kitchen, only breaking long enough to chat with Uncle Max, or be mocked by Fritz, or to walk along the beach. I even had fun packing everything up in the little boxes. But now I have to go out there and sell myself.

"You're still here?" Uncle Max asks, coming into the open living room from my dad's bedroom, which he has taken over. I can tell by his messy white hair, and from the pillow creases on the side of his face, that he's been napping in bed.

"It looks like I might just get this beach house after all," he says.

With that backhanded encouragement, I pick up one of my new coolers. It has *Help Yourself* written across it in green Sharpie marker. I was fixing to write it on there yesterday, but since Fritz knows calligraphy, he did the honors.

I begin to haul it down the stairs.

"Don't forget to drop that bag of goodies next door on your way out," Uncle Max says, pointing to the small shopping bag I packed for our neighbor. The one I met on the beach a few nights ago.

"Do you want to run it over there for me?" I ask. "I've sort of got my hands full right now. And since he was your brother's friend, he probably wants to give you his condolences."

"Oh no, not me," Uncle Max says. "I'm a homebody these days. Stay in and rest, you know. Doctor's orders." He grabs a pack of cigarettes off the side table and heads for the deck.

Fritz shakes his head when I look at him.

Phil and I have exchanged some nice love notes and recipes since I've been here, and we've had a few sweet phone talks. This time away from each other is turning out to be the highlight of our relationship. But the truth is: I don't mind delivering the goody bag next door.

I want to see Jack Morningstar up close again. Our kitchen window overlooks his deck, and since our deck is further forward, he can't see us. So it's a pretty convenient setup for spying. I haven't said so to Fritz or Uncle Max, so don't breathe a word, but Jack is gorgeous. I catch myself staring out my kitchen window when he's in view.

I feel a little guilty when I happen to be making a recipe that Phil taught me while at the same time stealing looks at Jack. Maybe that's part of why I've experimented with ingredients and done more inventing here in the past week than I've ever done before. It wouldn't feel right to pass someone else's dishes off as my own, either, so I have changed up all my old standbys at least a little, sometimes a lot. Now I can honestly say that this is my business and nobody else's. And do you know what? It all tastes wonderful. Maybe some things aren't as delicious as Phil might make them, but they're good enough for Uncle Max to rave about, and they're mine.

There's something else about Jack that draws my attention, now that I reflect on it. His shoulders sag, and he walks slow, like he's just plum given up. When I met Jack the other night, my big goal was to get him to smile. I thought maybe he would need rescuing, so I went down to the beach. It looked like he was in pretty deep. I'm not a great swimmer or anything, so I probably couldn't have helped him anyway, but I went outside just in case maybe I could.

His dog had been barking like crazy, and when she saw me, she ran right over. By then, Jack was making his way to shore. It was getting dark fast.

"Chaser, come on!" he yelled when he made it to the beach. I hoped he couldn't see me because if he could see me and he yelled in that tone, well, I wouldn't have liked it one bit.

Jack's sweet dog stayed by my side when he called for her. I wished she'd just go to him, but she stayed by me.

"Chaser!" he called again, sounding tired and fed up.

Since his dog wouldn't budge, I figured I'd have to take her on over to him. Chaser wagged her tail beside me and sort of pranced, like we were in a parade and she was the star of the show.

I had seen Jack before it got dark. I guess my eyes had adjusted to him because I could still make out his face all right. Sometimes it seemed to almost float over the darkness of his black wetsuit, and that was strange. But then I'd see his arm or leg catch some moonlight, and he'd snap into place as a whole man again.

I don't think he saw me at all, not until his dog led me up really close. I'm pretty sure I scared him, coming out of the darkness like that.

"Oh," he said.

"Hi there."

"I'm sorry my dog bothered you."

"Her? She's no bother. She's the prettiest dog I've ever seen. I can tell she wouldn't hurt a flea." It was true as rain.

He smiled. I was glad to be close enough to see it.

"She usually sticks right by me," he said.

He motioned for her to sit and she did. He gave another signal and she flopped down. It was comical how she went in less than a second from sitting at attention to completely flattened right to the ground, from her tail to her chin.

I laughed and clapped my hands together.

He smiled again. "I fell in love with Chaser the first time I saw her do that."

"Me too!" I said.

He took off his black glove and put out his hand. "I'm Jack Morningstar."

"I'm Merry Strand," I said.

We shook hands.

The waves crashed loud against the shore, so I had to stand close. "We were worried about you out there," I said.

He fell quiet for a minute.

"Do you live nearby?" he asked when he found his tongue again.

"Yes, sir. I live over there," I pointed to the house.

"With Claude?" he asked.

"No, sir. I'm afraid he passed away."

He nodded slowly. I heard him sigh in between the sound of waves hitting the shore.

This is no time for lollygagging or reminiscing! I finish hauling the coolers down and tuck them safely in the back of my borrowed SUV before I walk next door to Jack's house. I hear commotion inside when I ring the bell, and soon Chaser jumps against the door. She wags her tail and stares at me through the window, like she's sure the bag I'm holding is full of dog treats. Jack doesn't appear for so long that I figure maybe he's not there.

He doesn't have a garage, though, and his car is sitting right in the driveway. I would've noticed him go down to the beach since I can see his deck so well from the kitchen, where I've spent the whole morning. It's not my business, though, if he's napping or working or who knows what.

As I turn to leave, I see him come to the door. He looks like he doesn't know if he should open it.

I smile big.

He still doesn't seem sure. Maybe he thinks I'm going to try and sell him something. And when it comes right down to it, I suppose I am.

"Remember me? I'm your neighbor," I say through the door. "I brought you some food."

He motions for Chaser to sit and she does. He opens up.

"You brought me food?" he asks, like he's sure he misheard.

He has one of those voices, sort of deep and mellow, that just makes me want to keep listening. But I can't right now because he's quiet.

"Yes, sir," I say, handing over the bag.

"Thanks," he says, like it's a question.

I start walking away, feeling a little lighter now that I made my first delivery. I flash him another smile over my shoulder.

"Y'all are welcome!" I call. "I hope you like it!"

I hope everybody likes it, I think as I march up the sidewalk.

Chapter Twelve

IN WHICH FRITZ AND POLLYANNA SQUABBLE LIKE CHILDREN

As told by Fritz, at times in tones unmentionable

"So what's your normal job?" Merry asks.

She's standing at the kitchen counter preparing food, as usual. She is still working every night when I go to bed, and she is already working each morning when I wake up. I almost never see her sit down. Merry runs all over the region for ingredients, works countless hours in the kitchen, and then delivers food to the clients she has already managed to win over. She is a very busy woman.

I'm no shirker myself, mind you. I enjoy a hard day's work. But Merry is far more stubbornly determined than I would have guessed. I might not even mind it if she were somewhat less busy. Occasionally—rarely of course—I almost wish that I could spend a bit more time with her.

The old man has been passing his days either reading or dozing. Especially now that Merry cooks for us, he seems contented with very little. Like a baby, he eats and sleeps and doesn't appear to do much else. Merry's dishes, especially her chocolate cake, have certainly endeared her to him.

"You already know that I am an attorney," I say.

"Have you worked for my dad since you finished law school?" she asks while chopping vegetables.

"Yes. And every summer before that, as far back as I can remember."

"So you worked for him and grew up in his house, too? You must've known him really well then, huh?"

She looks up at me expectantly, with her knife poised above the cutting board. Merry asks open-ended questions constantly, as if they are as acceptable as comments about the weather. She should have learned by now that it won't get her far with me—I prefer not to be an open book.

"He must've been like a father to you," she says.

I sigh heavily and respond in a manner designed to shut her up. "I was the son of his maid. That's all."

She starts chopping again, since I've made it clear that I won't elaborate. I regret the fact that she often brings out my prickly side. I generally consider myself to be quite congenial, but Merry's incessant questions seem to be forever touching raw nerves. Then she acts shocked and hurt when I let her know she's gone too far, and I end up feeling a bit like an ass.

I suspect that she wants me to say that I loved Mr. Pershing and always wished he were my father. Well, I won't give her—his actual child—the satisfaction.

It is true that I wanted Mr. Pershing to be my father. Despite his fits of bad temper, his propensity toward using me as an accomplice in his white lies, his excesses with food and drink, and all his other faults. And perhaps a trifle because of them. From the beginning, from my earliest memories, I loved him like a father.

This is just the sort of embarrassing-to-admit tidbit that I know Merry is fishing for when she asks questions: There was a period of time, just prior to adolescence, when I watched the *Parent Trap* film over and over again and imagined ways in which I might successfully throw my mum and Mr. Pershing together. I even kept a secret notebook of plans.

Looking back, I can see that it was a ridiculous idea. Then, I didn't realize my mother was too matronly, and not intelligent enough in the ways he preferred, to ever attract Mr. Pershing's attention as a love interest. I thought everyone must see her as the generous, kind soul that I saw; I was blind to how anyone else might view my mother. Perhaps she doted on me too much, but I wasn't one of those boys who wanted to wriggle free and escape to play in the streets. I rather liked being coddled.

In that regard, I believe that Mr. Pershing and I were of the same mind. My mother treated us both like her sons in many respects. Though the man of the house complained about most things, I never once heard him complain that she was too solicitous for his comfort.

In short, she babied him. When she died, having made me promise that I would take care of Mr. Pershing in her absence, I knew it was too late to retrain him. He was already too ill; I couldn't attempt any sort of reprogramming. So I had no choice but to baby him, too.

"Do you think you can tell me some more about my dad later, Fritz? I love the way you tell the stories." Merry laughs a little. Sometimes, like now, she reminds me of Mr. Pershing at his most amiable, at his finest.

"You want to hear more nonsense about your illustrious parent, do you?" I ask, rolling my eyes like she's asking for the moon. But the truth is, I don't mind telling stories about him.

"Yes, sir, I do," she says.

She has still not gotten out of the habit of calling me sir. Like so many of Merry's little idiosyncrasies, it used to make me cringe. But lately there have been times—few and far between, of course—that I have actually found it a touch endearing.

"I want to know everything. Since I can't ever meet him, you're as close as I can get to my dad."

She has already finished her salad and packed up her cooler.

"By the way, I saw Jack Morningstar on his deck yesterday and was surprised he hadn't already gained twenty pounds from your cooking," I say.

"You saw him? I haven't seen him in days," she says, like the fact makes her sad.

"Oh, you've developed a bit of a crush, have you?" I ask.

"No, sir." Merry blushes. She looks quite sweet, hardly at all like the Dollywood hillbilly I brought here a month ago. "I have a boyfriend," she adds.

I scoff. "Phil the Neanderthal? Right, I forgot his romantic parting words. Something like: 'Go put on your uniform and get right back here, or else.'"

"He's gotten nicer since then. Even if I wasn't involved, it wouldn't make sense for me to have a crush on Jack Morningstar anyway."

"Why is that?"

"Because I never even get to step inside when I bring his food."

"Really?" I am surprised by this. Merry has been delivering delicious fare to Jack daily; I would have thought they'd have become friends, or started flirting, or something.

"Really. I thought maybe it was a good sign that he liked my cooking because you know the old saying."

"The one about the size of his feet?" I ask helpfully.

She laughs. "Shut up."

"Well, you're not asking for much. Not only was he your first, and continues to be your most consistent and easy customer—I mean, truly, what could be simpler than making extra when you cook for us and then running it next door?—but I take it that you would also like him to fall in love with you?"

"I don't have time for your nonsense," she says, lifting the heavy cooler with ease.

Now that it's evening and Merry has finished washing the dishes, we sit in the horrible living room. It looks somewhat less awful in lamplight, though the parrots in the upholstery will stare when I accidentally catch one's eye.

If I were alone, I would loosen my belt. Merry feeds us in a style that requires a great deal of restraint on my part. I was formerly in the habit of taking a morning jog on the sidewalk three days a week, but I've had to add an extra day due to Merry's meals.

On the positive side, I have picked up a bit of kitchen knowledge by observing her. Merry is a superb cook—a real artist, as Victor might say with reverence. Neither V nor I have ever willingly worn the apron in our relationship, and since I am in the doghouse for being here and not there, learning a few good recipes seems to me a wise course of action.

Tonight's mushroom lasagna took Merry so long to prepare and required so many steps, though, that it made my head ache. I assumed that it could never be worth all the fuss.

But it was.

Merry has taken up residence in the ugly pink recliner next to the old man's matching chair: two peas in a pod, as Merry might say.

He reaches for his cigarette pack, and she shakes her head no.

He grumbles and creaks and heads out to the deck for a smoke.

"I have some good news," Merry says.

She has chattered on at times about Phil's recent turnaround, how he has somehow seen the light and become a nice guy. I am more than a bit skeptical, believing if he has undergone a conversion, that it was surely of the television healer variety—all for show, which is to say very temporary indeed.

Merry has also mentioned, more than once, that he has asked to marry her. I dismissed the notion, of course, because the very idea of her cheerful smile and his angry red glower officially uniting is nothing short of absurd. I have come to think of Merry as a rather smart girl over the weeks that I have known her, so I haven't worried that she might actually accept him.

"What news is that?" I ask.

"It's time for you to check off my first task," she announces happily.

I exhale in relief before flatly telling her, "No."

"Why not? I have a few regular clients already. My marketing efforts seem to be panning out pretty well, and I'm going to run an ad in the paper next week."

"That's nice, but the answer is still no."

"But I'm in the black!"

"No."

"Yes, sir, I am!" She furrows her eyebrows and pouts like I popped her birthday balloon. "I'll show you my spreadsheet."

"Don't bother," I tell her.

"Why not? You don't want to admit that I'm right?"

"I'd have no trouble admitting it, if it were indeed the case."

"But it is! I've been tracking all my expenses against what I've earned, and, as of today, the second number is bigger than the first."

"What expenses are you tracking?"

"Ingredients, supplies, printing costs, gas money, and all that."

"Does the 'all that' include the rental cost of the SUV? The market cost of renting a kitchen, or, if you prefer, the prorated cost of renting this one? Heat? Electricity?" I stop there because Merry's somewhat crumpled posture tells me that she gets the point.

"I hadn't thought about those other things," she says. "But I guess you're right."

"I told you before, I usually am."

"Nice," she says, "that's really helpful."

"What's the name of your business again, Merry? It's called Help Yourself, and that's rather the point of all this. I suppose you thought I'd let you off easy."

"Easy?" she asks, looking at me with big, angry eyes. "Like your life has been? Growing up in *my* father's fancy house and going to expensive schools? *I* have never had it easy, and I haven't asked for anything to be easy, so don't act like I did!"

I wondered when little miss Pollyanna would show her jealousy of my relationship with her father. Of course, I knew it had to be in there somewhere, because I admit to some small moments of jealousy that she really is a Pershing and I'm not.

Our wayward smoker returns with impeccable timing. "What's going on here, children? You look like you've been squabbling," he says.

I sniff and turn away. Merry wipes her babyish tears with the back of her hand.

The old man squirms uncomfortably in his seat and motions for me to do something. I ignore him as long as I can.

"Didn't you mention to me that you were going to give

Merry her third task today, Fritz?"

She looks up at him. "He won't check off my second one."

"No, I won't. But, in the interest of time, while we're waiting for you to build up your business into a truly solvent enterprise, you can get started on the next task." I take a folded piece of paper from my pocket and throw it at her. Toward her, rather.

I don't want to sit here while she reads it, but I don't have any choice in the matter, which is the bloody story of my life right now. It doesn't help my mood that I am exceedingly mortified about this task. It is written in the silliest manner possible.

"Though it pains me, I suppose I must congratulate you on your success so far, Merry," the old man says, settling back into his horrendous pink chair. "It really has been lovely to see you cooking in this kitchen all day, and to be fed so well as a result, and to see your fledgling business start to fly, as it were."

She smiles at him in her ingratiating way, which I find quite annoying at the moment.

"On the other hand, of course," he says, clearing his throat, "it would be a bitter disappointment to me if you inherited this house. I've grown quite comfortable here."

She reaches out and pats his hand so earnestly that I could throw up. "If I get the house and decide to keep it," she tells him, "y'all can stay on as long as you want."

Y'all can stay as long as you want, I mock under my breath.

The old man shoots me a scolding glance, and I am tempted to say a few choice words.

"Read it out loud, Merry," he says quickly.

She reminds me of a politician running for office, the way she constantly smiles and so obviously wants everyone to like her. Of course she complies right away.

"Hello, Merry my dear," she reads. "I must congratulate you on making it thus far. The Pershing blood is a formidable substance, and I trust that being endowed with it will go a long way toward helping you achieve your goals."

I snort. Though I know it's immature of me, I frankly don't care. Merry skips the next line, which I remember refers to the infamous Pershing hemorrhoids, and despite my general annoyance with the entire situation, I admit that I am grateful for that omission.

"If you have inherited anything of my personality," she continues reading aloud, "I trust that you enjoy watching the ocean, spotting the dolphins, and perhaps walking along the beach. I hope so. It would help me rest easier somehow, in my present unpresent capacity, if you shared that affinity with me."

Merry pauses, sniffles, and wipes her eyes. The old man pats her shoulder.

I fold my arms. "Oh, get on with it," I say in a tone I'd rather not describe further.

Merry reads the next few lines in silence. They consist of juvenile insults about how difficult she must find it to put up with me, et cetera, followed by more mind-numbing ridiculousness about the magic of the sea, et cetera, which she also keeps to herself, thank *God*.

"Moving forward, then," she reads aloud, finally getting to the point. "Task number three: Find someone lonelier than you and befriend him. Look left. Look for a banana."

Merry giggles.

"What?" the old man asks.

"Well, it's a little strange, isn't it? I mean, do you suppose my dad was in his right mind?" She looks from the old man to me and back again.

He coughs, but soon regains the use of his black-lunged breath.

"All the Pershings have always been in their right minds," he asserts. "I think it's rather rude to suggest otherwise. That task makes perfect sense to me. In fact, it strikes me as quite cagey."

"Can you explain it then?" Merry asks. She reaches over and touches his hand again, apparently by way of apology for offending his—their, rather—bloodline.

"Perhaps it occurred to your father that you might benefit from a bit of innocent matchmaking?" He looks to me, and I get the impression that he would rather have me take over the explanation.

I don't.

"Matchmaking from the grave?" Merry says, shaking her head like she's finally gotten angry at something and forgotten to be Pollyanna-perfect. "I didn't mind coming here for the chance to know more about my father and to try and earn this house and help my family. I didn't mind getting a makeover. I didn't mind being challenged to try and make a career for myself. But being pushed away from Phil and toward someone else because some man who's never met me but happened to be my biological father thought it was a good idea? I mean, who the hell did my dad think he was?" She looks incredulously from me to the old man, who suddenly appears quite stricken.

"And Phil can be a nice guy when he wants to be. He's been visiting my relatives and bringing them over treats, which in my book is a very sweet thing to do!" Merry says.

Everyone is quiet for a minute.

"Who do you suppose he meant, anyway?" Merry asks.

"I believe it said to look left. Isn't that so? And to look for a banana," I helpfully remind them.

The old man shrugs his shoulders like he hasn't got a clue.

"Jack Morningstar lives to the left," I point out, to speed things up.

"Jack Morningstar? My father wanted me to befriend Jack…because he liked him so well, I suppose. And the part about a banana?"

"What color is Jack's surfboard, Merry? Isn't it yellow?" the old man asks.

Merry nods thoughtfully. "Then I think this means Fritz can already check off task number three. I'm already as much of a friend to Jack as he'll let me be."

The old man laughs heartily. "You may be right! What do you think, Fritz? What do you think Claude would say to Merry's point? You're his barrister; this is your show. What say you?"

I reply, again in a tone that wouldn't flatter me to elaborate upon, "If it were entirely up to me, we could check off all the tasks right now, Merry could take the deed to the house, and I could catch the next flight back to London."

The old man shoots me a look. "Well, that seems rather

drastic, and I would be left without any chance to gain this house. No, I think you had better stick to the plan you and your employer worked out. It wouldn't be very sporting to do otherwise. So I suggest you should simply check off task number three and continue on with the next one."

"Do you want it now?" I ask Merry, thinking how I might wrap it around a brick before gently tossing it in their general direction.

"Let's wait. I'll be fresher in the morning, I think, and more ready to tackle it. Would either of you like to go for a beach walk with me before the lasagna settles on our hips?"

"Perhaps tomorrow, my dear," the old man says.

I haven't seen him walk down to the beach a single time since he came here.

"Come on, Fritz. Come for a walk with me," she says, reaching out her hand and smiling in a placating sort of way.

"I truly despise the beach," I say, frankly not caring for the moment that neither this ludicrous situation nor my resultant foul mood is technically Merry's fault. "You ask me every single day, and I invariably say no. So let's spare ourselves this ritual going forward, shall we? I will never go down to the beach voluntarily. If the house caught fire and the street out front was likewise engulfed, then perhaps I might venture out to your beloved sand pit. But only then. Is that clear enough?"

Merry's short hair blows in the wind when she opens the door.

Chapter Thirteen

IN WHICH CHASER BRINGS
HOME A FRIEND

As told by our Jack, who has very mixed feelings

I have gotten used to letting Chaser run down to the beach to do her business because afterward she always comes right back up. But today she turns away from her potty spot and races toward the only person walking along the beach in either direction, as far as I can see.

"Chaser!" I call.

She ignores me. For such a well-trained, eager-to-please dog, she's developed a stubborn streak recently. She gallops in pursuit of the lone walker, and I already know that it's Merry. I can tell because of how determined Chaser is to catch up with her.

I confess that I have become a little partial to Merry as well. Especially her cooking, but her smile hasn't escaped my notice. It's hard not to appreciate an attractive woman who delivers delicious food to your door on a daily basis. If I were another man, in another phase of his life, I might chase after her on the beach, too. But of course I'm me, and it's now, and so any ideas of romance are out of the question.

"Chaser!" I call again.

The wind is with my yell, and Merry turns around. Chaser is already beside her.

Instead of ignoring my dog, which would help my efforts, Merry hugs and pets her. She smiles and waves to me, then turns around to continue her walk. Chaser stays by her side like they belong together.

I would go after them to teach Chaser that she can't just run off to anyone she wants anytime she feels like it. I don't think Merry would like to see me scold her four-legged friend, though, even if I had the time to do it.

I must finish reviewing the final Langdon Logistics proposal in the next hour or we'll miss our deadline for consideration. Martin spent months planning the details of this project, which would keep our staff busy and avoid the layoffs that have been looming over us like an ugly storm cloud. I've spent the last few weeks putting my stamp on the design. I'm just triple-checking the figures to make sure it's airtight.

I haven't had time to surf since the night Chaser introduced me to Merry. I also don't like the idea that she and Fritz might watch and fret from next door. I need fewer people worrying about me, not more.

I pour myself another cup of coffee to try to make up for my restless night. Katie has been absent from my dreams for weeks now, no matter how much I have pleaded for her. Sleep eventually comes, but she doesn't. I miss her so much that I wake up aching.

I came to this island, to this house, because we had made some of our best memories here. I stayed because Katie became real to me through the long nights that made the days bearable, only because they were followed by more nights. If she doesn't return to my dreams, there will be no reason for me to stay.

Chicago, with all its pain and chaos, doesn't feel like home now either.

I don't know where else I could go. Maybe there is no place for me anymore.

I finish checking the proposal and send it out via e-mail ten minutes before Jaycee's deadline. She plans to hand-deliver it to the client over dinner. I know this, along with the facts that her nanny's car is in the shop, her microwave broke last night in the middle of popcorn, and her son Graham's cold didn't keep him from scoring four points in his kindergarten-league basketball game yesterday.

It had made me dizzy for a second, listening to so much evidence of a real person's real life, in which she interacts with other real people out in the real world. In my isolation, it's easy to forget that the rest of society just continues on in the absence of Katie and me.

I hear footsteps on the exterior stairs and look up to see a windblown Merry standing on my deck, with Chaser beside her.

The house is a complete shambles. Instead of opening the door and inviting Merry inside, which seems like the polite thing to do, I step out and close the door behind me.

My arrangement with Merry, by design, hasn't involved interaction. She brings my daily bread in the middle of my workday. She comes around to the front of the house, puts food inside the cooler that now lives on the stoop, and rings the bell to let me know it's there.

I hired her to feed me after she woke up my taste buds with her bag of free samples. When I called the number on her menu and spoke with her about her cost and my convenience, I told her not to wait for me to answer the door when she makes her deliveries. I explained that, more often than not, I would be in an Internet meeting or on the phone when she came by. She leaves a bill with her Thursday deliveries, and I put a check in the cooler on Fridays.

Sometimes I step outside a minute after I hear the bell. I yell, "Thanks," and wave just as she's at her own front door, to be civil, and to see her smile. After three weeks of eating food she's made with her own two hands and brought to me like a present, I'm starting to feel bad that I haven't really spoken to her since the night we met.

Chaser seems determined for us to become friends. She races up to Merry on the beach every chance she gets. Tonight, apparently, she went so far as to lure Merry home.

"Your dog is a sweet walking partner."

Merry's accent is mellow and soothing. She takes her time with words like *sweet* and *partner*.

"I told her to go on home after our walk, but she wouldn't. So I thought I'd better bring her up. I wanted to make sure she made it back to you safe and sound."

My filthy house makes inviting Merry in for a drink impossible, along with about a thousand other reasons...or one. Chaser dances a full circle around her, though, as if she doesn't see any reason why we can't just bring her new best friend inside. She stares unblinkingly at Merry, like she expects her to throw a Frisbee at any moment.

"Why is this dog so taken with you?" I ask. "You must be feeding her."

Merry blushes.

I realize what I just said and feel stupid and hopeless. I sounded like I used to, back in my dating days, when I was an artless old flirt. That was a lifetime ago.

I look down at the deck floor, which is sandy from neglectful care. I look at Chaser, who hasn't had a bath, or even a brushing, since we came here.

Merry pushes back her hair.

"Was today's lasagna dry when y'all warmed it up?" she asks. "I should've told you to leave it in the oven five minutes less than I wrote. I hope it wasn't too dry."

Merry not only feeds me better than I have ever eaten, she writes out instructions on how to perfectly enjoy the day's offerings. She often puts a joke or a quote into her warm-up notes, always something that makes me smile or think. When I saw she wasn't *Mary*, but *Merry*, it just fit. I've never told her that I enjoy those little extras, but she keeps it up anyway.

"Dry?" I ask. "No. Honestly, I don't think I've ever tasted anything so good."

It's true. The memory of tonight's lasagna, along with Merry's prolonged smile, makes me pause.

"There was a dead pelican up a ways that Chaser was fixing to roll in. But when I told her no, she came right back to me. She's a good girl."

That's what Katie always called her. *Good, good girl.*

I pet Chaser on the head, feeling sick and empty inside.

"Well, now that she's back at home, I'll say goodnight," Merry says, already walking away.

Chapter Fourteen

IN WHICH FRITZ AND UNCLE MAX ARGUE CURIOUSLY

As told by Merry, the peacemaker wannabe

"Will you be stopping by a store while you're out, by chance?" Uncle Max asks. He just came back inside from having a smoke on the deck.

"Yes, sir. What can I get you?"

He hands me a list:

> *Hemorrhoid cream*
> *Cigarettes*

"Sure, no problem. Can you wait until later for these things, or should I make a quick run now?" I do the math and have just enough time. I made extra cookies and rolls to send to Mom and Grandma in Peaksy Falls, so I need to drop a box by the post office, too. I tucked an extra bag in there for the little ladies to bring to Missy Hancock; I know Mom and Grandma are just itching to see her babies again, but need an excuse to push them over their natural shyness.

"Later will be fine," Uncle Max says. He checks to see if the coast is clear. "I would have asked Fritz, but he's in a foul mood again this morning. He was the most cheerful boy…" Uncle Max looks off into the distance, as if he's watching a nice memory play out like an old home movie. Then he frowns. "But he started to have gloomy moods as a teenager. Not often, you know, only when he felt pressured, around exam time and suchlike. He hasn't been quite the same since his mother died." Uncle Max shakes his head solemnly.

"I didn't know you two knew each other so well. You said you weren't really close with your brother, and since Fritz lived with him…"

Uncle Max picks up one of the muffins cooling on the counter and takes a large bite.

Fritz sniffs from the top of the stairs behind me. I hadn't heard him come up.

"Right," he says. "Well, this Mr. Pershing was around quite a lot over the years, and we became acquainted. He with my 'gloomy moods,' and me with his, his, shall we say *personality*?"

"By 'personality,' you mean all my faults," Uncle Max says, looking stricken.

I suppose they're both still in mourning over my dad. It must've been really hard for Uncle Max to lose a brother and for Fritz to lose a father figure. They're probably each trying to deal with it. I'm sort of jealous, in a weird way, that they knew my dad well enough to miss him so much.

"We must be boring you, Merry," Uncle Max says.

He looks older and more worn out than he did when he first came into the room. His cough is downright scary at times, and he gets pale and sort of grayish. Whenever I ask any questions about how he's feeling, he calls *Poppycock!* When Fritz makes him take his medicine, Uncle Max calls him a *Henpecker*.

"Y'all can have a nice long chat any time you want, and don't worry about me," I say, trying to smooth things over.

I have really taken a shine to both of these men. Uncle Max is easy because he compliments my cooking till I blush. But I care a whole lot for Fritz, too.

I've got to focus on work now. I'm catering a school board meeting today. It's not a huge job, but I'm happy to have it. The lady who hired me has a daughter graduating from high school this spring, and she peppered me with questions about doing food for a hundred guests at the graduation party.

I also got a call out of the blue from somebody who liked my Asian pasta salad and ginger cookie samples. She asked if I can do an anniversary party for seventy-five guests in July.

I wish I could, but I just can't agree to do the big parties until I know that I'll be here to follow through on them. It wouldn't be right to take on work that far ahead, not knowing if I'll even be here. I might get kicked out long beforehand.

If I'm still here, though, I'd love those jobs. I'd have to hire some part-time help and invest in some bigger warming trays and other supplies. I'm already making a list, just in case.

I was supposed to get my fourth task this morning, but I don't want to bug Fritz for it right now. He's frowning toward Uncle Max, who's gone out on the deck to have another smoke.

Suddenly Uncle Max turns and knocks on the patio door. "Dolphins!" he shouts.

My uncle Max and I are in synch about the ocean: we both love it and stare out there any old chance we get. We especially love spotting dolphins. I never, ever get sick of the sight. A day hasn't passed without seeing some, but it somehow feels new and fresh every time.

"Come on, Fritz. Dolphins!" I say on my way out to watch the show.

He shakes his head. "Go ahead. You two can enjoy them well enough without me."

Fritz has paperwork spread out all over the kitchen table by the time I'm packed up and ready to go set up for the school board meeting.

"What're you working on?" I ask as I tape up the Peaksy Falls ladies' care package and slip Jack's instructions into his bag.

I always like to add little notes. Today in Jack's I added a quote by Abraham Lincoln I had noticed at the printer's shop. I liked it so well that I also wrote it out neatly and hung it in the corner of my bathroom mirror. It says: *Whatever you are, be a good one.* Inspiring, right?

Fritz sighs. "I'm paying bills for Mr. Pershing's London house and reviewing bids to get it ready to sell. It needs to have some painting done, and so forth, so that it's in tip-top shape."

"So it's going to be sold soon?"

"I still don't know for certain when I should have it listed, as the papers haven't been made available to me, which is rather a pain in my ass. An additional pain." He rubs his eyes like he's fixing to take them right out. "If you're hoping to inherit it, I'm afraid you'll be disappointed. I expect the directions will be to sell it and divide the proceeds among Mr. Pershing's favorite charities. I don't think any of that money will go to you."

"Good," I say.

"Good?" he asks, like he must've heard wrong.

"Well, I admit it was a welcome shock when you showed up and said I might have an inheritance coming. If I could earn it, that is. Especially now that I know the money could help my mom and grandma and Aunt Betty, I really hope I can make it through to the finish line. But this house and that money would be more than I ever dreamed of having."

"Of course," Fritz says. "That's precious. I almost forgot you are perpetually playing the part of a Disney princess, always kind and fair and looking on the bright side. Bloody hell."

I ignore his comments. I feel bad that he's determined to be angry all the time. I heard him arguing with Victor last night on the phone. I wasn't trying to listen, but I could hear. I was still up because I'd just had a similar conversation with Phil. He seems to have decided that since charming me back hasn't worked, he'll go ahead and try bullying me instead.

"I just hope that my dad left you something you cared about, Fritz. I can tell you loved him and that you were very good to him. You're still being good to him—more than he probably deserved—putting up with me and being away from home and all."

Fritz doesn't look up from his papers, but his jaw tightens, and I can guess the answer.

I want to believe that my father was a great man. I want to think that the quirks and failings Fritz likes to sum up in funny stories just go to show that he was on the eccentric side, but still had a big heart and a big soul.

But then some kernel of information comes along to make

me wonder. Like him insulting his sweet brother Max in his letters or not leaving anything to Fritz. I want to believe my dad was kind, and I wish every clue pointed that way.

"Want me to rent us a movie for later?" I ask. "You like Disney ones, you said?" I tease.

He doesn't look up as he replies. "If you'll stay with the old man tonight, I think I'll go into the city for some fresh air."

"Sure, no problem," I say. I place Jack's bag and the ladies' postage box on top of the cooler before I pick it up and begin to haul it downstairs.

I confess that our neighbor Jack has been on my mind all morning. Probably on account of how I saw him up close last night and talked to him for a while on his deck. Maybe my dad's nudging me toward him from the grave, too. Anyhow, I took bread from the oven while thinking of Jack. I thought of him while washing fruit and dicing vegetables. The dolphins swimming by made me think of the night he was out there in the deep water. I kind of wish I could say a few words to him this morning, in person.

But even if I want to, I know I won't see Jack when I drop off his food. I'll just have to leave it in the cooler, as usual, because that man is never going to invite me in.

I don't pull back into my space in the garage until eight o'clock, which is a lot later than I had planned. I got a last-minute call about catering an office party tomorrow, so I had to shop at the big grocery store in the city to get everything I'll need.

I left a message on Fritz's phone about what they should eat for dinner, since I wouldn't be there in time to serve them myself. Now I'm looking at several hours of work before I can shut my eyes. But that's OK; I'm inching closer to officially breaking even and getting my first task checked off. And, maybe more importantly in a way, I'm learning that I really can run my own business!

The luncheon today went so well that I was offered that graduation job. I need to talk it over with Fritz and see what he thinks about me scheduling work that is still months out. The way I'm starting to look at it is, even if I don't get this place, I want to keep my business going somehow.

Phil didn't send any messages today. I felt bad about our fight last night and kind of hoped he'd call or maybe send a sweet love note, but all I have are empty inboxes. Phil has been so familiar for so long that I suppose it's hard to not hear from him. Even a lumpy old pillow still feels good to rest your head on, especially if it's that or nothing. In Mom's last letter, she said they haven't seen hide nor hair of him for the past week.

When I hand over his bag with the cigarettes and cream in it, Uncle Max pulls a face that says I'm in big trouble. I look at the sofa to see Fritz sitting with his arms folded across his chest like he's spitting mad.

"What?" I ask as I unload the other bags I hauled up the three flights of stairs and hefted onto the counter.

Fritz doesn't answer.

It takes me a minute before I recall that I told him I'd stay here tonight so he could go out.

"Oh shoot, Fritz! I'm sorry I'm later than I thought I'd be. It seems like you could've left without me, though. You'd have been fine here, wouldn't you, Uncle Max?"

"I told Fritz that. I told him I didn't need a babysitter because I have a lingering cold. But he wouldn't listen."

"Don't wait up," Fritz mutters on his way down the stairs.

I go to the stairwell and call after him, "I'm sorry! I'll make it up to you."

I feel just awful about having ruined his night.

I finish carrying up and putting away all the groceries before I finally can give in to Uncle Max's begging for an extra piece of chocolate cake. First I drizzle chocolate sauce on the plate in a flower pattern. Then I set the slice carefully in the center, shave dark chocolate over the top, and sprinkle a little powdered sugar. This is just how he likes it. I drape a napkin over his lap to protect his clothes and serve it to him in his chair, along with his whiskey and a glass of milk.

Then I get started on prepping tomorrow's menu.

The doorbell rings and I step out onto the streetside deck to see down to the front door. "Hi, Jack!" I sort of squeal before I catch myself and try to sound calmer. "I'll be right down!"

I pat my hair and neaten my blouse on my way. I know I must look a mess because I've been working since dawn. I skip down the stairs anyway and give him a big smile when I reach the door.

He smiles back.

"Hi there, neighbor," I say. "You're just in time. I have one serving of chocolate cake left. So come on in!"

I move aside to make way, but he stays put.

"I don't want to get spoiled," he says, like he's a little shy. "The piece I had with my dinner was a slice of heaven," he adds.

"What can I do for you?"

"This was in with my food, but it wasn't meant for me." He hands me a piece of paper in my Help Yourself signature green color. The printer threw in a few notepads as freebies.

I feel my face turn red as a beet when I realize that I must've put his note in the box that I sent off to my mom and grandma in Peaksy Falls. Which means he read what I'd meant to say to them about my handsome neighbor.

"I'm sorry for the mix-up," I say quietly. I'm so humiliated I could just cry. "I got up so early, I guess maybe I wasn't awake yet."

"How is business going?"

"Really well," I say.

"I hope not so well that you stop taking the little jobs, like feeding me."

"I wouldn't do that." I'm still too embarrassed to look him in the eyes. I can't believe I gave him the wrong note!

"Good. Well, I better get back home. Chaser will be jealous that I saw you and she didn't." He turns to go. "Goodnight."

"Goodnight."

I chatter like a mortified magpie to Uncle Max on my way up the stairs, telling him about the dumb mistake I made. "... so Jack got the note I meant for them! Oh good Lord. And I'm sure those little ladies will be scratching their heads over why on earth I sent them an Abraham Lincoln quote. They'll probably believe it's a clue to the game show they think I'm working on…" But when I get to the top, I see that Uncle Max has already disappeared into his room.

Cake and all.

When I finally make it downstairs and am fixing to fall into bed, I notice an envelope on my pillow. It has *Fourth Task* written across it in Fritz's neat-as-a-pin writing.

I'm so tired that I'm tempted to just wait until tomorrow to open it up. But I have my alarm set for 5:00 a.m. as it is, and tomorrow is going to be filled to the brim. I stifle a yawn and take out two typewritten pieces of paper, figuring I may as well see what I'm up against.

Hello, Merry.

I hope that you are enjoying your stay at the ocean and that you are not working so hard that you forget to take time out to smell the air, to listen to the wild calls of the various sea birds, to feel the salty breezes, and to keep a keen watch out for dolphins.

I will make a posthumous confession to you: whenever I saw a dolphin jump out of the water (which often happens in what I can only believe is playfulness in its purest form), I made a wish. Because I loved to do so and because I wanted to believe in the efficacy of doing so, I made it a point to only wish for things that I was relatively certain would happen anyway. An example: "I wish for nice wine with my dinner this evening." This was a safe request, since I had an ample supply shipped from a lovely wine shop straight to my door each time I arrived on the island. Another: "I wish to sleep well tonight." This likewise was a virtual given, since I never slept as well as I did after spending a day at the sea.

I wished for easy things, in short, because I have always believed in setting myself up for success. Had I known about you earlier in your life, my dear Merry, I certainly would have wished to meet you, and I would have gone to the ends of the earth to ensure that my wish came true. And you can trust me when I say that, had I known about you earlier, I would have made it one of my life's highest priorities to help set you up for success as well.

I am tired and weak tonight, so I'll get on with it.

Task #4: Find out your mother's secret and see how far the apple falls from the tree.

I apologize that I cannot elaborate. As I said, I am tired. You have the energy of the young and the living, and I know you will wisely endeavor to figure the task out on your own or to enlist help where practicable and appropriate.

Yours belatedly, and with love,

Claude Pershing

(a.k.a. Dad)

Now what in the heck does that task mean, I wonder? I wish Fritz was here because I know there's got to be some mistake: there is absolutely no way in the world my mom has a secret!

Sometimes I get so frustrated because I feel like getting through these tasks is really life or death for me. A life of satisfying work in a place that I love and helping my family out of their terrible predicaments, or a slow death of going back to Peaksy Falls a failure, wondering if I could've succeeded if I would've just tried a little harder, worked a little longer.

A note in Fritz's handwriting at the bottom of the page doesn't help at all: *I e-mailed you a link to another one of your Aunt Betty's podcasts.*

He's got to be kidding me! Leaving me a cryptic task when he's not even here to answer questions and then saying, "By the way, you should hear what your kooky Aunt Betty has been saying on the radio."

Though I really, really don't want to hear it, I turn on my laptop and click the link to the podcast of my Aunt Betty's show. Because, let's face it, I won't be getting any sleep until Fritz gets home and I make him explain what in heaven's name I'm supposed to do before he'll check off task number four.

I hear the intro music I've heard a thousand times before and Aunt Betty's voice opening *The Betty Answers Show*. Then she launches right in.

My call lines are dark this morning. While we wait for someone to light them up, I'll philosophize on a question I recently saw in a magazine.

Sometimes I honestly can't believe that I ever found her interesting or smart at all.

The question was this: Why do you live where, and how, you live? Many people might scoff at such a question and write it off as silly. Those people are victims of inertia—they live where and how they do because life has happened to them and they have let it.

People who nod thoughtfully when such a question is asked have likely chosen their course and can explain it, if not completely defend it.

How do I live?

I live alone.

She can say that again! She's never even had a cat or a boyfriend that I can recall.

My sofa is modern and too rigid to be comfortable. I prefer to have only one inviting chair in my home: my own chair. The television provides me company, and I watch it almost all the time that I am home. I argue with talk show hosts and participants in dramas. I get to know them all in the limited, one-sided way that callers to my show get to know me.

Wait, she's telling the truth. And more of it than I've ever known her to do. Maybe she's not in her right mind today. Maybe she has a fever, and Fritz wanted me to listen because he thinks I should check on her or something.

When my head is very full of memories or worries, I turn on a Spanish-language soap opera. It soothes me, probably for the same reason I prefer speaking to nonnative English speakers: because there's very little nuance to it. All I get are the main ideas, and only if they are conveyed in an obvious enough way. Irony is lost, as is sarcasm and inflection; subtlety dashes out of the picture. I find it refreshing.

I wish I could exist that way in the world, only dealing in main ideas. No background or supporting imagery to muddy things, nothing for anyone to find by digging deeper or looking more carefully. Only the door slams, or the slaps in the face, or the bursting-into-tears of a Spanish soap. Only the surface-level, only the obvious.

Jesus Jenny! I wonder what my grandma and mom thought when they heard this show. I wonder if they were finally glad that she goes by a different last name and pretends she's not a relative. I know I am.

Someone close asked me a few years ago why I didn't just go live alone in the desert, or join a nunnery, or move to Antarctica. For how much I interact with other people, she said, I may as well go ahead and officially drop out of society instead of pretending to be in it, but not really.

I remember that show. It was my mom who called in, but of course Aunt Betty referred to her as "Darla."

I remember laughing lightly; it was on air, of course, and I also quoted her some of the more tolerable lines from my book.

I suppose that person is right, in a way. But only in the manner that someone outside a situation can feel that they know all about it. Though she is the person I have been most connected to in life, she still is not me. She thinks that because she knows all about me, my motivations, decisions, and their repercussions, that she really knows how I feel and what's best for me.

The problem is that she won't believe me when I say my life is really how I want it. Though it looks lonely and disconnected to her, it's my choice. Maybe I'm happy as can be; it isn't for her to say. I never explain anything, as anyone listening should know by now.

Look here, we have a caller.

Hello caller, are you there? This is Betty Answers, and you're live on The Betty Answers Show.

I close my browser after listening to the first caller, during which Aunt Betty turned back into her usual weirdo on-air self and stayed that way.

All my life, I never heard my aunt say more than two sentences about herself in a row, then lately she spills the beans every chance she gets. I don't know what to make of it.

It's embarrassing to remember, but I used to call in to her show when I was a kid. I'd set a tape recorder going in the loft next to the radio and call in from the kitchen. Later I'd listen to it back and giggle my head off. I used to love being in on the big secret that she was really my Aunt Betty, but we were keeping that fact from the listening audience. I imagined a million people out there, not the handful there really was. Anyway, back then I thought it was fun to playact like that.

I stopped calling when I was about thirteen. That's when I found out my friends who'd heard of it thought the show was dumb, and I realized it wasn't cool to call into an uncool show. I made excuses not to go out birthday shopping with Aunt Betty around then, too. Or for our yearly Christmas trip to the theater. I guess you could say I outgrew her.

Some long-forgotten image is sticking in my mind, and I stop to remember it.

There was another night, years ago, when Aunt Betty acted in the same odd way that she's been acting on the podcasts of her show. It was back when I was about to leave for college, and she insisted that I let her take me out to dinner. We went to a restaurant in the city that was supposed to be really great, but I hadn't been there yet since Mom and Grandma don't like going out, and it was too expensive for our budget anyway.

During dinner, Aunt Betty drank too much wine. Way too much wine. I could tell after the second glass that I'd be driving her home, and she still drank two more. That in itself was strange enough because she wasn't generally a drinker, or at least I'd never seen her drink.

That night she started telling me what it was like for her when she was my age and had moved away to college. I didn't really get to find out much because I was too embarrassed when she began to cry before dessert arrived, right in the middle of the restaurant, and I couldn't even eat my crème brûlée, which was supposed to be phenomenal.

I told Aunt Betty she could finish her story in the car and coaxed her out of there, with her leaning on me and still crying the whole way and people staring like we'd just landed our spaceship in the middle of the dining room.

When we got to the car and I had made her get in the passenger seat—I mean, duh—she became quiet. It was like she flipped a switch and was suddenly a different person. She went from saying too much to not saying anything at all in an instant.

All the way home that night, Aunt Betty refused to say another word.

Not even goodbye.

Tonight I figure I don't have anything to lose by calling her again. She said I could once, and I'd sort of like to make sure she's OK since she's been acting so loony. And maybe she might even have an idea about what secret my mom could possibly be keeping.

She answers her home phone on the first ring.

"Uh, hi, Aunt Betty. How are you?"

"I'm fine, thank you. And how are you?"

"I'm fine, too, ma'am. Are you sure you're well?"

"Yes, Merry."

"OK. Well, I wondered if you could help me with something then?"

"Possibly. What is it?"

"It's a long story, but basically I have to figure something out. I know this probably sounds funny, but I wondered if you happened to know of any secrets my mom might have?"

"Secrets?" she asks. She sounds a little worried, but it's hard to tell from a disembodied voice on the phone. Maybe she's staring at her television screen and some Spanish-speaking lady is about to faint or shoot someone.

"Yes. Apparently my mom has a secret, and I've got to find out what it is."

"Why is that, Merry?" Aunt Betty asks slowly, like I'm a really dumb caller to her show.

"Because that's what my father wanted me to do." I instantly regret saying it because I don't want to get into the whole story, but it just slipped out.

"Your father?" she asks. "Are you with him now? Is that where you've run off to?"

"I haven't run off," I tell her.

"Is he there with you now?"

"No, ma'am, he isn't even alive anymore."

"Your father is dead?" she asks, like she's suddenly trying to act a part in one of her dramas—excited one second, then nervous, then demanding, then sad.

I wish I had never called.

I sigh like Fritz.

"Yes, ma'am. I don't want you worrying Mom or Grandma about it because they don't really know the whole story, but basically he left some riddles for me to work through so I can earn an inheritance. I know it sounds pretty odd, but I have to find out about my mom's secret. I guess I should have called her, but she doesn't like talking on the phone much, except when she calls in to your show. And if she does have a secret, she won't necessarily want to tell it just because I ask. So do you know anything that might qualify as a secret?"

"Merry, where are you? The young Englishman who whisked you away refuses to tell me anything and doesn't even return my calls. I have been worried sick. Merry! You've got to tell me where you are and who you're with," Aunt Betty demands.

"I've *got* to?" I know I sound sassy, but so does she.

"Yes!"

"I'm a grown woman, and I'm safe, and I'm doing some good, honest work. That's all you need to know," I say before I hang up the phone.

I should have realized it would be a waste of time to call Aunt Betty. She never has good answers anyway.

Chapter Fifteen

IN WHICH JACK ACTS ON IMPULSE

As told by Mr. Morningstar, with
an assist from Mr. Copperfield

Chaser whines at the door. I let her out and she races down the steps to catch up with a lone, familiar figure walking in the distance. Of course it's Merry.

I have at times suspected Merry of slipping aphrodisiacs into my food. Why else would I find myself daydreaming about her?

It started with the note she mistakenly left in my cooler a week ago. It was effusive and funny and showed her to be a thoughtful and caring daughter. It also said, "I finally got to talk to my neighbor last night—I don't think I've ever seen a man so handsome."

It struck me as incredibly strange at first: the idea that someone might think of me that way. I haven't felt handsome, or even particularly human, in a long while. I wouldn't be surprised if I were completely invisible to others; I so often feel like a shadow.

Maybe that's why I felt the need to bring the note back to her. I wanted to make sure she could still see me. And I wanted to see her—to prove I hadn't imagined her somehow.

My days have been filled with long work hours. Since we delivered the Langdon proposal and are waiting for an answer, I've been catching up on other design work that has been piling up during these past few months. I'm plugging away, day by day, trying to regain my footing as well as my clients' confidence. Perhaps Merry also puts Prozac into my food because along with my satisfied stomach, intrusive thoughts of her, and a renewing work ethic, I feel less of an urge to exhaust my body and mind in the ocean.

Thoughts of Merry have not displaced thoughts of my wife. Katie is always somewhere in my mind. Often in the forefront, but sometimes in the background, when I'm only aware that she is there because I accidentally type her name in the middle of a business letter or hear myself say something out loud that makes Chaser perk up her ears and look at me with worried eyes.

Usually it's, *"Why?"*

Lately I've had to study pictures to remember certain details of her face. Sometimes I get up in the middle of the night to look at her.

Through the window I think I see Merry climbing the exterior stairs to my deck like she did a week ago. I'm not sure it's really her, though. Sometimes I have imagined her out there, only to become either relieved or disappointed to discover I was mistaken, depending on my mood. I have caught glimpses of her walking along the beach or entering her house again after dropping off my meals. At times, I have found myself watching for her without intending to.

Merry knocks on my sliding door. She's really there. This place is a pigsty, so I step outside and shut the door behind me.

"I brought back your sweet dog again," she says, looking wonderful: windblown, fresh, happy, and full of life.

"Thanks."

"How was your steak tonight?"

"Phenomenal," I say. "Truly."

Merry puts her hand on my arm. The warmth of it stirs something inside me. Like a lizard resting on a sunny rock, I feel myself start to come alive.

"I'm glad y'all liked it. I just wanted to make sure Chaser made it back to you, safe and sound," she says.

She takes her hand away and turns to go.

I don't want her to.

"Hey," I say.

She looks back and smiles.

"I'd invite you in, but honestly, I'm ashamed of the state of this house," I say.

She shakes her head, like it can't be *that* bad.

"You wouldn't want to come in. It smells," I confess.

"Really?"

"I wish I wasn't such a slob."

Her smile is gorgeous, but her skeptical frown is even better. What the hell did she put in my steak?

Her smile fades. I see that she thinks I'm trying to get rid of her by using a lame excuse. Of course she doesn't believe me because who would actually live the way I'm living?

"What if we went out for drinks?" I hear someone say, and half a beat later I am horrified to know it was me. I feel a rush of adrenaline. It's only partially excitement; the rest is panic.

She double-whammies me with a skeptical frown followed by a big, beautiful smile.

"I'll need to get my purse and put some shoes on. How about you pick me up next door when you're ready, in maybe fifteen minutes or so?"

An hour later, I finally leave my house through the front door. I took a shower right after I watched Merry walk down the steps toward the beach. It was supposed to be a quick one to sober me because I felt punch-drunk.

It was supposed to miraculously wake me up from the nightmare that began on October fifteenth. No, to transport me back further, to whenever it was that Katie began to be lost to me, so that I could change whatever needed changing, do whatever needed to be done. To keep her heart and mind connected to my heart and mind, and stop that first domino from falling that has led to this here and now instead of the one that should have been.

I started to think, and before I knew it, I was racked with sobs. I'm not sure exactly what brought them on: fear, guilt, mental exhaustion? Probably those and more, I don't know. If I knew my own head, I wouldn't be here, and maybe Katie would.

Christ, I'll break down again if I keep thinking.

I consider staying in. Calling Merry and making up an excuse. But the idea of doing that seems almost as hopeless as just going. I remember reading this line in one of my dad's psych magazines when I was younger: "Do something life-affirming: Call your grandmother, or plant some flowers, or walk your dog." I thought it was sage advice. How could it not be, set off in a square pink callout on a page that had an unshaven man in grayscale with his head in his hands? Now, trying to picture it, that man was a dead ringer for me.

It seems like a step in the right direction to have a drink with Merry, a good addition to the life-affirming list. It doesn't seem dangerous or evil. I don't understand why my legs feel like they're made of lead as I make my way across the driveway to my car. Logically, they should feel fine. I'm trying to affirm life here.

This house doesn't have a garage; instead, there are spaces under it to park. If Merry is watching out through her window, wondering why I'm so late, she can see me fill a plastic bag with debris from my small sports car. It's not as disgustingly unkempt as the house, but only because I rarely drive anywhere. I toss away old coffee cups, fast-food sandwich containers, newspapers from various places I passed through on my way here, and a broken umbrella.

I focus on the mechanics of getting into my car and driving next door.

I ring the bell.

Fritz opens up. "Finally," he says with his eyebrows raised, like I'm five hours late for a formal engagement.

"Hi, Fritz." I shake his hand. I feel guilty for my self-protectively cold reception of him when I arrived on the island. "I'm really sorry about Claude. He was quite a guy."

"Thanks," he says. We only fleetingly make eye contact, but

it is enough to make his voice become strained. "I'm sorry about Katie, too. She was lovely."

I want to thank him back, but my throat constricts. She was lovely.

"I'll get Merry," he says, heading upstairs.

I wonder who Fritz is in relation to Merry. From his irritation about my being late, I might guess that he is her brother. But they look completely different, and their accents couldn't be further apart.

"Hi, Jack!" Merry calls from above.

She skips down the stairs toward me, in a flutter of color and motion, until she's standing right in front of me. She smiles and I feel steadier.

When we first get inside the car, I think that I can imagine she's Katie, at least for the dark drive, if I put on some quiet music and we don't speak.

But Merry's perfume is different than my wife's, and she hums along with the music. She reaches over and pats my hand. "I'm glad y'all made it," she says quietly.

I can't say it aloud because I don't trust my voice, but even though this step is hard as hell, and I'm not sure how I'll feel five minutes from now, for this one moment I think I'm glad I made it, too.

Merry agrees to the first little island restaurant I point out as a possibility. It's dark inside, sort of damp-feeling, and covered from floor to ceiling with wood paneling. She leads me to a booth near the jukebox and a small dance floor.

There are a few fishermen seated at the bar, and two tables are filled with retirees. A young couple eats dinner in a booth across from us. Besides Merry and me, they all seem to be locals.

Everyone looked up when we came in and stared until they had apparently put us in whatever category they thought we fit into: maybe investors considering opening a business on the island before high season starts, or vacation home buyers sampling the quaint local fare after a day of home tours, or travelers just passing through on their way to someplace else.

Merry changed her clothes since she walked Chaser home

to me. She has on high boots with her jeans tucked into them and a soft-looking long blue sweater.

"I'll have the Pale Ale," Merry says brightly to the weary-looking waitress. She looks to me and asks, "Two?"

I nod.

I haven't had a drink since Katie died. I stayed away from alcohol at first because I knew that I was near the edge. I have never been a teetotaler for this long, but I've thought it wise to keep my head as clear as possible. It has been too thickly fogged by sadness and confusion to add any complicating chemicals to the toxic mix.

"I heard about your wife. I'm so sorry," Merry says, as if Katie's death is as valid a topic of conversation as the grease-stained menu.

I nod dismissively.

She looks at me fully for a minute.

"Mind if I talk about me?" she asks. "I know that when you're getting to know someone, you're supposed to ask lots of questions and keep your mouth shut. But I feel like talking tonight, if y'all don't mind."

I can tell she is doing this for me because I obviously don't want to open up. I'm grateful to her, and relieved.

"I'd love to hear all about y'all," I say.

Merry slaps my hand lightly for mimicking her accent. The beers come.

"Then drink up and leave the conversation to me."

Merry is true to her word. I enjoy listening. I watch her mouth move and her expressions change. She talks with her hands, motioning often to embellish a story and clapping them together when she reaches the end.

Each time she finishes telling me some little tale about her mountain town childhood and the characters from Peaksy Falls, she looks for a signal as to whether she should keep talking.

I want to keep listening, so I ask another question whenever she pauses. She obliges me by answering in her colorful, folksy, sweet way. I could listen to her accent all night long.

Merry talks so much that she doesn't have time to drink.

Listening gives me plenty. I drink three beers before she finishes one.

I missed the taste of beer, the attention of an attractive woman, and the light-headed optimism that comes with catching a buzz.

I notice Merry finally finish her drink.

"Would you like another one?" I ask.

"No, sir. I'll be the designated driver tonight."

"Can I ask how you're related to Fritz?" I ask because it popped into my head.

"We're not related," she says. "I like to pretend he's my brother sometimes, but he's not. It's a long story. I don't want to bore you with it," she says.

"I have all night."

I know I sound like the hopeless flirt I used to be, before I met Katie. We were married for five years and dated for two before that, so I am very out of practice with talking to another woman while enjoying a growing buzz.

After a little more prompting, Merry tells me the story of how she came to know Fritz and how he brought her to the island to claim her inheritance.

"You're making that up!" I say.

She assures me she isn't, but she laughs along with me. She lets her leg rest lightly against mine.

"So *you* knew my father and I didn't. How crazy is that?" she says.

"Pretty crazy," I agree.

I realize I have lost track of which beer I'm on. I know from experience that's never a good sign. They taste good, though, and I'm having fun for the first time since October fifteenth. Was that only a few months ago? Or yesterday? Or another lifetime?

I look down at my hands for a moment. I can still see the faint line where my wedding band used to be. It's been lost for months; I don't remember taking it off, and I haven't been able to find it anywhere. I'm on the brink of putting my head down on the table for a short cry.

Merry takes my hand, with its faint line. She holds it lightly and brings my attention back up to her face.

She tells me another story and I laugh. Maybe too loud.

When she tells me about her estranged boyfriend, I become jealous. That's another indication that maybe I'm getting drunk.

I excuse myself to use the bathroom. My tipsy walk down the long, narrow hall confirms my suspicion.

I tell myself that I shouldn't have gotten drunk, but I don't really believe it. I give a shitfaced grin to the mirror. I feel different than my normal self, and I was so sick of my normal self that I decide I'll never get sober again.

I return from the bathroom to find Merry choosing a song on the jukebox.

"Dance with me," I say.

She gives me her skeptical frown.

"Come on," I cajole. "Everyone has left but us." I put my arms around her, and we sway.

I like the music she chose. I don't recognize it, probably because Merry is younger than me by at least a few years, and Katie and I had been in a musical rut for a long time. Katie had a rapid style of speaking. She was also very thin and small-chested, a marathoner. It has been a long, long time since I've held a woman who is softer.

Katie's hair was long. She complained about it all the time, put it into a ponytail as soon as she got home from work, and always wore it back on weekends. Merry's hair is short and incredibly silky. I love the feel of it against my cheek.

I keep reminding myself to keep a respectable distance, but her body feels so good next to mine. I pull her closer; she's so warm and soft.

I stumble a little.

"Alrighty now," she says. "It's time to go home."

I begin to argue, but I hear my words slur so I stop. I let Merry lead me out after I pay for the drinks. She tries to pick up the tab, but I insist, or "inshist," I'm afraid.

She tucks me into the passenger seat of my car.

It's only a ten-minute ride back to my place, but Merry

has to wake me up in my driveway. I know I should feel very guilty, but she tells me it's OK so convincingly that I forget to be ashamed. She leads me out of the car and up the stairs, which keep moving.

I try to put my key in the lock, but it doesn't fit. I realize it's the car key and let out a comedic scream.

She takes the keys from my hand and opens the door for me. She leads me inside, but the rug shifts unexpectedly.

There's a certain passage in *David Copperfield* when Dickens (as David) describes being in a drunken state. It floors me every time. It's so funny, so absolutely hysterical…I laugh just thinking about it.

I have slurred my way through the passage several times over the years as I've tried to read it to inebriated companions. The first time I was fifteen and tried to read it to Martin. I whispered so that my parents wouldn't know we'd stolen a pint of Sloe Gin from their liquor cabinet before we'd gone to Janet Sturgeon's party down the street.

I ponder that Dickensian passage and my loyal old pal, drunken David.

"It was myself!" I snicker at one of my favorite lines.

I must not be telling it right because Merry doesn't laugh along with me. She's being a stick-in-the-mud, so I turn away from her.

"Only my hair looks drunk!" I tell my reflection in a window before doubling over.

I must read the passage to Merry. I know I'm not doing it justice by relating it in snatches. But when I look for the book, I can't find it.

Even the bookshelves are gone. Everything is different.

Then it dawns on me that none of my books are here. They're all back in Katie's and my Chicago apartment, neatly stacked and categorized.

Gathering dust.

I look around, confused, feeling like I've never seen this place before. I'm alarmed and saddened by how dirty it is. Katie will be angry.

Then I remember that Katie is no more. She is gone. Gathering dust.

I look at Merry and realize that I shouldn't have let her in here at all. My vision blurs, and I feel tears streaking down my face.

Now Merry seems to have gone away, too. I am sitting alone in the kitchen, slumped forward with my head on the table.

Merry is beside me again. I feel her hand on my shoulder.

"Come on, big guy. I found your room, and I'll help you get there."

I trip over Chaser and apologize profusely. Merry helps me navigate around the furniture, which is harder than it might sound because it keeps moving.

She helps me get through a doorway that has become alarmingly narrow. She pushes me down to sit on the bed. She takes my shoes off and removes my coat.

"I see what you're about," I say, suddenly very amorous. I'm confused regarding where I am for a moment and even who I am.

Merry smiles and I remember.

"No, sir," she says. "You need some sleep now."

I put my arms around her waist and lean back onto the bed, less gracefully than I meant. She lands on top of me.

I don't want to let go. I just want to feel the warmth of her. I want to feel her breathing.

Chapter Sixteen

IN WHICH FRITZ WEEPS
ACROSS THE OCEAN

As told by a very homesick Mr. Forth

I am tired, weary, beleaguered, and acutely aware of the clock slowly ticking off the seconds. My sleep machine can no longer muffle the ocean outside, let alone my myriad thoughts. It's the middle of the night here on this lonely island, morning in London. I wasn't able to reach Victor before he went off to his gig last night. Though I'm afraid I'll wake him up, I need, quite desperately, to hear his voice.

"Hello?"

Oh bloody hell, that's not V. I don't know how I could have reached the wrong number—he's at the top of my most frequently called list for heaven's sake; that shouldn't leave any room for error.

"Sorry," I mumble. I hang up and try again.

"Who is this?" the voice that isn't Victor's demands.

"I'm sorry, my phone must be wrong. I was calling for Victor Mercier."

"No, you're right then. This is his flat."

"Then who the hell is this?" I ask.

The most banished, supremely unwanted memory of my life floods back to me. I had just begun to see Victor. I was slowly getting used to the idea of dating a man openly, trying to negotiate the line between the formal, traditional manner in which I was raised and the overwhelmingly complex feeling of falling head-over-heels in love for the first time. Victor had been in love before. In fact, he was still in the process of breaking it off with his long-term beau.

He was performing at a club in Paris on a Friday night. He tried to talk me into taking the day off and going with him, but I had a hundred reasons why it was impossible. When he'd gone, though, I found that I couldn't concentrate on anything else but him.

I decided to surprise him in Paris. I am not an impulsive man, so the whole enterprise was a new experience for me. I found it exhilarating.

I wrapped up work early enough to make it to the end of the show. It had felt wonderful, sort of freewheeling and luxurious, to leave town with an overnight bag to meet my lead singer boyfriend after a performance.

When I arrived at the venue, which happened to be a small and smoky pub, I noticed Victor's old boyfriend, Michel. I knew Michel from many pictures in the photo album screensaver on V's computer. He was sitting in the audience, right at the front. I saw Victor sing to him. From my vantage point, I saw enough to break my heart.

I understand from books and films that there is sometimes a sort of limbo in between relationships, when one hasn't quite cooled down enough to put it away safely, but the new one hasn't heated up enough to warrant full and constant attention. That must have been the phenomenon I witnessed.

After the show, Victor saw me. His face lit up in proportion to Michel's face turning dark.

V and I enjoyed a wonderful night together, and we spent the next day in the lovely city before traveling back to London.

Being in Paris with Victor felt like being there for the first time. It was his city, where he had grown up, and he could take me places and show me things I would never have had access to without him. I loved listening to him speak French; I still love it when he talks to his parents on the telephone.

By the time we were back in London, I was able to forget how he had looked at Michel during the show. I thought I'd forgotten it completely, until this moment.

"I asked who the hell you are," I say again to the strange man who answered the telephone in Victor's tiny flat at an hour too early for legitimate guests.

V's voice comes on. "What's this? Why would you yell like that, Fritzie?"

"Who's there with you?"

"You can ask anything," he says in his thick French accent, "but please do not use that tone with me."

I take a deep breath and let it out. "Who's there, then?"

"You remember I told you we have a new band manager? It is him, Paul Bertrand. He came by early with good news: we may get a recording deal."

"Oh," I say.

I know I should say that it's fantastic, but, quite frankly, I don't believe it. Victor, like his parents, trusts there's a new opportunity around every corner, that all their hard work will finally pay off in the exhibition, recording contract, or book deal that will finally put them on the map. I have seen each of them at different times become hopeful over praise from a promising quarter, only to have their hopes dashed in the end. Somehow the encouragement, though ultimately fruitless, is still enough to keep them going. And since they each love their work, perhaps optimism such as theirs is valuable.

"That's great, V," I say.

"You don't believe it will happen."

I think he can read my thoughts sometimes.

"I believe in *you*. You know that. Whether a record company executive invests in you is beside the point. I know how talented you are."

"Perhaps it's beside the point for you, who have always had everything given on silver platters. For me it means more. No?"

"I hope that it happens this time, V. You know that I want what you want."

Mr. Pershing always disliked Victor's music to the point of extreme rudeness—if you agree that plugging his ears was extremely rude. He called *Poppycock* whenever V was hopeful about a lucrative gig or that long sought-after record deal, which seemed more and more like a mirage as the years passed. Mr. Pershing never missed an opportunity to predict that Victor would leave me if he ever became successful.

"Are you all right?" Victor asks. "Why is it that you are up now? Please tell me, has something happened?"

His voice can do anything from belt out glam rock at both extremes of the musical register, to soothe me like a caress in the middle of the night. Even across the cold, gray ocean.

I don't mean to, but I can't help it.

I weep into the phone.

I am reading a week-old copy of *The London Times* from cover to cover. I pretend that I am at home in London, ensconced in the front parlor, where in my former life I used to habitually consume the paper. I pretend I hear cars occasionally pass on the quiet street, and songbirds sing in the neatly trimmed hedges, and church bells ring out the half hours and the hours in the distance.

I pretend that if I look up, I'll see a proper room anchored by a rich red Indian carpet. I'll be surrounded by dark wood bookshelves and floor-to-ceiling mullioned windows. If I look to the left, I'll see a sofa covered in sumptuously rich upholstery. If I lean back, I'll feel the lovingly worn cognac leather of the chair upon which I sit.

I pretend that if I chose to, I could glance over to Victor's apartment window across the way, to see if his blinds are still shut tight. I'm a morning person, always have been. Due to my beloved's vocation, he's up most of the night trying to make his living in pubs or any other venue that will pay him to live out his rock-and-roll dream another day.

Sometimes, during my reading hour, Mr. Pershing would catch me wistfully looking for signs of life at Victor's flat. Then he seemed to feel that it was his responsibility to point out the differences between my beloved and myself. His attention to detail, unfortunately, was more impressive on this subject than on most.

Mr. Pershing commented on our styles of dress: I am a touch formal, while Victor prefers to look like a rock star, whether he's on stage or at home. Our schedules: I already mentioned they are not entirely compatible. Our upbringings: I had the benefits of education and home comforts that couldn't have been of higher quality if I were heir to Mr. Pershing instead of his servant's son, while Victor was raised by struggling artists. Our accents: mine is English, obviously, while Victor's is a romantic and expressive French. Very different, to be sure, as are our manners, which never seemed to escape Mr. Pershing's notice.

My benefactor/employer was always an instigator and a meddler. I knew this all too well, so I tried not to take it personally when he picked at Victor and me. My role was rather to smooth things over between the men I cared for most in the world. Luckily, Victor is actually far softer than I am. Though he talked a fine talk about how I should insist upon a good sight more respect from Mr. Pershing, V treated him with as much kindness and patience as I did.

Mr. Pershing was correct, of course, that Victor and I are very different people. I never argued otherwise.

But the late afternoons, after I finish my legal work and set my briefcase and tie aside, and after Victor sleeps off the night before, and showers the cigarette smoke from his hair and the driving beat from his mind in favor of an almost serene calmness...those few hours of each day are, quite simply, the best of my life.

My phone alarm goes off. I had been trying to tune out the sound and sight of the ocean, and any consciousness of sand, or the faded blue-gray nothingness of the oppressively open sky. I had shifted the newspaper strategically to hide the perversely staring parrots trapped within the quick-dry synthetic fabric of the sofa where I really sit.

I sigh and fold my paper.

"Come on, old man," I call toward the master bedroom. "It's time for your doctor's appointment. We have to leave here in ten minutes."

"You don't have to shout," he says, appearing in the doorway, fully dressed down to his overcoat and shoes. "I'll just have a smoke down by the car first."

He looks gray today.

"Can I help you down the stairs?" I ask, getting up.

"Help me down the damn stairs like an invalid?" he asks, appearing stronger for a moment.

"Go ahead then," I tell him, like I don't care whether he falls three flights or not. That it's of no concern to me.

But I watch his descent closely. When he is out of my line of sight, I hear Merry greet him cheerfully on the stairway before she appears at the top, with windblown hair and pink cheeks.

"It's so pretty out today!" she announces.

"Do you ever sleep?" I ask. She accosted me with questions when I arrived home at midnight, and I heard her alarm go off at a still-dark hour after Victor had talked me through my bout of homesickness, which was as painfully acute as any flu.

"Yes, sir, I sleep. Less than I might like to, some nights. But at least this way I'll know that if I fail your tasks, it won't be for any lack of trying on my part."

"I don't doubt it," I say. Merry tries harder than anyone I have ever seen.

"Can you give me any clues to figuring out that fourth task now?" she asks.

I shake my head a decisive no. I'm not helping with this one. The first two tasks were different. It was not only a benefit to Merry to get a makeover, but helping her repair her pitifully neglected appearance was in my best interest as well. After all, I've had to look at her every day since then. And it was almost a pleasure to help her get started with her catering business: to ensure that she was legally ready to launch, review her marketing materials, and sample her menus.

But the third task has rather soured me. Having had my own affairs meddled in, I feel increasingly uncomfortable meddling in Merry's. I agreed to see this project through, but that doesn't mean I have to like it.

Playing matchmaker between Merry and Jack Morningstar

had seemed like overstepping, but not horribly so, when it was simply words on a page. I didn't argue too hard against the third task for two reasons. First because I despise Phil, and second because I didn't think it would work anyway. Even if I believed that Merry and Jack might make a nice couple and perhaps help each other in many ways, I know that love is mysterious. Chemistry and mutual attraction can't be created out of thin air. Even if they could, perhaps the end result would be a broken heart on one side and more damage done than good.

And this fourth task? I wash my hands of it. "As I told you last night, you have to figure it out for yourself. I'm frankly not convinced these tasks are as helpful to you as your father thought."

"How can you say that? I've got my business going now. And even though I don't love the fact that my dad tried to play matchmaker, I do think that Jack is awfully sweet. If there really is a big secret in my family, I should probably know about it, right? Maybe it's important."

"Perhaps it is, perhaps it isn't," I say quietly, though I'm sick to death of being vague.

"Come on, if there was a big secret in your family, wouldn't you want to know?"

"Perhaps I would, perhaps I wouldn't."

"Oh, perhaps yourself! I know my mom, and trust me, she never did anything interesting enough to keep secret!"

Merry is violating my personal space again. She often acts as if we're children on a playground and she can grab my arm and pull me, or hug me, or smack me, or stand too close whenever she wants. I walk across the room to the other side of the dining table so that it's between us. Merry follows me like an annoying puppy.

"I mean, what on earth could there possibly be? It's not like if I dig around enough, I'll find out my mom has a double life. That under her cotton dress she's wearing leopard hot pants, and when I leave the house, she's the old mountain lady version of Hannah Montana!"

Merry's cell phone rings and I begin stealthily edging by her, hoping to be down the stairs and out the door by the time she's through talking.

"I told you I don't have time for this nonsense, Phil." she says.

I stop halfway down the first flight, not in such a hurry anymore.

"No," she says, facing away from me. "I will not marry you, so stop asking me. I told you, we're through."

I wish I could hear his side of the conversation, too, but I don't want to lean in and have her notice me lurking. And I doubt she'd comply if I simply asked her to turn on speakerphone.

"No," she says. "It's just over, Phil." She sounds kind of sad, but also quite resolute. I feel strangely proud of her, almost to the point of being choked up, which would be ridiculous, so it's probably allergies.

Well, there he goes, and now I don't need a speakerphone to hear him shouting.

"Why?" she asks. "You really want to know *why*?"

He can't possibly hear her, the way he's yelling. But that doesn't stop Merry. She opens her right hand and spreads her fingers out. "I'll give you five reasons," she says. Lowering her thumb: "For one, you're a bully." She lowers her pointer: "Two, you're a disrespectful son, and Amy Jo deserves better." Middle: "Three, you're self-centered and presumptuous." She holds the phone out a bit further and I hear him shrieking louder, so maybe he can hear her a bit after all. Merry lowers her ring finger: "Four, you're a hothead." I think he hangs up because it's suddenly quiet. "Five," she says to the empty air, and no one but me, the stairwell spy, hears: "I like somebody else."

She has crossed the room and gone out through the oceanside doors by the time the car horn beeps in the garage below. I watch her for a moment, sure that she's earnestly scanning the sea for a jumping dolphin to wish upon. Merry buys wholeheartedly into her father's feigned wisdom, into his rubbishy meddling nonsense. She won't wish for something easy, either, not if I know Merry! *Let Jack Morningstar fall madly in love with me so that we can live happily ever after*, she'll likely wish with dewy eyes and a trusting smile if she sees a dolphin jump.

I'll vehemently deny this, so you needn't bother mentioning it to anyone.

But damn it, I admit it: I hope that she sees one.

Chapter Seventeen

IN WHICH JACK HITS ROCK BOTTOM AND BEGINS TO RESURFACE

As told, in a whisper and wearing sunglasses, by an extremely mortified Mr. Morningstar

Chaser licks my face. My head pounds and my mouth feels like it's stuffed with old socks.

The last thing in the entire world I want to do is wake up and face my dog, the day, my life…everything or anything.

For a second, I think I remember having dreamed of Katie. A second later, I realize that a softer body graced my dreams. Then I begin to ask myself if I dreamed at all.

Memories of last night flood my mind, many of them blurry and confused. I half hope that when I open my eyes, I will see Merry beside me in the bed. I half hope that I won't.

More memories of last night come back to me, and I don't know how I'll ever face her again.

Maybe I should just pack up and leave the island this morning. Once my headache clears sufficiently to see straight, maybe I should move on.

Maybe it's time.

Getting out of bed will require many stages, I realize. I must take extreme care, or I will shatter all over the floor like glass. I have to adjust to each change of position, no matter how small. I inch the blanket off and acclimate to the feeling of cool air on my skin. I let my sensitive scalp adjust to it until my brain stops beating against my skull.

It takes approximately three years before I can slowly rise up to rest on my elbows.

It's an infinitely long process that brings me to a sitting position on the edge of the bed, with my feet on the floor.

Things look strange.

There are fewer piles of laundry lying around than I remember. I wonder if it's possible that I actually started to clean up last night.

I stand, very slowly. I shuffle, using extreme care, out to the kitchen. I find it so immaculate that I know there is absolutely no way in hell I could've done it.

It dawns on me, painfully and with stars, that I not only let Merry in here, but she actually cleaned up. Mortification stabs me as unapologetically as the sun shining through the window.

There is a note on the counter. I don't want to read it, even if it turns out that my eyes are capable.

Eventually I edge it closer.

> *Good morning, Sunshine!*
>
> *I thought y'all were kidding, but you were right: it actually smelled in here. I made a start because I didn't want to think of you eating my home cooking in a dirty kitchen.*
>
> *If you can have this house cleaned by Friday, I'll make dinner here. If you want. No worries if not, I just thought I'd ask, in case it sounded OK, and y'all were looking for an excuse to shovel the rest of this place out.*
>
> *Merry*
>
> *P.S. Please don't feel bad about last night. We've all gotten drunk and acted silly at one time or another. And don't worry about being fresh—you passed out before I could really get offended.*

It's a relief that Merry could find it in her heart to be sweet about it, but I am completely disgusted with myself.

It was a mistake to go out in the first place, followed by so many more mistakes…they're all adding up to make my head explode.

Chaser whines. The clock says that it's after ten.

"Sorry, girl."

I feel guilty about Chaser's bladder, along with everything else.

I can't take care of myself. I can't take care of my dog. My life is a shambles.

I let Chaser out to do her business and let her in again before I crawl back into bed. I ignore her nudges, her reminders that she needs water, and food, and eventually more exercise, and another potty break.

This is our arrangement, she seems to tell me. *We take care of each other. You can't just opt out one day because you feel sick and tired and hopeless. Get up!*

"Go away!" I yell, sounding stone-cold, like I hate her as much as I hate me.

Instead of whining or pouting, Chaser jumps into the bed.

She lies beside me for twenty hours.

When I occasionally wake and notice her, she is always in the same position. She watches me like a sentinel, or a guardian angel, or simply the good girl that she is.

Chaser, having seen me hit bottom, waits for me to come back up again, like she trusts me to do it. I guess she has no choice.

When I finally wake with my head feeling something like normal, Chaser wags her tail happily, like she not only forgives me, but she still loves me completely and will stick with me to the end.

I hug her coat and hold on.

Weak-kneed, dry, and hungry, I get out of bed. I feel light-headed, too, but in a good way, like my thoughts aren't so damn heavy for a minute. Possibly my bender and subsequent hibernation killed off exactly the right brain cells.

After taking Chaser for a walk, I head down to the cooler and pick up yesterday's food, follow Merry's instructions, and eat every single bite. *How are y'all feeling?* was written beside a smiley face with a cold compress on its head.

169

I spend the next few hours alternately getting chewed out by Jaycee for missing an important meeting yesterday and making it up to her by plowing through a stack of paperwork she has amassed for me.

The fact that Merry cleaned my kitchen basically shames me into manning up and going the rest of the way. I spend all afternoon and evening cleaning house.

My dad calls the next morning, and I don't know why, but I answer. Even knowing that it's him. Not only that, but I agree when he asks if we can Skype; he says he's been dying to try it on his new computer. I take my iPad around and show him the house. I turn the camera to Chaser.

"She's a beach dog if I ever saw one," Dad says. "It'll be tough for her to exchange the sand for the city streets again, won't it?"

I should have known he'd bring up my moving back, as if it's inevitable just because he wants it to happen.

"I can't get over your view!" he says. "I love Lake Michigan so much that I don't really think about the ocean. But she sure is something, isn't she?"

"I thought maybe I'd get tired of it, but I never do. Sometimes I think I could stay here forever," I say.

I can't help messing with him, taunting him a little. I never could resist. It's probably small of me and immature, but I can't help trying to throw him off center.

"Your place looks so clean," he says. "Katie would be proud to see how well you're doing. I know I am."

I am tempted to remind him that I'm not a three-year-old learning to use the potty by myself. Or thirteen, mowing the lawn on a Saturday afternoon without being hounded to death first. I'm thirty, for Christ's sake.

I silently and slowly count to ten before I speak. Another tidbit of advice I learned from one of Dad's psych magazines left in the bathroom during my childhood. A lot of the stuff seemed like voodoo or nonsense to me, more so as I grew older, but that one works when I remember to use it.

"Thanks, Dad," I make myself say.

"We'll have to do this again when your mom and Marty can be here," he suggests, as if that is a reasonable idea. His mild expression makes him look like he just had his brain removed, but has already forgiven the negligent surgeon.

"Not happening," I say.

"If you really think about it, buddy, you'll agree it's a good idea. We can break the ice as a family, then you and Martin can spend some one-on-one time."

I've always thought my dad would've made a great preacher's assistant. He couldn't yell in a fire-and-brimstone way, but he'd be perfect for all the insinuating, ingratiating, fly-on-the-wall ministrations.

"It's definitely not happening, Dad."

"Martin really needs your forgiveness, buddy."

"Is that right?" I ask, like he just gave me a minor stock tip or a trick for getting water stains off a coffee table. "Interesting."

"You can pretend you don't care. I know that's a defense mechanism you often employ. I'm not blaming you for it or trying to make you ashamed of how you cope. I'm only saying what's best for you."

"Really? I thought you were saying what was best for Martin."

I should have counted to ten, twenty, to three hundred if I'd had to. I'm out of practice with my dad. I should have known better than to engage him.

"It's all one and the same, Jack," he says, leaning back in his desk chair and getting comfortable for a long, one-sided discussion.

"Got to go, Dad. I hear my doorbell!"

Yesterday I must have missed Merry's delivery because I couldn't hear the bell over the vacuum cleaner, which I ran for hours on end. Today I disconnect from my dad and race down to catch her.

She hasn't even made it to the bottom of the stairs after placing my food in the cooler when I open the door.

"Hey!"

She turns around and smiles. It makes my knees go weak.

"I could kiss you," I say. I don't know where the hell that came from, but it's true.

"You already did," she says in her smooth, slow accent.

"I wish I could remember it better," I confess.

She surprises me by coming back up the stairs and kissing me quickly on the mouth.

"There. Now why are y'all in such a good mood today?"

"Come in and I'll tell you."

She looks at her watch and hesitates. "I can't stay long. Are you sure it's safe to go inside?"

I open the door wide for her to pass in ahead of me.

"Wow!" she says, looking all around. "Once you put your mind to something, I guess you go all out."

"That's true," I admit. From both a positive and a negative standpoint, that fact has always been true. Whatever I do, I do it all the way.

"I was horrified to realize you'd seen the state of the house. When I found that you'd cleaned the kitchen, I was ashamed enough to segue that into a full housecleaning. The place obviously needed it. I needed it."

"Just because it was needed didn't mean it would get done. Good for you!" she says. Her eyes actually sparkle. Her wind-tousled hair and pink cheeks are magazine-cover gorgeous.

"You gave me a good incentive by promising that if I did, you'd come back on Friday. Do you still plan to?"

"Yes, sir! Any requests on what I should make?"

"Come here for a drink first, then we'll go out to dinner. You can take the night off."

"Really? Are y'all sick of my meals? Don't tell me this is a good news/bad news thing, and you're firing me…"

"Don't even joke about that. I love your cooking."

She pets Chaser. I do, too, until my hand touches hers and I hold onto it. I look down at our hands together, and at the empty, fading line where my wedding band used to be. I suddenly feel very uncertain.

"This is a little strange for me," I say.

"Because of your wife?" Merry asks.

"I still have trouble believing she's gone."

"I'm so sorry. I can tell that you loved her very much."

I nod. I know that I'm giving the impression of a happy marriage. I don't want to be dishonest, but I don't want to be a revisionist historian either. I really believed that Katie's and my marriage was as perfect as a marriage could be. "It's just so complicated," I say.

Merry squeezes my hand a bit. "Show me something worthwhile that isn't."

I don't know what possesses me, but I kiss her. Gently, not like last time. Slow and short, but with meaning. And she was right: it was incredibly complicated.

Chapter Eighteen

IN WHICH JACK TALKS
AND THEN CLAMS UP

As told by Merry, who listens while she can

Jack is handsome in that manly way that makes it easy for me to imagine him chopping wood, or carrying a child on his shoulders, or setting up a tent without breaking a sweat or a nail.

I know that Jack's in mourning. I also know that he drank too much the other night, and that's a red flag. But I'm partly to blame there; I could tell he was wound tight, and I figured that if he wanted to let off steam, I'd be there to drive him home afterward. I didn't tell the waitress to stop bringing him beer when it seemed like maybe he'd gone tipsy. But I promise you I didn't realize he was all-out drunk until we danced.

I don't think I ever talked about myself so much in one night. Or even in my entire relationship with Phil, and I've known him forever and a day. Jack asked good questions, and he seemed interested in everything I said. I suppose that was a new and fresh experience for me. I found out I really like being listened to!

But I can't let thoughts of Jack distract me from focusing on the tasks ahead. No, sir.

I wish Fritz would at least give me a hint about my mom's secret so I'd know where to start looking. I'd ask Uncle Max if he has any bright ideas, but his bronchitis has gotten worse, and now he's on new medicine that makes him nap even more than usual. He and Fritz had seemed to be getting on one another's nerves something awful for a while there, but lately they're nicer to each other. I've been working out of the house a lot, getting home with only enough time to serve them dinner and reward myself for a day well spent by taking a long walk on the beach.

I love the ocean so much! Even more than I dreamed I would.

I've begun to fantasize sometimes about how amazing it would be to spend the rest of my days in this house. I know, that's really getting the cart before the horse, right? But a girl can dream.

Even if I did earn the house, I know I'd have to sell it off and get something smaller that I could afford to keep up. Fritz is right that a business like mine won't earn me enough to live in a five-bedroom house on the Atlantic Ocean. Unless maybe I managed the stipend smartly…but I don't know if that's a nickel or a million dollars, and none of it is mine yet anyway. And it won't ever be if I just sit here dreaming.

I do know one thing: I want to stay on this island, no matter what happens. Maybe I'll find a small place across the street with a nice, bright kitchen, where I might still be able to see the dolphins through binoculars from a window or two, and the pelicans flying over. The island is a pretty lonely place in the winter, but I hear it really gets busy in the other seasons. That's good for me since I like people, and it should be good for business, too.

If I do get my inheritance, my first priority will be to help out my mom and grandma and Aunt Betty (though she's a loon). Thinking of folks back in Peaksy Falls, I also can't help but think of Phil.

I got a message from Amy Jo yesterday. It was just about as sweet as pie, as I'd expect from her, but I could also tell she was sad about having to tell me that Phil's former girlfriend is going to take my old job. I'll bet Sarah will make the dishes on the menu just the way Phil likes them. She'll probably never try to swap Dijon mustard for regular or anything that got me in trouble from time to time.

• • •

Friday is finally here, and I'm looking forward to tonight. Though I love it, it'll be sort of nice to have a night off from cooking. Fritz and Uncle Max are having pizza—which Max grumbled about until I promised him an extra slice of chocolate cake.

I don't know where Jack plans to take me. I'm glad he's not making dinner himself. The only guys I ever dated were good in the kitchen. Jack is so different from the others, and I suppose I want him to stay that way. Plus he's older, and more experienced, and very successful with his business and all. I think it's good that I'm better than he is at something.

I put on a nice outfit and spend extra time on my makeup. I put some mousse in my ultra-short hairdo, which I made time to get touched up a few days ago after Fritz pointed out that my roots were fixing to show. I love my hair! It always looks better after a beach walk, which seems just about perfect for me. I put on some lipstick and really go for broke with the mascara.

When I get to Jack's house, he has to let Chaser out, so I join him on the deck. The ocean is in a jumble. The night that I met Jack was wild like this, and he'd actually been out in it. I look at the churning, forceful waves and shiver at the thought. "I'm glad you'll be having dinner with me instead of surfing," I say.

"I might have if you weren't here."

He looks into my eyes. His gaze is intense. He pulls me into a hug and we stand that way, our hair and clothes blowing in the wind.

Jack pours me a glass of wine once we're inside, but he has to take a call, so I sip alone. He goes into another room and soon I can hear him speaking loudly. He sounds upset. I hear him curse out someone named Martin.

"Who's Martin?" I ask when he rejoins me.

"An old friend."

"I suppose there's more to the story?"

He sighs and takes my hand. "Do you really want to know?"

"Yes, sir."

"Here's the abridged version: Martin had an affair with my

wife. They were together the night she died. She had just left his place when she pulled in front of a semi without its lights on. She was broadsided."

"Oh my God. So why were you talking to him?" I ask.

"We're business partners."

"Wow." I mean *wow*. I put my hand on Jack's shoulder and feel how incredibly tense he is.

"I'm sorry to lay that all on you," he says. "We better get going or we'll be late for our reservation."

"How is your project going?" he asks me on the drive.

"Are you sure you want to hear me babble on about it?"

"Positive. Please distract me," he says. He reaches over and pats my leg.

"All right. Well, I'm supposed to figure out what secret my mom has been keeping. And I can't imagine her ever having had a single secret."

"No?" he asks.

"She makes all her own clothes. Did I tell you that?"

He actually laughs a little. It sounds like the purest sugar. "Yes, I believe that you did."

"I know, right?" I shake my head and laugh a little, too. "But honestly, I don't have any idea where to start. I called her to see if I could find out anything, but she acted like she didn't understand my question at all."

"What did she say?"

"Nothing helpful, that's for sure. I asked, 'Are there any secrets you're hiding, ma'am, because you know I love you and I don't care about any skeletons in your closet; I just want to help you drag them out.' And she replied, I kid you not, 'Oh, Grandma is doing just fine. The crocuses are up. The weather lately couldn't be any nicer.'"

He chuckles. "Is that really true?"

I put my hand across my heart. "I swear."

The restaurant is off the island, on the outskirts of the city. I have passed by it several times, and it always makes me think of the Mountainside. Of course it's not on a mountain, and it isn't made of logs or surrounded by acres upon acres of trees.

I suppose the only way that Cascade is like the Mountainside is that it seems to belong right where it is.

Inside there's a much more chic and elegant feel than anyplace else I've been around here. I wish I could sample everything on the menu. My mouth waters at a few of the descriptions, and others have me just plain curious. I suspect somebody in the kitchen really knows what she's doing.

I order the house red, and Jack orders a soda.

"I don't want you to get the idea that I drink too much," he tells me.

"Good," I say.

I dated one excessive drinker in my life, and it was more than enough, thank you very much. I take a sip of my wine. "It's your turn to talk tonight," I remind him.

For a minute I'm afraid he's going to shut down and I'll have to fill the quiet air.

"What do you want to know?" he asks.

"Everything," I say. "Start at the beginning."

And to my surprise, he does.

According to Jack, his parents had waited a long time for a baby. They had wanted one so much that when he was born, neither of them could hardly believe their luck. They loved him near to death.

He told me this like it was a hardship somehow. I said I couldn't help wondering how great it must've been to have a mom and dad, both of whom were madly in love with me. It almost seemed too good to imagine.

He said he knew he was lucky.

I was tempted to say that I didn't think he really knew, but I held my tongue. It was my turn to listen, and probably I'd said some things when I told my life story that made him raise his eyebrows, but he still let me have my say. To Jack, having both a mom and dad that loved him was just the way it was.

Martin showed up pretty early in Jack's story.

One time soon after they met, Jack said the two of them

brought Martin's muddy bike into Martin's house to wash it, brought it right on into the shower. Martin's parents nearly had heart attacks! Martin spent the rest of the weekend at Jack's to let them cool down, and Jack said that was the beginning.

Jack told the story like he knew it was supposed to be funny and remembered that it had always been funny, but he didn't quite think it was funny anymore.

Then he was quiet for a while.

But after he ate his salad, he seemed ready to start in again.

I suppose it might have been kinder of me to stop him. I could tell it wasn't the most comfortable thing for him to do, to sit there and tell me about his life. But I asked questions and listened because it seemed sort of helpful for him to talk things through.

The first few stories he told appeared to be well-rehearsed, like he'd told them at parties over the years and had polished them to a shine. He knew when to pause for effect, to make a face, or laugh.

Then he seemed to go off the script of his history and to stop telling it to me the way he had always told it to people. He became more matter-of-fact.

He seemed to take a step back and describe his life as if it had all happened to somebody else, though he still used "me" and "I" language. He talked about meeting his wife, falling in love, and what their marriage was like. He talked about their careers, their home, and friends. It seemed like he was trying to relay the facts only.

I know that Jack is an emotional man. Already, I have seen him wear his emotions out in the open. Already, I know they run deep and forceful.

He just seemed steely determined to get through the important facts tonight, to lay all of them out for me. Because I'd done the same for him, and because he said he would.

"I think those are the basics. That's my full disclosure," he says during dessert. He has gotten us up to the here and now, having talked every spare second he wasn't chewing.

"I think you forgot to say your favorite color," I tease.

"What would you call the color of your hair?"

I feel my face turn warm.

"No," he says, "the color of your cheeks, right now. That's my favorite."

I shake my head.

"So there you have my history: the good, the bad, and the tragic. If you want to hightail it back to your ex-boyfriend, I won't blame you."

"We're through for good," I say, like I'm not too brokenhearted about it. And I'm not.

"Good. Well, if you want to go back to putting my food in a cooler and never see me again, I guess I'll understand."

"Are you kidding?" I ask. "From the very first day, I hoped that you'd ask me in."

He takes my hand in his and looks into my eyes. "Well, you're in now."

Back at Jack's house, Chaser cries at the patio door and I let her out while he lights some candles. Chaser races down the steps to the beach. She dances there, running up to meet the waves and running back again when they soak her feet. Her joy reminds me of the first night I felt the ocean water, when I couldn't help twirling in the moonlight because I was just so happy to be here. Chaser's golden blond hair shows through the darkness. So do the waves, breaking white and frothy as they reach up to cover a little more sand each time. The tide is coming in.

The beach is like life, I suppose: it never stays the same for too long at a stretch.

Chaser runs back up to meet me. I open the door just enough to ask Jack for a towel so I can dry her feet off before I let her in. Jack brings one out and sits down in a chair to wipe Chaser down. He takes my hand and we go back into the house, where he has poured out two glasses of Malbec.

"I forgot to mention that your hair looks nice," I say.

It's cut short and neat. I liked him disheveled, but I like him even more now.

"Thanks," he says, smiling. He crouches in front of the fire, fixing to light it.

"Can I help?" I ask.

He reaches back to me for a second and pats my leg. He has a wonderful touch.

"Have a seat and drink your wine," he says.

I sit on the couch across from the fireplace so I can watch him. Chaser circles a few times before she lies on the floor beside me. She puts her head onto her front legs, stretched way out. She sighs a big, contented sigh.

Jack joins me on the couch once the fire catches.

He eases down with his back in the corner, resting on the arm, facing me. He pats his chest and opens his arms.

I lean back onto him. It feels amazing and natural, like this isn't our second date but our hundredth.

We watch the fire and sip our wine. Neither of us talk. I think we're all talked out.

We sit for a long time. When I see that our glasses are empty, I take them into the kitchen and refresh them.

I planned to sit back down in the same spot, to lean on him again, with the dog lying on the wooden floor beside us, while the waves make a peaceful soundtrack to our night.

But when I look into Jack's eyes, I change my plans. I set our wineglasses on a side table and smile.

He reaches out and takes my hands.

I bend down and kiss him.

We adjust ourselves until we lay next to each other.

I have pined for guys before. I followed at their heels, begging for scraps of attention. Often these have been my bosses. Cooks or, as I progressed, head chefs in restaurants where I worked. When they finally showed interest, I couldn't help but wonder if it had been worth it.

One smelled of garlic. I guess it isn't surprising, since it was an important ingredient in our most popular dishes. But when we kissed, woo wee; it was like he chewed garlic cloves instead of gum. Another was an instant groper. He had been the hardest to interest, but as soon as he decided to give me the time of day, he threw everything into it: his hands, arms, mouth, tongue, teeth, legs.

Phil and I had a more complicated history because we practically grew up together in the same small schools and all. But I sought him out like the other guys, and he was the one in charge. I loved Phil in my own way. He was familiar and convenient, but he didn't ever make me feel sentimental and tender just by looking at me.

The way Jack does.

"You feel so good. So soft and warm," he whispers in my ear.

He kisses my neck, sending shivers up my spine.

My whole body feels alive with electricity. I run my fingers through Jack's short hair. I know it tends to curl when it's longer, and it's thick and soft. His cheek is just the tiniest bit rough. It feels like heaven. So do his lips.

I put my hand under his chin and raise it up so I can kiss him on the mouth again.

Chaser barks at the patio door, startling us both. I giggle. I feel like we're teenagers on his parent's couch, about to get busted.

"Shhh, girl," he says.

She barks again.

He sighs. I make room for him to get up. We're both flushed and disheveled. We share a smile. He picks up my hand and kisses it.

"I'll be right back," he says. He gives me my wine glass from the side table. Chaser dances excitedly as he opens the deck door.

The wind rushes in. It feels colder. Jack closes the door.

I sip my wine and curl up to erase the chill.

In a minute, he opens the door and pokes his head in.

"Chaser ran after someone with a flashlight way down the beach." He reaches inside and takes her leash from a hook. "I've got to go after her. Please stay right there; I'll be back."

"Yes, sir."

A minute after Jack goes, I'm startled by a knock on the

door. I peek outside and can't hardly believe my eyes.

"What are you doing here?" I ask Phil.

"I came to ask you to marry me again," he says, holding out a velvet ring box.

"How did you find me?" I ask, completely dumbfounded and frazzled.

"Your mom gave me the address, and that guy you ran off with said I could find you here. So what do you say, Merry?" he kneels in front of the fire.

A cold wind blows in. Jack shuts the door and stares at us.

Phil stays kneeling, the big oaf!

"Who the hell are you?" Jack demands.

"I'm Merry's new fiancé."

"Oh, no you're not!" I say. I am torn between laughing and crying.

"Come on, Merry. You know what we've been through together. I love you, and we make beautiful meals together."

Jack grabs Phil by the arm and hefts him to standing. He turns his arm behind his back.

Phil kicks backward at him. "You son of a bitch, get your hands off me!"

Jack doesn't seem to hear; he tightens his grip and marches Phil to the door. I run ahead and open it.

"Go next door, Phil. I will talk to you there," I say.

Phil turns on Jack as soon as his arm is free, but I stand between them. "Go next door!" I holler. Phil finally saunters off, with the little ring box still in his hand.

"You said you two weren't dating anymore," Jack says in a very jealous, very possessive way.

"We're not," I say.

"Then how do you explain his proposal?" Jack yells.

I stare at him a minute, hoping he'll cool down. I touch his arm, but he shakes my hand off.

"Listen to me," I say. "I never lied to you. I never cheated on you or anyone else. I have been honest from the get-go."

"How can I believe you?" he says. He seems less angry now, more confused.

"I guess you have to trust me," I say softly.

"Trust you?" he asks. He slumps down on the sofa and puts his head in his hands.

I kneel down and try to hug him. He won't let me; he turns away.

I wait a few minutes, hoping that he'll come out of his haze, that he'll look at me, and speak to me. But it doesn't happen.

I pour my wine down the sink on my way out the door.

Chapter Nineteen

IN WHICH JACK TASTES BLOOD

As told by Jack, who comes to a decision, perhaps too late

I don't know how to explain my behavior last night. It may be as easy, or as complicated, as saying that I was jealous when I walked in on Merry's surprise proposal in my living room last night. I'm not sure what the appropriate reaction would have been for that occasion—I doubt that Emily Post ever took it on—but I realize now that mine was unfair.

With a day's hindsight, I could tell Merry that I know I was wrong, that I shouldn't have gotten angry with her. I could promise that I'll never be jealous again.

It might be easy enough to say that. It's only a series of words, after all. I was able to explain the general facts of my sordid history to her yesterday. Those were far worse, and I just laid them out straight.

I could assure Merry that I'm ready to move on. I could promise that she can trust me to act reasonably, and that I'll never again assume she's lying just because my wife did.

I feel like I'm standing in a doorway. On one side is my history with Katie, which I thought was wonderful, but the facts tell me otherwise, and my friendship with Martin, which was one of the solid truths of my life, until it was revealed to be a lie.

On the other side is the future, with the possibility of happiness and discovery, sadness, and love. Merry is standing on that side.

I don't know if I'm capable of passing from one to the other.

Last night I felt trapped in that metaphorical doorway. I wasn't wholly in the realm of the past, nor was I able to take another step toward the future. I was an unhappy spirit, condemned to walk between the worlds of the living and the dead, unable to fully commune with either one.

The phone rings.

"We need to talk," Martin says on the line.

"Will you please stop calling me? Jesus Christ! Don't you have any shame at all?"

"No. I don't have any shame, or pride, or anything," he says.

Something about his tone pulls at my gut.

Katie's casket was closed during the wake. They couldn't make her presentable, not even for a family viewing. Martin was the only one, besides the semi driver, the paramedics, and the presiding emergency room doctors and nurses, to have seen her broken. I try not to acknowledge, even to myself, that this is his tragedy, too.

"You have to forgive me, Jack. I can't live like this."

I feel incredibly weary all of the sudden. I sit down on the floor with my back against the wall, my elbows on my knees.

"I forgive you," I say, because I want him to stop doing this.

"No, you don't."

"I just said I did."

"But you don't."

"No, I don't!" I yell.

I take a deep breath and let it out. I try to speak more calmly.

"Continuing to torture yourself is bad for business. It's bad for my parents. And it annoys the living shit right out of me. Would you please stop now?"

"I keep thinking that if Katie hadn't come to my place that night, she wouldn't be dead. If she hadn't agreed to help me train for the marathon, we wouldn't have started the affair. I loved her so much, Jack. Oh my God, I still can't believe that she's gone…"

He dissolves into racking sobs.

I sometimes believed that I wanted to know what had happened. How and when I had lost her, and him, in order to try and understand this terrible tragedy. I have an analytical mind. I thought I wanted to break it down and study it.

I realize that I don't. That I can't.

It's over, and no amount of dissection and analysis will change the bottom line: she's gone. We're here. Sometimes I envy Katie, my beautiful, strong, cheating, warm, haunting, vibrant, dead, young wife.

I try to push away memories of the late nights Katie said she spent working. Her proud expression as she crossed a finish line. I try to let the ocean drown out the sound of Martin's tears.

And mine.

I watch rain lash against the windows. It's wild out there today. It looks beckoningly cold.

"I know you hate me, but it can't be as much as I hate myself. Katie's gone. I can't believe she's gone…"

His voice rises to a wail.

I hang up the phone and put my hands over my ears to drown out the echo of Martin's voice, pressing so hard that I hear the blood pumping in my body: my own inner rhythm like the ocean that calls to me.

When I cleaned the house, I hosed off my wetsuit and hung it in my shower to dry. I take off my clothes now and put it on.

Through the window, I see the sky is gray again. It could be noon, maybe later; I don't know or care. The ocean is a chaotic storm, mirroring my mind. I want to plunge into the cold water and feel its energy. I want to let it overtake my thoughts and emotions until I'm completely exhausted by it, with nothing left to feel or think. I grab my surfboard from the outdoor wooden shower on the landing and head down to the water.

The wind lashes me and pulls at my surfboard, like it's trying to wrench it free and hurl it out of my hands into the dune.

I hold it tight.

I walk into the water, which seeps inside my suit. I know it will eventually warm to my body temperature and protect me from the elements, but first it chills me to the core. I welcome the raw cutting edge of its pure frigidity.

Currents rush and whorl around my ankles with a force that pulls and warns me at once, from every direction.

I keep walking.

I feel pressure on my calves, then my thighs, then my waist. I throw myself onto my board and paddle with my hands out to deeper water.

I don't argue with myself today, or with any ghosts, or memories of what was and what wasn't. I need all my mental and physical energy. For breathing, and for getting to the surface when I'm thrown under the freezing chaos of water, which rushes in every direction to create a force I've never known.

Its violence staggers and exhausts me.

My muscles burn and ache with the overburdened effort of keeping my body upright, my head above the hostile surface that seems determined to bury me.

I gasp for breath each time my head clears the water, but I take in as much sea as air. The waves and currents are unpredictable and unforgiving.

I find myself at the decision point that always comes.

Do I fight to drag myself toward shore? Or do I let the ocean carry me wherever it may?

A seabird soars close by, screaming. I look up and watch it fly toward shore, up past Merry's deck.

I see her there.

She's far away, but I can tell by her posture that she's watching closely, that she's anxious.

I remember how warm and soft she felt, leaning on me in front of the fire. How sweet her mouth tasted.

A wave crashes over my head, burying me in icy water.

I want to go to shore.

I want to be with Merry, to feel her body next to mine, thawing me. To see her smile.

I surface again. I look for her on the deck, but I only see Fritz and Claude. I remember Claude is dead, though… Maybe my decision was made for me. Maybe I'm gone, too.

A wall of churning sea encompasses me. I overcome it to

see Merry rushing down the stairs toward the beach.

Another wave hits, and this time my head smacks my board. I taste blood.

I push toward shore. It feels very, very far away. Too far.

I hear Merry yell out.

"Ja-ack!"

She runs across the beach as fast as the sand allows. Her voice gets closer. I try to help close the distance, but it's so hard. Impossibly hard. I realize with a sudden horror that I am growing weaker and weaker.

"Ja-ack! Ja-ack!"

Chaser barks and runs to the water's edge. I touch my face and see blood on my hand before the ocean carries it off.

I don't feel specific pain; the water is so cold that I just feel a generalized, numb ache throughout my body. My lungs struggle for air.

I'm in shallow enough water now to stand. I manage, though it's difficult.

I wave to Merry.

She looks horrified; I put my hand up to my face again. There is so much blood… I feel my teeth; though my hands are numb and my mouth is numb, I can tell there are no gaps. Maybe my nose is broken.

I struggle for breath as I try to wave again, to reassure Merry.

She screams.

It pierces me and I freeze.

I feel, rather than see, an enormous wave bearing down on me from behind. It cracks me like a hundred baseball bats. I fall forward to connect again with my surfboard.

I hear Merry scream again before everything goes black.

Chapter Twenty

IN WHICH MERRY ANSWERS THE MILLION-DOLLAR QUESTION

As told by Merry, who couldn't have done it without Fritz

A fisherman lifts Jack in his arms like he's a child who might've just fallen asleep on the couch watching a television show. Instead of loose popcorn falling on a family room carpet, though, blood drips from Jack's open gash and disappears into the swirling water.

Fritz runs toward us, catching up to help form a sorrowful parade across the sand. The breaking waves provide the music for our slow, hard shuffle. The fisherman walks silently. I sob and Fritz rambles. Jack won't wake up.

When we reach the stairs, the fisherman lays Jack across the walkway. I support his head on my lap.

Fritz throws off his own jacket and removes his white button-front shirt. He rolls it up and wraps it tightly around Jack's head wound.

Blood blooms through before they can even pick him up again. The fisherman carries Jack's arms, and Fritz carries his legs up the wooden staircase.

"Straight to the driveway," Fritz says. I open the gate for them to cross over the dune. "Call an ambulance."

Inside Jack's house, I speak calmly enough to convince the emergency operator that we need medical help. That she needs to send somebody quickly. *Please.*

Chaser is at the door. I let her in and towel her off. She has blood all down the side of her golden coat. Jack's blood, which had poured from his handsome head.

I hug her. She pants and whines. I give her fresh food and water. I try to focus on being useful. I see Jack's wallet on the counter and grab it on my way out the front door, where Fritz hovers over Jack's quiet body in the driveway.

The ambulance screams its way up the street.

I give the wallet to one of the paramedics before Jack is lifted on a gurney and pushed through the open back doors. I want to ride in the ambulance, but they say they need room to attend to Jack.

We watch the ambulance drive away, until even the sound is gone, and the silence is broken only by our breathing.

"Let's follow them," I say.

"Wash the blood off yourself first. Put on dry clothes and shoes," Fritz says, taking charge. "I'll clean up, too, and drive us to the hospital. I know exactly where it is."

I look down and am surprised to see blood all over me. The driveway is bloody. And I saw blood hit the sand on the beach to form an awful paste.

I try not to add it all up.

Fritz sounds calm, but he looks pale and near frozen with his shirt off. I wonder if he's adding up all that blood, too.

When I've finished changing, I hear Fritz talking to Uncle Max upstairs, trying to reassure him. I hear enough to know that he watched the drama unfold.

"You'd better come up a minute," Fritz says. "The old man wants to make sure you're all right."

Uncle Max is slumped in his chair. He looks like hell, like he partied last night and every night of his life, and it all just caught up with him. His hair is messy and stands on end.

"You're OK?" he asks, clutching my hand.

"Yes, sir. I'm fine."

"You're OK?" he asks Fritz. He clutches his hand, too.

Fritz shocks me by bending down and kissing Uncle Max's meringue hair.

"Of course I am," Fritz says. He turns to me, "Are you able to drive to the hospital?"

I nod.

"I'll stay here with Mr. Pershing, then."

I hug Fritz tightly.

I feel like we've been through so much together, and we're not done yet.

He hugs me just as close. "Call and keep us posted," he says.

I follow Fritz's example and kiss my Uncle Max on the top of his cotton candy head. "There's still one slice of cake left for you," I tell him. "Make sure Fritz serves it right."

"He will. He does everything I ask, whether he wants to or not."

Fritz clears his throat and goes into the kitchen. He starts to fill the teakettle.

I can tell he's hiding tears. This past hour has been the most stressful of my entire life. I know that for Fritz, living here has been a constant challenge, not to mention what he must have gone through watching his mother die, and my dad. Now he's saddled with me and Uncle Max. I'd hug him again, but he's keeping his back to me. I know he wants his privacy, that he is doing his best to keep a stiff upper lip.

I remember all the blood and take a deep breath to gather strength. I grab my purse and keys and head for the door.

Pacing the hall, I think of Chaser on the beach. She ran up and whined at Jack, a dead weight in the fisherman's arms. Then she ran off again, barking up and down the beach, as if she was asking for help or casting desperate prayers into the wind.

The nurse told me that Jack regained consciousness in the ambulance on the way over. She said they are "cautiously optimistic."

He lost a lot of blood, though. They gave him some and

sewed him up. She said they are doing a whole slew of tests, and she'll let me know when she has more information.

I don't think I ever saw a clock move so slowly as the clock on this waiting room wall.

Time seems to have bended in the weirdest way—I can't believe it was only last night that Phil showed up with a ring. It took me an hour to convince him I'd *never* say yes before he went away again. I'd thought those minutes were painful, but I had no idea.

A nurse finally appears. "Are you Merry?"

"Yes."

"He wanted me to let you know, if you were here, that he's awake."

"Of course I'm here. Can I see him?"

"In an hour or two, after we finish our tests."

"Will he be OK?"

"I think so."

I sit down again in a waiting room chair because my legs are very wobbly. I have never felt relief in such a physical way before. My lungs expand to let in more air, and I realize I must've been holding my breath.

I pull out my phone to call Fritz. I imagine him back at the house, kissing Max's old white head.

Suddenly Fritz isn't on my mind, but in the waiting room next to me.

"What happened? Are you OK?" I ask. He looks just awful.

"We have to hurry, Merry. The old man is fading fast. He wants to see you right away, while there's still time."

"Uncle Max is here? What do you mean he's fading fast?" I ask.

Though Fritz tries to pull me, I plant my feet and wait for his answer.

"He's dying of lung cancer, Merry. He's the most stubborn man! He could have fought it, but when the doctors gave him his odds, he said he wanted to die on his own terms."

"He's *dying*? Right now?" I ask.

Today the big picture has been shifting violently and

erratically, like a toy boat pitched into the ocean. I can't tell where the next wave will come from, if we'll capsize after all.

"Should we call someone?" I ask.

"Who would we call?"

"You only know him because of my father, and I only know him because he wanted to get the house…"

"Merry," Fritz says, suddenly very tender. "We're all he has."

"I know he never married and had kids, but he must have friends or neighbors…I mean, someone has to care that he's about to leave the world."

"Only us, Merry."

Fritz looks at me hard, like he thinks I'm on the cusp of some deep understanding, like I'm about to answer the million-dollar question on a game show.

"What?" I ask.

"Haven't you figured it out?"

I shake my head no, but many things come back to me at once: the strangeness of the will, Uncle Max's interest in me, his happiness at my small successes, and his seeming not to really care after a while about inheriting the house.

Fritz said he wanted to die on his own terms, which meant living at the ocean, with Fritz, and with me…

Fritz must have followed my expressions. He nods when I get to the end.

He puts out his hand and I take it. Together we head toward the dying man—my father—whom I barely know, but also love so much that my heart might burst.

A man who only has Fritz and me in all the world.

Chapter Twenty-One

IN WHICH FRITZ IS
RENDERED SPEECHLESS

As told by Fritz Forth, man of property

Perhaps after all that I've been through in the past year, nothing should surprise me. But Mr. Pershing could pull a live elephant from his chest pocket, or belch "God Save the Queen" in perfect pitch, and I wouldn't be as surprised as I am by what he's doing now.

He is being frank. He's simply telling the truth. I have never seen him behave so shockingly out of character.

He is talking straight to Merry, as if he has always been capable of doing so, as if after seventy-five years of lying through his teeth as often as not, he suddenly finds it very tiresome and decides not to bother with it anymore.

He shrugged his shoulders at me, as if to say, *why not?* He tossed aside his Max persona as casually as an outdated coat.

"...so I invented a brother. Max is actually short for my middle name: Claude Maxwell Pershing is what I was called at my christening."

The old man laughs a little, like he thinks he's incredibly clever. Merry sits in a chair beside his bed and continues to listen to him, holding his hand and smiling through her silent tears when he says something she's supposed to think is funny. I marvel at her ability to put up with other people's nonsense without pointing out how really silly and selfish they are.

"I've been a cagey old bastard, haven't I?" he asks.

Merry nods thoughtfully. "Why couldn't you just say?" she asks.

"Oh, I didn't know what sort of a girl you'd be. If you were a stick-in-the-mud, or pinch-faced, or dim-witted, I could have slipped away as Max. That bit was in case we didn't hit it off. But we did! Famously."

He coughs and she moves his Styrofoam cup of ice chips and water close enough for him to reach the straw.

"But when you realized you liked me, you could have told the truth," she says.

"I was afraid you would get angry and leave if you knew you'd been hoodwinked," he says.

When someone has been strong and powerful your whole life, it hurts like hell to see him vulnerable. But Merry never knew Mr. Pershing when he was in his prime. She looks down at his withered, liver-spotted hand in her smooth, young one. She doesn't reply. Perhaps she doesn't want to argue with a man on his deathbed, even if he so clearly deserves it. Perhaps she doesn't know what she would have done.

She looks up at him again. "What were all the tasks for?"

"I was trying to make up for all the influence I hadn't been able to have on you. You know, the wisdom I hadn't imparted and suchlike. I had Fritz to help me, and you know that fellow is cleverer than me by far.

"He went down to meet you. He played private investigator until he was able to think of exactly the right things to have you do. Things that would help you get on your own two feet, realize your potential, and all that sort of thing. Then we wrote them up as clever tasks, and I slipped in the one about Jack Morningstar when I thought of it. How did we do?"

Merry looks at me.

I'm standing against the wall, near the door. I tried to leave them alone, but they both insisted that I stay. I feel guilty. I know Merry should be angry with me, but I hope she isn't. I hate to admit something so pathetically sappy, but I have come to regard her as a sister.

"I think you did really well," she says. "I feel better than I ever did before, I love the catering work, and I'm so glad I got to know you, and Fritz, and Jack…" her voice weakens a bit, and Mr. Pershing pats her hand.

"What about your last task?" he asks.

Merry shakes her head. "I haven't had any luck with it yet. Can you give me the answer?"

"I'm afraid not, my dear. The important thing is that you keep on trying to figure things out for yourself. But perhaps we ought to waive some of the original requirements of your inheritance. In the interest of time, you know. What do you think, Fritz?"

Typical Claude Pershing—setting up parameters and rules only to move or bend them as need or whim dictates. He is ashen, and his voice is getting quieter. I know he's near the end. I try to keep my voice steady.

"Whatever you say, Mr. Pershing."

"Good. Well done."

He turns to Merry again.

"Of course, you get the beach house. I thought I noticed that you came to rather enjoy the place?"

Merry nods. "Very much," she whispers.

"Oh, good. Good. You also get your money. Now don't cry anymore, my dear. It makes your nose red."

He kisses her hand and motions for me to come over. Merry gives me her chair and takes my place near the door, weeping quietly.

"Now you, young sir, are another story entirely," he says. "Having had the good fortune to know you from the very beginning, I've had a tremendous amount of pleasure in seeing you grow into a fine, fine man. I couldn't be more proud of you, Fritz, if you were my own son."

His voice breaks, and I hand him a tissue to dry his tears. I take one for myself as well.

"You must have thought me an ungrateful ass for not making provisions for you, dear boy. But now I have the satisfaction of telling you something profound."

Mr. Pershing asks Merry to take papers from the pocket

of his jacket, which is hanging on a hook behind her. She gives them to him. He hands them instantly to me.

Unfolding the papers, I see a copy of the deed to the London house. It has been transferred to my name.

"If I had more to give, I would give you more," Mr. Pershing says in a broken whisper.

In a world full of them, I find that there are no words to express how I feel.

There is a second page behind the deed. It is handwritten.

"Oh, you found the last task," the old man says. "Don't read it now! It's for the two of you to complete together. I thought it up by myself, and I'm sure you'll agree that it's quite ingenious. Don't read it now, you know. Save it for another day. I'm so tired, I really must nap."

"Merry…" He reaches for her, and she takes his hand. "We heard from one of our nurses that my friend, the handsome widower, will recover. I'm glad for it. Go and see him and give him my regards. Take Fritz along. Go now."

He takes my hand once again before waving us away with a force of will that leaves us no choice but to do as he says.

I cast one last look over my shoulder to see him lean back heavily on his pillow.

"I think he'll get better," Merry says as we make our way down the hall. "He was able to talk so much and everything. He doesn't seem like he's about to die. Who told you he was, Fritz?"

"Many doctors have told us, both in London and here, Merry. I had tried to talk him into going back to London for an experimental treatment, but he wanted to meet you instead. I know he made the right choice."

I do. Though I hated to stand helplessly by and watch him grow weaker, I respect his choice. Several weeks of hospitals, needles, and ultimate death anyway, versus time spent at his favorite place in the world with Merry and me…I know it was an easy decision for him, and I'm immeasurably glad that he made it.

"He wanted me to be sure and tell you, if he forgot to tell you himself, that he ate his last slice of cake today. He said he never enjoyed anything so much in his life."

"I'll make him another cake tomorrow," she says with that determined optimism that is her trademark.

I don't want to break it to her, but I don't believe there will be time for more cakes.

I'm afraid that it's already too late.

Chapter Twenty-Two

IN WHICH THE OLD MAN GIVES A FINAL TASK, JACK RESEMBLES FRANKENSTEIN, AND BETTY ANSWERS EXPLAINS EVERYTHING

As told by Merry, who you could have knocked over with a feather

My father died on the same day that Jack was hurt, which was the same day he told me he was really my father. What a day: so sad, and so happy, and so sad.

After Claude Pershing passed, and Fritz and I had just about cried our eyes out, we remembered the handwritten paper. "What does it say?" I asked. He took it out and we both read it together.

> *Last Task:*
>
> *Spread my ashes where you know I will want them. You two are certainly clever enough to figure it out!*
>
> *I wish I could have done better by both of you and many others. I hope I did my best sometimes.*
>
> *I have had the utmost pleasure in witnessing the growing admiration between you two. I know you will remain friends and be a gift to one another throughout your long lives. If either of you ever have children, I humbly suggest that you consider the name Claude. Or Maxwell, for a girl.*
>
> *Sincerely and belatedly, and with all the love one can give the*

> *children of his heart, which I confess has rather staggered me,*
> *I remain (though I really am dead this time)*
> *Yours truly,*
> *Claude Pershing*

At sunset, if the wind is right, we plan to let his ashes free from the deck. Fritz will take what's left to London, to bury near a tree in the backyard, which used to hold a hammock.

When Fritz talks about London, he's like that fateful day we lost my dad: he's both happy and sad. He's sad when he imagines how different the house will be without "the old man," but happy that he'll be able to live there forever. He hasn't told Victor yet that the grand old London house is his. He wants to tell him in person, and he also doesn't want to steal Victor's thunder.

Because guess what? Cryptodynamite got a record deal! Victor is coming to help Fritz pack up here just as soon as the contract is signed. Then they'll fly off into the sunset together. Isn't it so romantic?

I'm savoring these last days with Fritz. I will miss him something awful. But I'm glad he'll finally get to be with the man he loves.

Speaking of lovable men, I need to tell you about Jack's progress. When I first saw him in the hospital, I admit to thinking he looked a little like Frankenstein. He had so many stitches and bruises that I nearly cried at the sight of him. Well, I already was crying on account of my father, but I nearly cried a whole new set of tears because of how sore Jack looked and how much pain I was sure he was in.

But he smiled and reached out his hand to me. And I smiled, too.

It will take a while, but his bruises will fade from the deep eggplant they are now, to a green maybe a shade or two weaker than the Help Yourself color that Fritz picked out when I first came here. And then, one day, we'll look to find that the bruises have disappeared altogether.

That day will come.

Then Jack will only have tiny railroad track scars where the stitches are now. They won't bother me a bit, although Fritz might still sometimes hum the theme from *Beauty and the Beast* to try and get my goat. I'm so grateful that Jack is alive and all right, I can't even say.

"I have an idea about that third task," I tell Fritz after a dinner for two that he helped me make. He wrote out instructions on an index card so that he can recreate it for Victor.

"You do?" he asks.

"Yes, sir. Aunt Betty acted so strange when I asked if she knew what my mom's secret could be, like she knew something but didn't want to spill it, that I've decided to call her on it again."

"Are you sure you want to dig up an old secret, Merry? Remember the saying: *What you don't know can't hurt you.*"

"I don't know if I agree with that saying. Anyway, I want the truth, even if it hurts a little."

"Then I have no doubt you'll find it," Fritz says. "You're the most determined person I've ever met."

I get up and hug him before I start clearing the table.

"No, no. I'll tidy up tonight," he says. I suppose there's a first time for everything!

"Then I'll meet you back here at sunset," I tell him.

I sit on my bed and look through the sliding glass doors at the ocean. I dial Aunt Betty at home. For the first ten minutes, she grills me on the basic facts of my recent adventure. I answer her questions because I don't have anything to hide, and it's sort of amazing to list all the things that have happened in such a short time. Then it's my turn to ask questions.

"Aunt Betty, I want you to tell me what you know about my mom's secret. I'm sure you know something, so please just tell me."

"You know very well that I don't explain anything."

"Oh, for heaven's sake, would you quit with that crap?" I ask. "Ma'am," I add.

She's quiet for a while. I watch a string of pelicans fly just above the wave tops.

"I'm sorry about your father," Aunt Betty says, out of the blue. "He was charming."

"Wait. You knew him?" I ask.

"Yes, Merry."

"How did you know him? When?"

I hear her take a deep breath and let it out.

"Do you know what I've been doing tonight, Merry?" she asks.

I don't say it out loud, but I guess she's been sitting in her one and only comfortable chair in her all-white living room watching a Spanish-language drama.

"No, ma'am," I say.

"I've been going through a file folder that I keep locked in a desk drawer. Do you know what's in it?"

"No, ma'am."

"Dozens of pictures of you, Merry, from the time you were a baby until now. One of my favorites is you as a newborn. You were so pink and helpless, so terrifying. I thought it would be the only picture of you I would ever have."

She pauses, but I don't say anything.

"Every one of these photographs is precious to me. But I'll shut the file now and put it back into the drawer, next to a copy of the letter that I sent to your father. I can't indulge in the pictures anymore tonight because I think it's finally time for me to explain everything to you."

You could knock me over with a feather!

"You sent a letter to Claude Pershing?" I ask. Pieces of a puzzle are beginning to fall into place. I wish I could stop them.

"I did, and that's what originally sent Fritz to you, though I didn't know for certain that the two things were related at first. I didn't expect such a convoluted chain reaction from what I'd tried to frame as a straightforward note, only a few lines long. I only wanted to make sure that you and Fanny and your grandmother didn't lose your home. I would have preferred a simple yes or no answer."

"So you sent a letter to my father asking for money?"

"If you can please try not to interrupt me, Merry, I'll tell you everything," she says. And she launches right in.

"I turned nineteen years old the summer before college began. My mom had originally held me back from school for a year, which may have contributed to my boredom. At least she didn't hold me back for life, like she's done to poor Fanny.

"Though I turned nineteen, I looked much older than my years. I think my age finally caught up to my face when I turned forty; it took that long. I had saved money from babysitting and working in the ice cream parlor for years on end and had accumulated enough to move to Wilmington early. I wanted to spend the summer having a little fun before the dorms claimed me as an academic scholarship student to the University of North Carolina–Wilmington.

"I sublet a tiny apartment overlooking the Cape Fear River. Though my mom and Fanny strongly urged and pleaded that I stay home until college began, until the last possible moment, I went.

"I first saw Claude Pershing as he sauntered along the river walk below my apartment balcony. I was up there reading and sipping a gin and tonic. He was distinguished and very upright, with a jaunty air about him. Though I could see he was very old compared to me, I was instantly drawn to him.

"I had dated boys, of course, but I suppose I thought I was ready for a real relationship, perhaps even overdue to fall in love. I called down to him and we talked that way, like Romeo and Juliet."

A much younger Aunt Betty and a much younger Claude; it's strange to picture either of them at all, let alone together.

"That summer, Claude seemed more essential to me than air. I never felt more free, or happy, or alive, than that one summer when I was in love."

In love...

"I had been attempting to write a short story when I met Claude. He saw the evidence of it and assumed I was a struggling writer waiting for a break. I didn't correct him; it saved me from having to confess how young I was. He was nearly fifty then, you see, and I feared he would balk if he knew my age.

"Claude didn't ask a lot of questions. He preferred to talk about himself, which suited me, because there wasn't a more fascinating subject in the entire world. We spent a great deal of time together over the course of that summer, but if I'd had my wish, we would have spent all day, every day, all night, every night. He was a busy man, though, who only happened to be in North Carolina on business.

"Claude fell in love that summer, too. Not with me, but with an island down the coast. He purchased a large lot on which he planned to have a vacation home built."

I look around the room, through the patio doors to the ocean, at the sun getting lower in the sky.

"I knew Claude was rich. I suppose, looking back, that was part of his original appeal to me. I loved the way he carried himself, too, and his accent, and his sense of humor, and his passionate temper. He often spoke of London, where he had grown up and where he still lived. It sounded cultured and sophisticated. I dreamed of him taking me back to England with him and marrying me. I dreamed we would visit the ocean house on holidays. I would, of course, attend college; I knew I had a good mind, and I didn't want to waste it."

I want to keep the pieces of the puzzle apart, but I've already seen the image, so it's too late. "Can we cut to the chase, Aunt Betty?" I say, my voice shaking a bit.

"Please let me finish, Merry. I want you to know how it was. May I continue?"

Outside the window, a family is walking their black lab along the beach. The dad throws a Frisbee and the dog runs, jumps high into the air, and catches it.

"Go ahead," I whisper.

"Well, that summer I was very much in love, and as the time drew nearer for me to move to the dorms, I knew I had to explain my situation to Claude. I kept putting it off, though. He stopped by my apartment unexpectedly one day and said he was leaving for London, having concluded his business earlier than expected. I asked when he would be back. He said he would return in the spring, when the ocean house was finished. He said he would love to see me then, if I liked.

"He kissed me in a gentlemanly way. I remember trying to absorb what he'd said. It was hard to catch my breath. I pasted on a smile because he smiled, and apparently that was the polite way to break up. He couldn't even stay for a drink. He had to catch a flight.

"I had spent the better part of the summer with him, marrying him in my mind, traveling the world with him, and caring for him in his old age. Then, as a lonely widow, consoling myself with how much we had loved each other and how we never let the thirty-year difference in our ages come between us.

"The one consolation I've had all these years is that I didn't tell him how I felt. I didn't beg him to stay. I didn't let him know that he was my first—perhaps he'd be my only—love. I didn't tell him about the castles I had made in the air for us and how they were floating away as he stood there, making hasty excuses and then disappearing before my tear-filled eyes."

She sounds far away, like she's watching the scene play out in her mind. The family on the beach has passed out of my view. I watch the sun slowly sink lower in the sky while I wait for Aunt Betty to continue.

"I realized I was pregnant during my second month of school," she finally says.

Though I knew something to that effect was coming, the world still shifts before me at these words. I close my eyes because I'm suddenly dizzy.

"My first month had kept me so busy getting to know the lay of the land, establishing myself as first in every class, and nursing my broken heart, that I didn't really notice that I missed my period. When my breasts became tender, I began to suspect. I went to a clinic and had my fears confirmed.

"I only considered telling Claude for one evening. I indulged a fantasy wherein he was in love with me after all and agreed that the baby I carried was cosmic proof we should be together. I imagined us marrying and him whisking me off to London to live in a modified, diaper-filled version of the dreams I had harbored all summer.

"By the time I laid my head on my dorm room pillow that night, I knew it wouldn't work out that way. Claude had had a fling with me. It was over as far as he was concerned. I knew that. He might help out financially, but having his child wasn't going to make him fall in love with me any more than all the time we shared over the summer had.

"I wasn't ready to be a mother. Abortion was out of the question for me; it seemed like punishing someone else for my own naivety. I didn't have the stomach for it. And so you were born three days after spring term ended."

I open my eyes to see a framed picture on the desk: my mom and grandma are standing in front of our cabin, wearing cotton dresses and smiling. They have always loved me, and they have always been right there for me. I look at my reflection in the mirror. I see a full-grown, stylish woman, with a good career started and a home of her own. How I began doesn't matter as much as who I am now.

"Are you still there?" Aunt Betty asks.

"Yes, ma'am."

"Do you have any questions?" she asks.

"Why did you give me to my mom?"

"Mother and Fanny begged. I had planned to use an adoption agency, but they hounded me and wanted you so much. Finally I said yes. You were legally adopted; Fanny is really your mother."

"I know she's my mother," I say. The motion of the waves outside the window steadies me. "I suppose I do have a question or two."

"I'll answer if I can."

"Why did you change your name?"

"I stayed away from Peaksy Falls, and from you and Fanny and Mother, for five years. When I returned, I was a new woman. As Betty Answers, I moved to the nearest city that had enough people so that I could blend in. I have been Betty Answers for more than twenty years. I barely remembered my former self until you went away and I began to relive our history and to question the wisdom of having sent the letter in the first place."

I'm glad she sent the letter—too glad to even express it. And I'm glad that I will never feel the way she did. Though I have changed a lot in a short time, I am still the same old me inside.

"Why did you want to come back to live near Peaksy Falls?" I ask.

"I thought that if I were nearer, I might offer advice and guidance to Fanny and Mother and financial assistance when necessary. We set up our ground rules right away. I was to always be Betty Answers, even in private. I'm not going to second-guess if it was too drastic, or silly, or anything else I have been accused of since I took on my new identity. I did it, and I'm not going to look back.

"I set up the barriers I needed, and Fanny and Mother respected them because it was also their secret to protect. I suppose the old girls were scared that I would try to take you from them, which is the nightmare of every adoptive parent. But I never felt equipped to be a mother; I'm amazed anyone ever does.

"Fanny always referred to you as my niece, as her daughter, which was legally true. I have tried to see you that way, too. I think I succeeded as well as I could.

"Occasionally, though, I have felt the loss of you like a road not taken, one that might have led to sunshine and happiness. I sometimes wonder if that path might have branched out into a million others."

I hear her voice catch.

"It's OK, Aunt Betty," I say, because I hate hearing anybody cry, no matter the reasons.

"When financial woes threatened everything, I wrote to Claude, explaining that he had a biological daughter. I wanted him to give you monetary assistance if he could. I hoped he might save your home since it appeared that I would fail to do so in the end. You know what happened next far better than I do."

"I'm glad you finally told me all this, ma'am."

"I'm sorry it took so long. Are you well and happy, Merry?" she asks.

"Very well and very happy," I answer.

"I'm so pleased."

"I have to go now, though, because I have something important to do at sunset."

"I'll let you go then," she says. "Goodbye."

"I see you're reverting back to your old ways," Fritz says, motioning toward my Dollywood T-shirt when I reach the top of the stairs. He has the kitchen polished to a shine.

"No, sir, but I never want to forget who I am, either," I say. I didn't think I was sad or anything, but somehow I feel tears on my cheeks.

He comes over and hugs me. "That would be a terrible tragedy indeed," he says.

I point to the sky through the windows. "It's almost sunset."

"We can wait until tomorrow if you like," he suggests.

"Look how gorgeous the colors are! He would love this view." I tuck some dried coconut flakes into my pocket and pick up the urn from the bookshelf very carefully.

Fritz opens the door to the deck and shuts it behind us.

Our clothes blow in the wind. Our short hairstyles are mussed by it.

I hand the urn to Fritz and toss some of the flakes into the air to test the wind. We watch them fly in the direction of the waves. Some probably only make it to the dune, others to the soft sand, and others soar so high and far that I'm sure they dive straight into the ocean.

Chapter Twenty-Three

IN WHICH JACK DRAMATICALLY RE-DUCES HIS REAL ESTATE HOLDINGS

As told by lucky Jack Morningstar

"We have big news," Jaycee says.

"Why do you have me on speakerphone?" I ask.

"Because Martin is here, too. He's back in the office."

"Ok. So what's the news?"

"We got the Langdon Logistics contract!" Jaycee yells.

This is huge for our company. To have landed this lucrative software project, which we've been working on in turn for months, is a huge relief to me. And I'm sure to Martin. And to everyone else on down to the student interns. Jaycee worked the hardest, and we all know it.

"I'm ready to throw myself into work," Martin says.

"Can you help out, too, Jack?" Jaycee asks.

"I'll work remotely. I know it hasn't been optimal, but I'm committed to really focusing on the company again. It'll be so seamless you'll forget I'm not across the hall."

"I'm taking your office," she says.

"Do it," I tell her, seizing at the idea because it seems so obviously right. "Really, Jay, you deserve it. Move on over there."

"I was kidding…"

"I'm not. I don't know if I ever want to work nine-to-five in Chicago again, and if I do, we can duke it out then."

"I understand you knocked your head pretty hard. I'll wait until your concussion is gone and then see if you're still singing the same song."

"That's fine; if you don't want it, I'll give it to that skinny intern with the goatee. What's his name again? Aaron? Owen?"

"OK, fine, I'll take it."

I can almost see her packing up a cardboard box right now. I bet she has moved over to the big office by the end of the day.

I have a sudden thought. "Are you still interested in my apartment, Jay?"

"Just how bad were you conked, Jack?"

I close my eyes for a moment and see Katie's perfectly organized closet. Her shoes lined up on shelves and all her clothes…I know they are arranged by color, I remember that, but I can only see them in gray tones in my mind. Every visual image of the apartment that comes to me is black and white.

I know there's nothing there that I can't live without.

"I'm serious, Jay. Once it's emptied, you can take over my lease."

"Why don't you think that one over for a while, Jack?" Jaycee suggests.

"I've decided to let it go anyway. If you want the place, you better take it."

"If you're sure you're ready to move on…" she says.

"I am."

I am.

When we finish our business and I hang up the phone, I go straight next door. I need to bask in joy and positive energy, rays of sunshine and saturated color, and the most beautiful smile that has ever been seen.

I need Merry.

She has amazed me over and over again. She has been through so much, yet never complained, never threatened to throw in the towel, never stopped working hard and trying harder.

She has had more curveballs and revelations hurled at her in the past few months than most people deal with in a lifetime, but she has absorbed them and moved on. She has started a business, found out that her father was dead, then alive, then dead again, that her aunt is really her mother, and that maybe she's in love with a man who isn't sure he can ever deserve her, but would really love to try.

Merry hasn't confined her tireless optimism to her own life, either. She has agreed to visit my parents with me next month. Though it means I'll also have to see Martin, Merry has convinced me that I'll likely survive it. And she didn't even blink when she found out that Phil, her ex, got engaged to a girl named Sarah the day after she turned him down. She baked them some cookies.

Merry is a mermaid, a sorceress in the kitchen, and she's impossible to resist. And I am the luckiest guy in the world.

Chapter Twenty-Four

IN WHICH FRITZ'S WISH COMES TRUE

As told by Fritz Forth, who says: "Yes, sir"

I have helped Merry with all the financial legalities and paperwork regarding her mum, grandmother, and Betty Answers. To prove the maxim that no good deed goes unpunished, the three of them have descended upon us en masse. They claim that three nights is a short visit (two down, one to go), but I humbly beg to differ.

Bless their cotton-frocked hearts, the mountain ladies haven't quite managed to get it through their heads that Merry didn't win the beach house in a game show. I know they realize that technically Merry inherited it from her father, and they now also admit, albeit in a decidedly twitchy way, that Betty is Merry's biological mother. Infuriatingly, though, they still seem to believe a game show was somehow involved in Merry's procurement of this house.

I have tried to explain otherwise, and I have seen Merry try, and Betty. But whenever we're sure they finally understand, one of them says something frustratingly silly, like, "What network will it be on?"

"Finish up soon so we can get that table set," Merry says as she works in the kitchen. She shooed Jack out of her way an hour ago, and now he's playing Yahtzee with the ladies. It's clear that they find him nearly as charming as Merry does. He'd had to coax them to choose a board game from the stack of tattered boxes on the bookshelf, but now they're showing their competitive spirits and talking a bit of trash.

I wish Victor could be here, too, but I can't complain since he's due to arrive late tomorrow.

I hear the doorbell ring when I'm boxing things up in Mr. Pershing's room. I come out to hear voices in the stairwell and don't believe my ears at first. But as the laughter and chatter grows louder and closer, I catch my breath.

"Victor!"

"Oh my God," he says, scooping me into a hug that lasts forever, but not long enough, followed by a kiss that continues the trend.

"Oh, dear," Betty says, fanning herself with her scorecard.

I can't believe he's actually here. My knees go weak.

I thought I remembered every strand of his hair, every angle of his face and shoulder blades, but I feel nervous and speechless in his presence. He has never looked so good to me. Or sounded so good. Or felt so good.

"Introduce me!" Victor says, turning to face the tableful of ladies and one gentleman, keeping an arm around me.

"I already met your Merry; she is so lovely!" he says, pointing to her.

She smiles and blushes, obviously smitten with my beau. I can't imagine that there's anyone in the entire world who wouldn't be. It's not just his French accent, or his stature, or his tastefully understated violet eyeliner. It's everything: he's the entire package.

I go around the table calling out names. He follows me, kissing hands and making ceremoniously extended eye contact as he goes, so that all the ladies are fanning themselves with their scorecards by the time he's through with them.

"And, finally, this is Jack Morningstar," I say.

Victor shakes his hand before reaching out to lightly touch his stitches.

"I wonder, can I do that with makeup?" he asks. "Do you mind if I take some photographs? We have a zombie song in writing, and I would love to have this look."

"Oh my!" Merry's mother says.

"And this beautiful house, it is magnifique! Fritzie, why have you said it was not perfect? It would be amazing for the music video. No?"

"For the zombie song?" Jack asks.

"No, no, of course not the zombie song!" Victor laughs. "It would be perfect for the sunshine song! Can we?"

"Ask Merry," I say. "It's her house."

"Yes, sir," she says. "But nobody can smoke in here or anything like that."

Victor laughs. I imagine the Bandmaidens walking along the beach during breaks from the video shoot, with their overdyed black hair and black clothes and glorified combat boots, each of them smoking like a factory.

"And I must sample that sound—the ocean! It would be lovely," V says.

"For the sunshine song?" Betty asks.

"No, no! For the song called 'Marry Me.'"

He turns and looks at me intently. So does everyone else.

"You've been writing a lot," I say, in an attempt to make light.

"I wrote that one only for you, Fritzie."

"The zombie one?" I ask.

"Marry me."

I hear Merry gasp and clap her hands together. I don't want to look at her face. She is a hopeless, optimistic romantic. She misunderstands him, I'm sure. Out of the corner of my eye I see her mom and grandma clutch each other's arms and stare expectantly.

I know they'll all be disappointed.

I have pushed for a formal commitment from Victor, but he has shied away. He has maintained that he doesn't want to be dependent on me financially. I have repeatedly said that I don't mind, that it doesn't matter to me who makes more money. I only want us to be together, happily ever after.

The thought goes through my mind that it might just be possible, he might actually be serious. Perhaps his record deal makes the difference between dependent and coequal that has always been so important to him.

I still can't look at him, though, because I'm afraid I'm wrong. I wish he hadn't started this mortifying scene in front of an audience. But Victor loves an audience.

He takes my hand and gets down on one knee.

I can't help it anymore. I look into his eyes.

Oh my *God*.

He means it.

I feel my eyes fill with tears and bite my lip to stop them.

Victor leans on Mr. Pershing's chair to steady himself before taking a spectacular platinum band out of his pocket. I know in my heart the old man would approve. He loved me enough to want me to be happy. And nothing could make me happier than this!

"Will you marry me?" Victor asks.

I can't hold my tears back anymore. I kneel down, too, and we embrace in a hug that isn't at all elegant, but is perfect nonetheless.

"You have to answer!" Merry calls out in her slow twang. "Y'all didn't answer him yet."

I pull back and smile at Victor. He's crying, too.

"Yes, sir," I say.

Chapter Twenty-Five

IN WHICH WE BID ADIEU

As told by Merry, our hostess

We are about to sit down to our farewell dinner.

The stove timer goes off, and I take Jack's favorite dish out of the oven. On the table are salads, bread, and wine. My three ladies are perched across from Victor, who is drumming his forks on the table while quietly composing something in French.

On the counter is the cherished Pershing chocolate cake. "Maybe I should retire the recipe as a tribute?" I say to Fritz and Jack, who are helping me bring the hot dishes to the table.

"No!" they say together.

"Do you need a hand over there?" my mom asks.

"Y'all sit tight," I tell her.

I'm glad my family came, but I'm even gladder they'll be leaving in the morning. The happy couple will head home to London the next day. Jack's and my world is getting smaller and smaller. Pretty soon it'll be down to the two of us and Chaser.

"So you're staying on the island for a while?" Fritz asks Jack with a frown.

I know for a fact he really likes Jack, but that he also wants to look out for me. He seems to think he really is my big brother now.

"I have to be out of the house by Memorial Day weekend. It's booked up for the entire season after that. I'll stay there until the end of May, but then I have to figure out what to do."

Jack winks at me.

I am so in love with that man.

He says I'm more beautiful every single day and that I feel more perfect on his skin each time he touches me. He makes me blush, especially since I can tell he really means the sweet things he says.

"I just wish I could find someone with a little extra room among her five bedrooms that might be coaxed into renting me some space," he says.

I roll my eyes, but I can't help but smile. I haven't said yes, but if things keep going like they're going, I will say it when the time comes.

Fritz shakes his head like he doesn't approve, but I can see that he does. He knows about love.

We have just enough room to fit everything on the table and everybody around it. My father would be proud to see us all here. He'd be tickled pink to know how well his meddling worked out.

"I'd like to make a toast," I say.

I raise my glass, and so does everybody else.

"To Claude Pershing."

Fritz and Victor lean into each other. Aunt Betty wipes the corners of her eyes with a napkin. I pretend not to hear my grandma whisper, "Is he the host of Merry's new show?" before we clink our glasses together and Fritz repeats:

"To Claude Pershing."

I close my eyes and savor my sip. I am so darn grateful, for everything.

"I'd like to make a toast, too," Jack says, standing up. "To Fritz and Victor. May you grow old together."

We all touch glasses and drink our toasts: "To Fritz and Victor."

Fritz stands at his place at the head of the table. He gazes around at each of us and clears his throat like he's going to make a very long and formal speech. I look at the lasagna and bite my lip, wondering how long it will stay hot.

"Alrighty then," he says in a truly awful impression of my accent. "Y'all need to join me in a toast to our purdy little host and chef." He raises his glass high: "To Merry!"

"To Merry!" Glasses clink together.

I smack Fritz lightly and lean over to kiss him on the cheek when he sits back down. Victor laughs and picks up a serving spoon. "Can we begin?" he asks.

"Yes," I say. "Help yourself!"

as is

Gwendolyn Golden and Armand Leopold have been America's go-to couple for home decorating tips, letting the cameras into their So Perfect house, their So Perfect life, their So Perfect marriage.

One problem: it's all an act.

Actually, two problems: America just found out it's all an act.

When a picture of Armand kissing another man hits the newsstands, everyone knows the jig is up. Both are evicted from their home and eviscerated by the press. While Armand deals with his very private life becoming very public, Gwen Golden returns home to Riveredge, a quiet town where her sick father, her angry sister, and the guy who got away still live.

After years of pretending, Gwen has to rebuild her life for real. But while turning a new house into a home, and starting the next chapter of her life will be tough, reconnecting with the man she once loved may prove to be the most difficult of all.

With humor and charm to burn, Rachel Michael Arends has written a beautiful novel of rekindled romance, home improvement, and how only the truth can really set you free.